Howling Dead

M. H. Bonham

Dragon
Moon

www.dragonmoonpress.com
www.howlingdead.com

Howling Dead

M. H. Bonham

ISBN 10 1-896944-93-0 Print Edition
ISBN 13 978-1-896944-93-7

Dragon Moon Press is an Imprint of Hades Publications Inc.
P.O. Box 1714, Calgary, Alberta, T2P 2L7, Canada

Printed and bound in the United States
www.dragonmoonpress.com
www.howlingdead.com

Dedication
To Larry, as always.
And in memory of my parents, B. Albert and Betty
M. Holowinski.

Acknowledgments
A huge thanks to the following people: Gwen Gades
my publisher, Gabrielle Harbowy my editor, Larry
Bonham, Phyllis Irene Radford and Joyce Reynolds-
Ward for reading this. Andrew Burt, for really coining the
name "spiders." And Mike Fowlkes, who graciously allowed
me to tuckerize him in a book. Congrats, dude!

1

Hunger.

The creature felt the desire deep within; the need to drink blood, and to tear flesh and muscle from bone. The hunger had been an ache — a dull throb — for some time. But now it screamed at him. The hunger must be fed.

The creature snuffed the air. It was cool that evening, and here in the dark alleyways, he was safe. Safe enough from the cops who patrolled the streets. Safe enough from the throngs of humans who inhabited the city. His senses were far beyond human — he would hear and smell anything long before it arrived.

He licked his lips in anticipation of the hunt. Others had this hunger. Most kept it in check with the thin veneer that was civilization. Normally he would, too. But the full moon was overhead and it screamed for blood. Neither he nor others like him could deny the burning within.

He trotted forward, ignoring the drunks who lay passed out next to the Dumpsters, their bodies reeking of sweat, puke, and alcohol. Not long ago, the creature would've sated himself on those unfortunate men, but tonight was different. Tonight there was new quarry.

He halted in the darkness of the alleyway. Darkness was always his friend. He lay down now, his nose wrinkling at the smells of filth, tar, and human excrement on the pavement. It couldn't be helped. Not if he were to catch his prey. He waited with anticipation.

It would be soon. Very soon.

"I'm going to kill him!" Kira Walker grumbled. In the dim light, the screen reflected her blue eyes. She sat back and sighed. "I think I found our problem."

"What's wrong?" Susan asked, peering over the gray cubicle wall.

"Bob."

Susan groaned. She scooted her wheeled chair around the low wall and over to Kira's cubicle. "Now what?"

"I found our little security breach." Kira ran her hands through her blonde hair. "Man, oh, man! I'm glad I get paid overtime for this crap."

"What'd he do?" Susan asked, peering intently with her hazel eyes.

"He NIS'ed all the machines together with a stupid password file. He then distributed the main password file to all his machines using rdist. Get this — he gave superuser a password anyone could crack," Kira said. "I bet he uses it on all his accounts. Boy, are the execs are going to be pissed."

"What is it?" Susan asked.

Kira looked sideways. "I'm a man." She pointed to the screen where she had cracked the password. IM-A-MAN stared back at them.

Susan burst out in a fit of giggles and Kira began to laugh, too. "I guess he needs the reminder," Susan gasped between bouts of laughter. "I wonder how he made lead UNIX systems administrator."

"Maybe he's a suck-up," Kira suggested.

"They seem to like that, here."

"I wish Bob had let us evaluate his systems earlier," said Kira. "I had no idea how many backdoors he put on these suckers until tonight. No wonder the hackers got in and deleted the database."

"Do we have backups?" Susan asked hopefully.

Kira stood up and stretched. "Do we *trust* the backups?" She looked at her watch. "Christ, it's ten already. No wonder I'm hungry. You think anything's open?"

"Maybe on the 16th Street Mall," Susan said. "There's always the vending machines."

"Oooh, yeah, doughnuts. Nice, good dinner." Kira spread her arms to simulate an expanding waistband.

"Makes a growing girl," Susan snickered. "Hey, why don't we start a build on the NIS Server, grab dinner, and then restore the backups? I think the Paramount Café is still open."

Kira nodded and popped a CD into the CDROM drive. She waved her hand. "Go away," she told the computer as she rebooted it. She booted the computer off the CDROM and began the reinstallation. "What password should I give superuser?" she asked at the prompt.

"You're a wimp?" Susan quipped. "UR-A-WIMP?"

"Naw, how about 'DEADBOB' with a zero instead of an oh?" Kira asked.

"Works for me. I wonder..." Susan paused. "I better check — oh man!"

"What?" Kira peered over.

"The backdoor SNMP passwords on all the machines are original. A hacker could get in that way, too."

"DEADBOB," Kira said firmly.

Susan laughed and entered the new password. DEADB0B.

Alaric snuffed the air. He could smell humans, a few feral cats and assorted rodents, but none of his kind. Good. He didn't expect to find anyone here — at least, not yet. Alaric was hunting tonight, but his prey was a predator.

In this body, Alaric's senses were heightened and his strength was greater than any human's. Overhead, the full moon glinted off the high-rises, feeding his power. His sinews rippled beneath his black hair as he walked slowly, carefully on asphalt that was now cool beneath his feet from the night air. He felt the blood-lust of his ancestors and turned it aside.

The wind changed and Alaric caught a familiar scent. His hackles rose as he walked stiff-legged toward the smell. Just within the moonlight, he saw the hulking shape of his second-in-command.

Cathal, he said.

The wolf hesitated and turned to Alaric. *My liege,* the wolf said, not bothering to disguise the unbridled hatred in his eyes.

Have you seen anything? Alaric asked, ignoring the hateful stare.

Monkeys...

Humans, Alaric corrected him with a low growl. *They are humans.*

They are primates, Cathal snarled. *They aren't what we are.*

Many of our kind were human before becoming like us, Alaric reminded him. *You will not call them that.*

Anger glinted dangerously in Cathal's eyes. *Yes, my liege,* he said.

What have you found? Alaric demanded.

Nothing. None of the wolves are here, save us, Cathal said. *It appears your monkey-kil — I mean, human-killer is nowhere. He must've gotten wind of your plans.*

Damn, thought Alaric.

Is that all? Cathal asked.

Keep watch. Alert me to anything unusual, Alaric replied. His second-in-command left and Alaric pondered what he'd just learned. Alaric had been afraid that the rogue movement had grown, but now he had confirmation of it. The killer was now wise to Alaric and would now avoid the Alpha.

Cathal was dangerous, Alaric reflected. But the pack hierarchy wasn't built on loyalty, but on strength. For all Alaric knew, Cathal might indeed be the rogue he was seeking. But somehow, Alaric doubted it.

He snuffed the night wind and waited, hoping for some sign...

It was ten-thirty when Kira and Susan walked out of the Intermountain Telecom building on 17th Street in Denver. Although this was technically a workday, Fridays were casual days, which meant jeans and t-shirts even for contractors. It was still cool out, typical for a May night in Denver, and they had both put on the Intermountain Telecom jackets they had received as SWAG (Some-What-A-Gift) from the VP. The jackets had been thanks for keeping the computers up for more than a week.

The streetlights cast their fluorescent glow next to the big buildings. The glow from the Qwest sign rivaled Intermountain Telecom's in intensity. Overhead, a full moon was cresting the tops of the skyscrapers.

"I'm going to be so glad to finish this job and leave here," Susan said with a heavy sigh. "I want to go back to San Jose so bad."

Kira shook her head. "Not me. No jobs there, since it's all been outsourced. I kind of like Denver. It's pretty here and the people are nice enough. And we haven't been to the mountains yet."

Susan snorted. "Who has the time? It's 'fix Bob's system' here, 'Can you do a restore on the backups' there. I swear, if we weren't getting overtime I'd have quit a long time ago."

"Well, it's no worse than any Silicon Valley gig we've had," Kira remarked. "Anyway, did you check out the new wireless Intermountain's been putting up? They say they'll have a completely wireless Internet in two years; revolutionize the way we think about it."

"Yeah well," said Susan. "Not sure if it's all that revolutionary. I mean, Christ, Kira, we've had wireless since the 90s."

"This is something Randy concocted."

"Randy? You mean Green at MIT?"

"Yeah."

"Loser!" Susan made an "L" with her thumb and index finger and put it to her forehead. "God, Kira, why did you hang around with such assholes?"

"They're smart assholes," Kira said. She paused as she looked where Susan was leading her. They stopped at a dark alleyway between 17th Street and the 16th Street Mall. "Hey, I thought we were going to the Paramount."

"We are. This way's faster," Susan said.

Kira hesitated.

"What's wrong?" Susan asked.

"It's dark," Kira said. She caught Susan's smirk. "No, really. Why don't we go around?"

"If we run into anyone, they'll just be homeless. They're mostly harmless." Susan started into the alley. Kira hesitated for a moment and then followed reluctantly. They walked past the Dumpsters and toward the welcoming glow of the Paramount Café's marquee. "I swear, Kira, you're such a weenie when it comes to—"

A dark form leapt from behind a Dumpster. Kira turned and for a split second, she saw a face. Not quite human, but not animal either. Something in-between. Then, fur, teeth, and claws were on top of Kira. She screamed, flinging her arm up at the last minute as the wolf tore into her.

Five hundred pounds per inch of bone-crushing force tore into her arm. Blood burned in Kira's nostrils and filled her mouth. As teeth slid through flesh, there was pain. Kira heard another scream — it could've been Susan's, or it might have come from her own mouth.

The wolf shook its head from side-to-side, shaking her like a rag doll. Blood sprayed everywhere. Kira could feel the bones snap and her body shake. Kira brought her legs up and kicked and kicked, but the force of her legs did nothing to dissuade the brute from its prey.

Kira could see the lights of the Mall just beyond, lit up like daylight. So close, and yet, so far. "Susan, run!" she tried to shout, but the words came out in a gurgle. Her face lay against the cold, rough concrete of the alley. It was slick with oil or blood. Maybe both. She wondered if they'd mix.

The wolf released her mangled arm. It was completely useless now. Through the blood and the haze of pain, she could see the raw meat and stark white broken bones. Kira looked into the unholy yellow eyes and saw sentience far beyond anything canine. Kira gasped, unable to tear her eyes away. The wolf opened its maw and she smelled the hot copper breath as it bore down to rip her throat out.

"Oh my GOD!" Kira heard Susan scream. The wolf hesitated from its quarry and it turned. Susan stood there, transfixed by the grisly sight.

"Run! Susan! Run!" Kira tried to shout again, but the words came out as a hoarse croak. For a split second, Susan stood there, not knowing what to do. The wolf leapt on the startled woman and within moments had her by the throat. As it bit into her, the body went limp. A sickening snap told Kira the beast had broken Susan's spine.

Kira tried to stand, but she had lost too much blood. Her stomach churned in nausea as she realized that not only was her best friend dead, but that Kira would soon be joining her. As she started to fade into unconsciousness, she thought she heard a police siren and the sounds of gunshots. Then the world spun into blackness.

ONE MONTH LATER

It's too hot, man, time to bug out, Lizard said.

Spaz stared at the message on the palm top and felt a trickle of sweat run through his close-cropped straight hair and down his brown skin. He wiped his forehead and shivered slightly — the cold breeze from the plane's air vent chilled him. He closed his eyes and tried to relax. The receivers worked best when his thoughts were clear.

Not quite Asian, and not quite African, Spaz had inherited his Japanese features from his father and his coloring from his African American mother. He had also inherited his father's ability to crack just about any machine out there...

Spaz could see the pathway if he focused properly. The Forest was like that — you needed to be focused if you used it. Spaz pulled the data once again. At that moment, he saw Lizard's avatar appear. It was a green gecko, reminiscent of the car insurance ads.

Knock, knock, Spaz Boy, said Lizard.

Go away, Spaz said. *You'll lead the werewolves right to me.*

They're already circling, Spaz Boy, Lizard said. *I'm just here to watch the fun.*

Wrong, said Spaz and began rerouting the links. *Maybe you'll give in, but I won't.* His fingers flew over the PDA pad faster than he could realistically form his thoughts into the right algorithm. That was the problem with prototype interfaces — as gee-whiz and Buck Rodgers as the public would like to think they were, the reality was that they had to compensate for an enormous amount of human frailties. One of them was the lack of ability to stay focused in a logical way. The human mind naturally made associations — associations which boggled even the biggest supercomputers. Spaz slammed the door on the Lizard and began to establish a secure session with the Denver database. He pulled up the *whois* files and started looking for a name.

They can't find me if you can't, he thought smugly.

One record popped up. Kira Walker, age 32, blonde hair, blue eyes, stared back at him from the photo. *Damn, you're looking good,* Spaz thought. When he had looked her up previously, he had half-expected that she'd be married with three kids and settled down somewhere in Iowa. Instead, he found her in the most unlikely place — at Intermountain Telecom and right where he needed her to be. He only hoped she wasn't a stik.

He pulled up Susan Baker's photo. *Susie-Woozy,* he remembered teasing her back in college but he couldn't remember a time when she *ever* got woozy. Susie was 32, brunette, and miss-goody-two-shoes. Where Kira had a bit of a wild streak in her, Susie was all no-nonsense. She hated Spaz and hated when he called her Susie.

Susie, Susie, Susie, Spaz told the photo. The interface replied that the command was invalid. He needed to reprogram it to have a sense of humor.

"Excuse me, Mr. Barnes?" A flight attendant was staring at Spaz. "We need all electronic devices turned off or put in plane-safe mode for take-off."

It took Spaz a few seconds to look up. He had already forgotten his identity. What was it again? Jeremy Barnes from Chicago.

Not that his current identity really mattered to him. It might matter to Jeremy though — once he got the bill.

Spaz muttered something noncommittal and put the palm in plane-safe. He took the headset off and stared out the window. The transmissions might interfere with the plane's communications and even if they didn't, he didn't want to draw any more attention to himself than he already had, ordering first class seats off Jeremy's platinum American Express.

It was probably best he was no longer online. If the werewolves had found Lizard and shut him down, they'd be looking for him. Then again, it might not be werewolves after all, but the stiks from the FBI. Regardless, it paid to lay low for a while, at least until the FBI stiks or wolves moved on. There were plenty of other targets out there besides him.

His mind drifted back to Kira again. Now that his operative within Intermountain had turned wolf, he needed another. He had one backdoor — all good spiders did, when the shit hit the proverbial fan — but he wasn't sure if it could be trusted. Intermountain was a lynchpin for the Forest, and at the moment his operative was leaving it open. But for how long?

That was where Kira and Susie came in.

They were working right in the Forest, only Spaz would bet they hadn't noticed. Kira might, if she found something non-sequitur with the network, but that was Cathal Murphy's department and Spaz doubted Cathal would let her sniff around. Still, the computer layout probably looked a little strange, and Kira might question it — or might simply think it was one of the myriad bad attempts by an inept administrator to maintain job security.

Spaz wondered how much of a stik Kira had become. Susie was a stik and it was bound to rub off, but Kira was no doubt a spider at heart. All Spaz had to do was play to Kira's curiosity.

In the meantime, he had gotten a piss-ant job at a cybercafé called *Axioms*. The pay wasn't much more than minimum wage, but it gave him a good enough cover that no one would question unless they looked closely. But that was the role of a spider — you crawled between the cracks and spun your little webs, and for the most part were unseen and unnoticed. You didn't do much damage, either.

He sat back and ordered a scotch straight up, snaked the iPod into his ears and turned on some tunes and relaxed in the first class seat. It was going to be a long trip and he'd have a lot of work once he got to Denver.

3

The apartment doorbell buzzed. Kira closed her eyes and leaned back in her chair. She rubbed her eyes after having stared at the screen for so long. Her arm twinged — it was still painful from the mauling. The stitches were out and she was wearing a soft cast, but the pins would always remain in place. No doubt, she would set off metal detectors at airports from now on.

"Coming!" Kira grumbled as she glanced once more at the Denver Post jobsite. Today had been a new experience for her. She had received a phone call from Intermountain Telecom, telling her that her services as a contractor were no longer required. She filed for unemployment online and posted her resume on Monster.com. All-in-all, a new experience.

Kira peered through the security peephole and saw a man standing outside. He had black hair and was wearing dark clothes. A salesman? she wondered. "I'm not interested!" she called through the door.

"Ma'am, I'm Detective Walking Bear of the Denver police," he called back.

Kira unlocked and cracked the door, still keeping the security chain on. "Walking Bear?" she asked in amusement as she peered out. No sooner had the words left her lips than she regretted them. Before her stood a man of about thirty with short black hair and dark eyes. His skin was the color of the sun-baked Arizona sand and his face and body were that of a warrior. Sharp-chiseled jaw — beardless, of course — with a strong nose, high cheekbones, and moderately arched brow, Kira could imagine this man riding a horse and hunting buffalo more than she could picture him riding in a police cruiser. He held out his Denver police badge for her to inspect. "I'm sorry, you're Native American," she said lamely.

A slight smile played across his lips. "May I come in? I'd like to get a statement from you."

"Certainly," Kira said, unlocking the chain on the door. "I'm sorry — I haven't been in good form lately — I'm still on painkillers."

The detective glanced around the apartment and Kira grimaced. Kira and Susan had rented a small apartment in LoDo (the fashionable term for lower downtown Denver). Empty Dominoes Pizza boxes still sat on the coffee table next to the brown couch (covered with newspapers) and the orange peel beef takeout from P.F. Chang's from two nights ago was adding its aroma from the kitchen counter.

Kira nudged the pile of ubiquitous O'Reilly books with her toe to try to make room for the officer to come in and almost toppled the book pile near the door. *TCP/IP Network Administration* and *Firewalls* went skittering into a stack of *UNIX Systems Administration Today*. "I'm sorry — I'm not much of a housekeeper."

"It's okay," Walking Bear said, carefully picking his way among the landmines of spare computer parts, books, and computer printouts. "You've been recuperating."

Kira met his gaze as she cleared off the couch with her good arm. "Yeah, I should keep the sling so I've got that excuse when guests come by." She paused. "You want coffee?"

The detective smiled and sat down on the only clear spot on the couch. "No, I'm fine."

"So, you want to talk about the wolf?" Kira asked. She poured a mug of dark roasted coffee into a Dilbert mug, ignoring the growing biological experiment in her sink, and walked back into the living room. "The officer who took my statement said that it was a wolf or something."

"That's what we think," said Walking Bear. "A wolf or wolf-hybrid of some sort. I was hoping you'd have more information, being the only one who has survived these attacks."

"Attacks?" Kira repeated. She carefully balanced the Dilbert mug on top of the pizza boxes and shoved some papers on the floor from the chair. "Oh, hey! There's that board," she muttered. She held up a circuit board wrapped in a silver anti-static bag and tears welled up in her eyes. "Susan was big into Sun UltraSparcs — she was going to replace the motherboard in her Sun 'cause it was kind of flaky." She set it down. "I guess she won't be needing it." She turned her head and blinked away the tears. "I'm sorry, I can't believe she's gone."

The detective shifted uncomfortably. "I'm sorry your friend died, but we believe that whoever was responsible for your attack has been responsible for the others."

"There were others?" She took a swig of the coffee. It had been sitting too long in the pot and tasted burnt.

"I thought the police put it down as a wolf-hybrid attack," Kira said.

"That's what they say," he said evenly. "But there have been four attacks in the past six months. You're the only one who survived."

Kira ran her left finger along her jaw line. Bruises still marked where the stitches had been. "Four?"

"At least four that we could see a pattern in."

"And you didn't do anything about it?"

The detective hesitated. "That's what we're doing now. Who do you know that owns a wolf or wolf-hybrid?"

Kira stared at him for a moment. Did he think *she* had something to do with all this? "No one."

"What about Ms. Baker?"

"Susan came with me from So-Cal. I don't think she knew anyone except me and the people we worked with."

A silence ensued as the detective took notes on a white pad of paper. He looked up expectantly. "Is that all?"

"What more can I say?" Kira tasted the coffee again and found it just as bitter. Those dark eyes continued to stare at her; unnerving her. Why was he making her feel so uncomfortable? Wasn't *she* the victim? This wasn't her fault — it couldn't be. Maybe he was trying to get her to admit that they shouldn't have gone down that alley. Okay, maybe they shouldn't have — but that wasn't the point, was it? Who'd expect a wolf to attack?

"Why were you out so late?"

"Ten-thirty on a Friday isn't late." She snorted in disgust. "Unless you believe they should roll up the sidewalks after six."

"Seems a little odd you'd be working so late."

"Look, we were fixing the systems at Intermountain, okay? We're admins, okay? We have weird hours. It was ten-thirty and we were hungry and made a dash to the mall. Some wolf-thing attacked us. There's nothing more than that!"

Another silence ensued and Kira realized she had stood up and was yelling. She fell silent and felt the tears well in her eyes again. She dropped back in the chair.

"Easy, ma'am," the detective said, meeting her gaze. He had the darkest eyes Kira had ever seen. Kira took a deep breath. "I'm not accusing you of anything," he continued. "I simply want to get a full description, that's all." He stood up. "We'll talk more in a few days. In the meantime, here's my card — if you remember anything."

He handed her his card and picked his way through the piles of computer printouts, books, and parts. "I'll call you in a few days." He let himself out and Kira locked the door behind him. She stared at the mess and then returned to her computer.

Kira sighed and shuddered as she tried to find a place on her desk to put the detective's card without it getting lost. Her outburst must have been due to the pain and the painkillers, she decided. She didn't usually have a hair-trigger temper, but there had been something in the way Detective Walking Bear had asked the questions. She glanced at his card. Sergeant James Walking Bear. James. She wondered if he went by "Jim." She pulled a piece of tape from a dispenser and taped the card below the 20-inch monitor.

Kira's computer was a PC running Red Hat Linux. She glanced at the table next to it, and at Susan's old UltraSparc. Susan hated PCs — said they were works of the devil — and insisted on a Sun. Kira hadn't been quite as picky but chose a less standard operating system. Kira and Susan had networked the computers together and were running a T-1 link to the network off of the Intermountain Telecom backbone. Her mailbox indicated new mail, so she flopped down in the chair and double-clicked the icon.

Two new messages and spam. Kira opened the spam and smirked — Mrs. Jewel Taylor was offering her Liberian husband's bank account of 15 million dollars to be shared, of course, with to whom it may concern for just a bank account number. Kira noted the address, tracked it through the headers and found it came from an address she hadn't blocked yet. Too bad she no longer worked at Intermountain — their customers could benefit from the blocking.

The next message was from *bmarks@intermtntel.com.* She opened the message:

I cleaned up your desk—come by and pick up your stuff. Bob.

Kira grimaced. Not even, "Sorry you lost your job." Not "Hahahaha! Bitch!" Nothing.

"Asshole," Kira muttered as she deleted it. It was just like Bob to be unfeeling and uncaring.

She paused at the last message. The subject was blank and it held a curious address: *wolfbane@den-wolfpack.com.* Rather than dismissing it as spam, she opened it. A chill ran down her spine as she read the message:

WATCH YOUR BACK AND STAY INDOORS ON FULL MOONS.

Kira caught her breath and shivered. Pinpricks ran along her injured arm where the wolf's teeth had torn in.

Kira found herself trembling as she stared at the message. Watch Your Back And Stay Indoors On Full Moons. What sick bastard would email her that? Somebody who knew that she had been attacked a month ago? Someone who knew her email address?

She looked at the email address again.

Wolfbane@den-wolfpack.com was the sender and the recipient was the same. A classic setup for spammers. Looking at the IP addresses, Kira could tell that the address was forged. She recognized a few of the paths coming from Intermountain Telecom, but that was no surprise. As an ISP — Internet Service Provider — they owned a piece of the Internet backbone. The mail could have come from anywhere.

She let the mouse hover over the delete button on her mail browser, but then changed her mind and saved the message to a folder. She didn't feel like tracing it right now and she had more important things to do. Namely, find a job.

She entered the website address for Dominoes Pizza online and ordered a medium with pepperoni and mushrooms before returning to the Denver Post website. Entering a few choice keywords, Kira looked for a UNIX Systems Administrator job.

"Shit." Three ads from last Sunday popped up on the screen. One was an ad with a post office box; the other was an ad for "bettering one's career." The third required Oracle database and PeopleSoft — two skills Kira didn't have. A buzz in the intercom broke her from her reverie. Dominoes arrived and Kira left to pay for the pizza.

"It's time," said Alaric softly to himself as he stood in the doorway and looked into the nights sky. He could feel the pull of the moon — as he had for countless years before. Each year — each tens of years, each century — made him more resistant to its power. But its power still held sway over him. Inevitably, he could not resist the call of Hecate.

Hecate, Diana, Artemis, Luna, Selene, Chandra — the goddess went by thousands of names, both known and unknown to Normals. But she was also a he — Mani, Thoth, Mah, Sin — and countless other male names as well. Not even Alaric knew all the names.

According to the legends handed down from werewolf to werewolf over generations, it was Artemis who first granted the wolf his sentience. At the time, Alaric's people called the moon Mani — a male god — and yet, Alaric had always thought of the deity as a she. Fickle, the goddess changed with the days, exerting her pull on the oceans and those who had come from them so long ago.

A curse to some and a power to others, being a shapeshifter had been his life for as many moons as he could remember. The goddess had given him power — great power — and yet that power came with a price. Whether he chose to or not, he had to become a wolf when Hecate danced full overhead.

Alaric felt a pang of guilt as he remembered that there was one who would change this night for the first time. He had not caught the murderer that night, and had only had hints of his whereabouts since. The girl would not know what had happened to her and would be alone tonight. He had to find her first.

A lone howl echoed through the canyons of Denver. They were no longer canyons of sage and scrub, but of concrete, glass, and steel. How far was this from his homeland? He closed his eyes and tried to remember the smell of the sea; its bitter tang in his mouth. He let the transformation take him.

Alaric had done it countless times before. He couldn't remember the last time the transmutation actually hurt him. Maybe it never had. He could feel certain bones elongating and others shortening. His skin grew fur as his nose and mouth lengthened and became a snout. When he was done, he was in his wolf form.

A howl issued from his throat and he trotted into the back alley and into the street. He had to find the girl before the murderer found her and finished the job.

I t was nearly midnight when Kira glanced at the clock on the computer screen. She yawned and stretched. Her job search had uncovered nothing new in the Denver area and California looked even worse for systems administrators. Outsourcing was a dirty word to computer professionals. The computer jobs were going offshore to other countries where similar work could be had for thousands less. As she stared at the screen, everything started to blur. Her arm was prickling, and it felt as though her eyes wouldn't stay open. *I'm tired,* Kira decided. She stumbled into the bedroom and collapsed on the bed. She felt groggy — not quite asleep, but not awake either.

As Kira lay there, she thought she heard a howl from a wolf. Again, she shivered. *This is a dream,* she told herself. *The windows are closed and the door is locked. There are no wolves here.*

The thought, however, gave her no comfort. In her dream, she began to worry and she stood up and went to the front door. She checked the door and found it difficult to unlock it, remove the chain, or grasp the doorknob. Her fingers were growing stubby and unresponsive. *This is a dream,* she thought, *Why would my fingers be stubby?* As she moved, through the airlock and down the stairwell, her clothes fell away from her. With a last attempt at the front door, she was out on the street, looking up at the midnight sky.

Kira stared at the moon overhead. It was full — as bright as the Intermountain Telecom and Qwest signs that ruled the skies over downtown Denver. She raised her head and a lone howl issued from her throat. Kira stopped and blinked.

Looking down, she saw her legs were no longer human. They were gangly long things with big spread paws and black curved nails. Gray fur ran down her legs and changed to white as it met the wrists and the paws. They were the legs of a dog — or a wolf. She counted her toes — four, not five. She looked back at her body and saw a gray canine form with agouti fur and a plume tail. The back legs were canine too.

Kira gasped and a very canine whine escaped her lips. *Damn that cop!* she thought. *He's giving me nightmares about wolves again.* Her dreams after the attack had been about wolves, but they had been about wolves attacking her. Never about herself becoming a wolf.

Kira looked back up at the moon. Her throat tightened and a small, mournful howl escaped her lips. Kira sat on the sidewalk. Whatever this dream was, she wanted to wake up. She heard another howl. Involuntarily, a howl burbled up in her throat. It seemed to convey the misery she was feeling at losing her best friend, her job, and being unemployed.

The answering howl relayed a message. *Come here, I want to meet you.*

Kira hesitated. *This is a dream,* she reminded herself. *I can't die.* She stood up and trotted toward 16th Street. The businesses and apartments that lined Wazee Street were extraordinarily quiet. The homeless Kira were used to seeing along the streets had disappeared with the ghostly sentinel overhead. She walked silently, her paw pads making no noise on the cold concrete beneath her feet.

She halted at 16th Street and looked south. She could see the sign for the LoDo Tattered Cover Bookstore and her mouth watered as her sensitive nose picked up the wafting aromas of the Mongolian Barbeque and Mexican restaurants nearby. She paused and slunk into a nearby alleyway as she heard bar patrons come out of one of the establishments, chattering loudly. Two women and two men stopped to talk outside. Kira watched in fascination.

Something cold and wet pressed against her cheek. She jumped away and yipped in surprise, nearly leaping out into the street again. She turned and saw another wolf looking at her. A large gray male wolf.

A wolf! Kira froze in terror. The brute was huge by her reckoning, with those terrifying yellow eyes and gray agouti fur. She wanted to back up and run, but there was nowhere else to go. If she ran to the people, they would think she was a wolf and would run away, or they would call the cops, who would kill her.

You're new, the wolf said.

Kira yipped in fear and ran down the alleyway, trying to get away.

The wolf loped beside her. *It's okay,* he said. *I didn't mean to startle you.*

This is a hell of a dream, Kira thought. She wanted to wake up. *Wake up; I've got to wake up!*

It's not a dream — you're here with us.

Kira shook her head. *No, this is a dream.* She turned, leaving the gray wolf dumbfounded. He began to follow her.

Say, don't I know you?

I don't think so, Kira replied. *Not unless you bit me.*

You're Kira Walker — the girl who got bit by a rogue wolf, the wolf replied.

Fine, whatever.

Alpha wants to meet you. He sidled up to her and tried to sniff her.

Kira snarled and the wolf backed off. *Leave me alone! Go away!* When was she going to wake up? Not only was this a wolf, but he was a rude pest as well. Kira wanted to wake up and find herself in her own bed. Maybe if she tried thinking about something else the dream would go that direction.

The wolf flashed a smiled and lowered his head. *As you wish.*

Kira trotted deeper into the alleyway that separated 15th and 16th Streets. She noticed that her newfound acquaintance was following her, but she ignored him. As she walked down the alleyway, she found that she could see well even though it was night. The acrid smells of oil, garbage, and dirt filled her nostrils as she strode through the alley. Popping out on 15th Street, she noted it was nearly deserted and started toward Blake Street. The strange wolf dogged her every move.

This is not real, she reminded herself. *There is no wolf. I'm safe in bed.* Maybe this dream needed her to confront it.

Kira turned around snarling. *I said, go away!*

The strange wolf lowered his head beneath hers and cocked it slightly to the side, exposing a small portion of his neck. His tongue darted between his teeth, licking her lower jaw and he raised his paw as if in supplication. Kira snarled and swatted him in the head. Instead of fighting, he allowed her to flip him over and continued to lick her chin.

Kira was disgusted. The fawning, the lip licking, the apparent lack of pride was revolting and she snarled louder and bit into his neck. He whimpered but licked her muzzle.

Is he bothering you?

Kira looked up to see a large male black wolf standing a few feet away. She caught her breath. Never before had she seen such a magnificent animal. He was nearly twice her size and his sleek, black coat glistened in the moonlight. His golden eyes seemed to penetrate her very being. He was powerful. Even with the thick coat, she could see the muscle ripple underneath.

Even in her fear, Kira would appreciate the wolf. As terrified as she ought to be, the black wolf was strangely enticing. She could sense the unbridled power the black wolf held and yet, as she looked on him, found she was no longer afraid.

The other male wolf lay at her feet, whimpering and forgotten. Kira had released him in her surprise. When she remembered to breathe, Kira looked down at him in disgust.

He's a pest; nothing more.

The black wolf nodded. *Come with me.*

Kira stepped over the prone wolf without looking. The black wolf grinned and took off. Kira hesitated and for a moment looked back at the wolf lying on the ground, still looking up at her in adoration.

Come on! she heard the black wolf say.

Kira ran north, following the black wolf toward Commons Park. At first, it felt strange to run on all fours, and yet, as she ran, she found herself stretching out into a full lope. She hardly touched the sidewalks beneath her as she followed the black wolf to the park. Once her feet touched the grass, she howled in delight. The black wolf stopped. She could see by the light of the moon the impish grin on his face. He nipped at her neck and took off with her following.

Kira laughed as she chased him around the park; her laugher came out as throaty growls and yips of delight. He was faster than she could imagine, but he was just as quick to let her catch him and soon she was it in a merry game of tag. When at last they were both out of breath, she lay down and he flopped down beside her. Kira nipped at his legs and he rolled over and let her wrestle with him a while. Soon, their energy was spent and Kira lay beside him as they both panted.

Now that she had a chance to look around, she saw other wolves in the park. Most were lying in the grass, but a few were playing or investigating something on the ground. There were small makeshift shacks down near the Platte River where some homeless men camped. Kira noted that the wolves didn't approach them.

The black wolf nuzzled her affectionately and then sniffed the air. The lights of the city drowned out the starry sky, but Kira could see the pale glow in the east. The moon was beginning its trek across the western sky toward the Rocky Mountains.

It'll soon be light, he said. *You'd better go back.*

Go back? Kira asked. *You mean that I'll wake up?*

The black wolf considered her. *This is your first time — as a wolf, I mean,* he added when he caught her sharp look.

This is my first dream of being a wolf, she replied.

A gleam shone in the black wolf's eyes as he appeared to consider something. Kira cocked her ear toward him, but he made a very human-like gesture, shaking his head as though discounting the thought. *Go home, Kira,* he said. *I will see you again soon, I believe.*

Go home? she repeated.

The black wolf snuffed the air. *You don't have much time — not until you learn to control it. Go home.*

Kira stood up and for a moment was about to argue. Then, she got up and trotted off without a word. Dreams were like that, she decided. She followed 15th Street back to Wazee. Turning onto Wazee, she saw the first glimmer of the sun's rays as it crested the eastern horizon, turning the buildings a rosy pink with its light. She passed a group of street workers preparing to work on a small patch of Wazee.

Kira looked at the doors to her apartment complex, wondering how she was going to open them. It was at that moment that she started to shiver from the early morning cool breeze.

"Whoo-whoo-whoo-whoo!" one of the road workers shouted. "Nice ass!"

"Let's see your tits!"

Kira turned to see the road workers gawking and whistling at her. She looked down at her arm and saw pink skin prickled with goose bumps. She was no longer the wolf in her dream, but human. Kira was standing at the door to her apartment complex — completely naked.

Alaric paused as he watched the sun crest the lower buildings of downtown, changing the skyline to a pinkish-orange. It was time to return to human form, and yet, at the moment, he had no desire to. His mind was on the gray wolf he had spent the evening with.

Besotted, came a voice.

Alaric turned to see a small gray wolf standing not far from him. *Isn't that a bit archaic, Megan?*

Megan laughed—the laughter coming out as a series of yips. *Perhaps, but I haven't seen you so taken with a bitch*—she paused—*ever. The term suits you well, Alaric.*

She's the girl who just got bit, isn't she?

Yes, Megan said.

Find her, he said. *I want to meet her in human form.*

Megan nodded. *I think she's one of Trevor's tenants. It'd be his job to talk to her.*

Trevor? He hesitated. *Can he handle it?*

Maybe, but I doubt it. She might hit him—I know I would. I'll go bring her in. She turned to leave.

Oh, and Megan? he asked.

The wolf bitch paused. *Yes?*

Be discreet.

"Shit!" Kira yanked open the main door. The men had dropped their tools and were whistling and shouting at her. She slammed the heavy door. Even it couldn't silence the catcalls.

"Heya, Hot mama! You want some?"

"Come on, baby! I'll show you a good time!"

Trevor. Trevor, Kira thought. Yes, that was the name of her creepy landlord. She stared at the buttons but her eyes wouldn't focus. "Damn! Damn! Damn!" she shouted at them. There was no Trevor listed. Of course, he wouldn't be listed under his first name, but his last. What in the hell was it? She glanced out of the side panel windows and saw that men were approaching. The main door had no lock, allowing anyone entry into the airlock.

Kira punched a button. The name said Smith. "Answer!" she whispered in panic as she glanced outside. The men were almost at the door. She looked down and saw a wedge — used to prop open the door — and shoved it between the door and the weatherstrip. She prayed that it would hold.

One of the workmen pushed on the door. It cracked open, but the wedge held. He was a big man with a potbelly and had scraggy, unshaven black stubble. The undershirt he was wearing beneath the flannel shirt was gray from sweat. He smiled at her with broken teeth stained yellow from too much chewing tobacco as he got a good view. "Heya sweetie!" he grinned.

Kira smacked the door and slammed it shut.

"Hello?" came a sleepy voice from the intercom.

"I lost my keys. This is Kira Walker in apartment two-twelve. Can you let me in?"

"You need to talk to Trevor about that."

The intercom went dead.

"Fuck!" Kira shouted. Now there were several men trying

to push open the door. She shoved hard against the door, not expecting to hold them back, but the wedge bit in and held. Kira punched the button again. "Trevor, who?" she shouted.

She heard no reply. "Asshole." Then, suddenly she saw a button on the panel that said *Manager*. She hit the button.

Nothing. The door inched open and Yellow Teeth got a meaty paw through. Kira screamed and threw herself against the door. The door slammed forward and Kira heard a sickening snap. Yellow Teeth screamed as his arm went limp and flopped at a bizarre angle.

"Gawddamn bitch!" the man bellowed.

"Hello?" said the intercom.

"Trevor, it's Kira Walker," Kira shrieked. "Let me in! Let me in! I left my keys!"

"Hold on," Trevor's voice said. "I'll meet you at your apartment."

The door buzzed.

Kira leapt to the second door and sprinted through, slamming it behind her. She didn't care what the workmen were doing now. She leapt up the stairs two at a time. When she got to her apartment door, she found her clothes on the floor. "Thank God," she whispered and shimmied into them.

"Hey Kira!"

Kira turned and saw Trevor as he walked up the stairs. *Creepy*, she thought immediately. He had gold eyes and spiked gold hair. He had dyed the ends fuchsia and had multiple earrings in both ears, and a nose ring. His torn sweatshirt and sweatpants sported the logo of *The Grey Wolf Bar*. She hardly expected someone pushing forty to look like this. He was still barefoot, as if just getting up.

"You know what that's all about?" he asked, pointing with his thumb over his shoulder back toward the front door. "Some road workers are saying some naked bitch broke this guy's arm."

Kira found herself shaking. "I don't know what you're talking about." She sounded steadier than she felt.

Trevor considered her with those inscrutable yellow eyes as if pondering something. He shook his head. "I told 'em to get lost before I called the cops." He stepped up to the door and sorted through the multiple keys on his ring before pulling the right one out and inserting it in the lock. "So, out for a moonlit stroll, eh?" he asked. His eyes glinted with amusement.

"What is that supposed to mean?" Kira demanded. Did he know what happened? Did he see her naked?

Trevor smirked. "Hey, no growling. Since you're new at this, you might want to take a look in the mirror sometime. Let me know if you figure it out."

Kira stared at him for a moment. "Thanks," she muttered and slid into her apartment.

"Hey, if you want, I'll leave a spare..." Trevor began.

Kira slammed the door.

"Or not," she heard Trevor mutter as he left.

7

Kira stared at her apartment. It was much as she had left it last night before going to bed. The pizza boxes were still on the coffee table; the newspapers were still on the couch. The piles of sysadmin books were still next to the computer magazines. Her computer's screen saver — various pictures of the mountains and extreme sports — was still cycling. Only the dead Chinese food had changed, and was stinking up the apartment even more.

Kira shivered and closed her eyes. What had happened was weird — too weird. She had heard about people sleepwalking, but she had never done it. What was really creepy was that she had dreamt she was a wolf. A wolf! How strange was that? What would Freud say? What would *any* shrink say?

The next door neighbors' TV was blaring and broke her from her reverie — it sounded like cartoons. Funny; the neighbors were normally quiet. Kira walked over to her computer and moved the mouse to check the time — it was six-thirty. She frowned. Christ, didn't these people know how early it was? Kira decided that she'd have to complain to Trevor.

Trevor — *there* was a creep. It wasn't just his hair or nose ring or multiple earrings. Hell, she wouldn't give a second glance to tattoos, either. It was those stare-straight-through-you gold eyes. She had seen those eyes before, but she couldn't place them.

What in the hell was Trevor's last name? Something simple. Like Smith or Brown. It was then Kira noticed the icon flashing on her computer saying that she had email and one voicemail.

She clicked on the voicemail icon and turned up the volume on her speakers.

"Hi Kira!" came her mother's voice. "Your dad and I are calling from Peru — sorry we missed you. The Egyptian grant fell through, so we're excavating some Inca ruins instead. I'll contact you later this month. Love you!"

Kira smiled at the voice. "You don't even know, do you?" she said to the voice. It was probably best. The last thing she needed right now was her parents flying back from Macchu Piccu or wherever they were to wring their hands over her. That was one small blessing, having parents who were archaeologists and who also eschewed cell phones (and most technology, like email). At the same time, if the wolf had killed her, it probably would have been a month or more before her parents had found out.

How odd was it that their daughter was technologically savvy when they were practically Luddites? Kira grinned at that. She listened to the phone message again; this time hearing the background nuances. She could pick up a low rumble of chatter and occasional roar from traffic. *A payphone?* she wondered. *Maybe in a market.*

Kira sat in the chair and double clicked the message to listen to it again and again. She closed her eyes as she listened to her mom's voice and realized how tired and lonely she was. Without a job and without Susan, Denver was just another fucking dot-com bust town.

Maybe I should get a pet, Kira thought. Or maybe she should just move out. But where to? Susan had wanted to go back to So-Cal, but the jobs just weren't there for those who amounted to white-collar migrant workers. She had some savings — all good contractors did — but the cost of LoDo wasn't exactly cheap.

Maybe it was time to go through her PDA's address book and pull in some favors. If anyone could help her right now. The high-tech market was shit.

She stared at the houseplant in the corner with its thick bulbous leaves and stem. It was Susan's. Susan's family had claimed most everything of hers, leaving the second bedroom empty, but had left the plant in the corner. What the hell was it? Something Jade. Kira was surprised Susan had bought it, but she had felt the apartment needed brightening up. It was ugly and Kira would have gotten rid of it, except that it had been Susan's. Kira felt as though she'd be disrespecting the dead if she threw it out now.

Kira stood up, stretched, and walked into the kitchen. There wasn't anything edible in the fridge, so she opened the cupboard and pulled out the box of double fudge Poptarts. She shook the empty box and opened it to find a single empty silver wrapper, and sighed. The coffee can was empty, too. She'd have to go to the local coffee shop for breakfast.

Instead, Kira went into the bathroom and turned on the shower. Her feet were black from asphalt. As she scrubbed herself down, she tried to remember the wolf dream again. Why would she dream that she was a wolf? And why would she sleepwalk? She guessed that maybe that officer's questions brought it on. After all, Detective Walking Bear hadn't been very pleasant, even if he was kind of cute.

Kira leaned against the shower wall and carefully scrubbed one foot and then the other. She was amazed how much she stank of city — the oil, grime, dirt, and exhaust. She relaxed a bit under the hot water and then washed her hair. Odd, she'd never noticed how much she smelled of the city before. She stepped out of the shower and dried herself. As the bathroom fan took away the steam, she stared at her body in the mirror.

Kira had been working out, but she hadn't really noticed how muscular she had become. Her biceps and triceps were well defined and her muscles rippled along her legs. Funny, she didn't remember being this cut from the workouts. She admitted ruefully that she had given the road workers quite an eyeful today.

As more of the steam dissipated, she stared at her face. Her blue eyes were now gold.

8

Brass eyes. Wolf eyes.

"Shit," Kira said. She stared at them. They were a light gold color, almost amber. And definitely not human. She tried to laugh it off. Maybe she needed to see an optometrist or something.

Since you're new at this, you might want to take a look in the mirror sometime, that creep Trevor had said. He had gold eyes just like hers. Did he know something about this that she didn't? A chill ran up her spine and she shuddered.

Maybe this was some bizarre thing that altitude did to you, she wondered. After all, she was a mile high in elevation. She had heard of altitude sickness even this low. She sure had felt the altitude when she moved here. Even now, she was still trying to get used to it. Maybe it changed your eye color or something.

There had to be a logical explanation.

Kira dried her hair and threw on jeans and a sweatshirt. She tied her wet hair back and spent a few minutes looking for her apartment keys, finally finding them buried under a stack of printouts, and slid her wallet in her back pocket. She'd talk with Trevor before getting a coffee and a scone, she decided.

Kira left her apartment and walked down to the first floor. If she remembered correctly, Trevor lived in the first apartment on the right past the door. Kira frowned as she approached it. In her panic, she'd forgotten he was there — she could've just looked him up under his apartment number.

"Stupid, stupid, stupid," she muttered and knocked on the door. She was doing a lot of stupid things lately. Walking through dark alleys, sleepwalking naked, living in LoDo without a job, to name a few.

"Yeah, hold on." Trevor's voice came from somewhere inside. Kira fidgeted.

Trevor opened the door and sighed. "Oh, it's you." He was still in his torn t-shirt and sweatpants. Still barefoot, too, but now holding a mug of hot, frothy coffee. "Want a latte?"

"No, thanks," Kira said. "You know what's been going on, don't you?"

A gleam entered his eyes, but he shook his head. "What in the hell are you talking about, Kira?"

"My eyes! You said to look in the mirror sometime and I saw them. What in the hell is happening to me?"

"Inside!" Trevor said, pulling the door back so she could enter. The shades were dark over the windows. The walls were filled with metallic bookshelves and the black leather couch had a metal frame as well. Dark, Kira thought. And spooky, too. There was a dark sword mounted on the wall near the kitchen, not far from the metallic table. A movie poster for *The Wolf Man* with Lon Chaney Jr. hung over the couch.

Kira frowned. She didn't find it at all comforting. "Why have my eyes turned this color? Why do I have dreams about being a wolf? What's going on here?"

Trevor ran his hand nervously through his blonde hair. "Why did it have to be me?" he muttered. "Look, Kira, I think you'd better sit down."

"I'd rather stand."

"Okay." He sipped the latte nervously. "Are you sure? I mean, it might be better if you sat..."

"I'm fine!"

Trevor winced. "Okay, no growling. Look, Kira, you're one of us now."

"Us?" Kira looked at him and then glanced at the apartment. "What, Goths?"

Trevor laughed nervously. "Nah, the Goths sort of followed our lead. I mean, if you saw a bunch of us, you might think we're Goths, but we're not."

Kira felt her temper rise. "What in the hell are you babbling about?"

"Well, it's not that easy to explain."

"All right, what's happening?" She crossed her arms.

"Welcome to the pack, bitch."

Kira's mouth dropped open. Without even thinking, she felt her fist close and she swung hard. Knuckles impacted nose. Trevor yelped and fell backward; blood spurting everywhere. His latte flew from his hands and splattered across the carpet. Kira turned on her heels and marched out, slamming the door behind her.

"Goddamn bitch!" she heard him yell. "I should've left you to rot with those road workers!"

Kira ran down the hall and out the door. What was she thinking? She stared at the blood on her knuckles. She could smell the acrid copper reek from it. Odd, she'd never noticed the smell of blood until recently.

But today had been a day of firsts. First sleepwalking; then breaking a guy's arm. Then discovering her gold eyes. And now hitting Trevor. She'd never hit anyone before — not even Bob. She smiled slightly. It *felt* good. It really did. So what if she got evicted? She was tired of this fucking town anyway.

Kira stepped out of the building and saw that the road workers were still patching part of the section across the street. She did a quick turn and ran in the opposite direction. Her face began to burn as she heard the catcalls.

"Damn, I've got to move," she muttered. Between Trevor and the road workers, she decided that she'd look for another place in

Denver. She stared up at the crystal blue sky. The sun was warm as it shone above the buildings in LoDo. She walked up Wazee Street toward 15th Street. If she recalled correctly, there was a coffee shop on the corner. As she walked, her head spun with everything that happened — the dream, Trevor, the sleepwalking, the black wolf—too much to think about before her first cup of coffee. *"Welcome to the pack, bitch,"* Trevor had said. What in the hell did *that* mean?

As she walked, the sound of footsteps broke her from her reverie. She turned sharply and looked around, but found herself alone. Still, something prickled the hairs on the back of her neck and for a moment, she thought she caught motion out of the corner of her eye. She took a few steps backwards. Had one of the creepy road workers followed her?

As she continued to walk toward toward the coffee shop, she peered into the alleyways. She saw a few homeless men, huddled by a Dumpster and sleeping off the night's booze. She hurried by as one man looked up at her with gold eyes and snuffed the air. She shivered and ran to the coffee house and opened the door.

The warm scent of java was overpowering and downright heady as she walked into the Uncommon Grounds. The coffee shop was typical for LoDo, with tables arranged for patrons and a bar along the wall and storefront. Shelves of coffee and tea were available for sale along the back where the baristas worked. Kira had been to the Uncommon Grounds twice before. It was a free wireless Hot Spot, which meant geeks with laptops could plug into the wireless network and surf the Internet or conduct business or whatever. It hooked into the main Intermountain wireless connection and had a separate broadcast that anyone within range of the coffee shop could hook into. Kira generally eschewed Hot Spots only because her work was so heavy in security and the Hot Spots were unsecured networks. She'd also have to set up web pages that allowed her access — something she was loath to do at any company. Giving people a backdoor on the Internet just never seemed a good idea, even if all the executroids thought it was great for business.

But now, she felt comfortable here. There were plenty of geeks with laptops, appropriately wired on coffee and unwired with equipment. She took another big breath and let the aroma pound her sinuses.

Man, you could get high just hanging out in a place like this, Kira thought. She got in the line of people waiting to be served. They had pastries, too, and Kira had already decided on a cinnamon scone and a Brazilian mocha latte with a double shot. She paid for the coffee and waited in the line for the barista to make her drink.

The barista was a small man with short-cropped hair, two earrings, and a tattoo on his cheek of a Celtic knot. He was growing his beard out, Kira noticed, no doubt trying to hide the tattoo now that he was in his twenties.

"Here's your Brazilian mocha latte double shot," he said and met her gaze with brass-colored eyes.

Kira caught her breath and stared at him. He grinned and winked at her, setting the cup down. When she recovered her voice, he was already busy mixing another coffee and another barista — a kid with red hair, still in his teens — pushed another drink on the bar. "Large mocha cappuccino. Large Brazilian mocha latte with a double shot!" A businessman jostled forward and scooped up the cappuccino, bumping into Kira. Kira glared and he sidled away. She picked up her coffee and headed over to an empty table. Maybe when the guy was less busy, she'd be able to ask him about his eyes...

Kira sipped the coffee, nibbled the scone, and closed her eyes. As she did, she found she could pick out snatches of conversation. Geek conversation, to be sure.

"I can't wait to get our network on IP6 — I've got a couple of Cisco routers that are bitchin'..."

"Microsoft's due out with the new Windows. We're the beta..."

"You try SNMP with Linux yet?"

The bells attached to the coffee shop door tinkled and Kira

opened her eyes to see a blonde woman enter the shop. Kira cocked a quizzical eyebrow at her. She was about Kira's age or a little younger — about the same build, as well — wearing what looked like aqua scrubs as though she'd come from a hospital or clinic. Freckles splashed across her fair skin. But what was startling was that the woman had golden eyes.

Her eyes met Kira's and she made her way over to Kira's table. She sat down opposite Kira. Kira stared at her.

"You're Kira Walker, aren't you? You're the girl who got bit by the lycanthrope last month," she said.

W ho the hell are you?" demanded Kira. She looked at the woman skeptically. The scrubs she wore suggested a hospital. Maybe she was an escapee from a mental ward. Just my luck, Kira thought. I'm being followed by a nut case.

"Alpha sent me as backup — he told me you're alone. Trevor was supposed to tell you, but Trevor is an idiot. I told Alpha that, but Alpha said that Trevor knew you and it'd be easier if he told you," the woman chattered.

"Whoa! Slow down!" Kira said. The girl was babbling excitedly about nonsense. "What in the hell is an Alpha? What's Trevor supposed to tell me?"

"Trevor didn't tell you?"

"Tell me what? He called me a bitch and I punched him in the face."

The woman grinned. "Good for you! I've been wanting to do that for some time, myself. Anyway, kiddo, I've got some news for you. You're a werewolf."

Kira felt the coffee cup slip from her hands, but caught it before it spilled. "I'm a — what?"

"A werewolf — a lycanthrope. Someone who can shape-shift between human and wolf," she said. "By the way, I'm Megan

Olson. I'm a Beta female of the Denver wolf pack."

Kira smothered a laugh. Was this woman serious? She tried to look for a hint of a joke, but the woman looked earnest. "Are you Trevor's girlfriend?"

"Oh heavens no!" Megan said. "He's gay, you know."

"No, I didn't," Kira said. "Did he send you after me to play this joke?"

"This isn't a joke, Kira. A member of the rogue pack attacked you and your friend. You somehow survived — you're the first victim to have done so. Unfortunately, it's left you lycanthrope. Alpha's been trying to find the rogue pack for a long while. You're his first lead — you're the only one who's gotten a good look at one of them."

Kira wrapped up the half-eaten scone. "You're nuts," she said. The conversation had taken away her appetite. She wanted to get far away from this gold-eyed woman. "Good-bye." She picked up her coffee, stood up, and walked out.

Kira didn't bother to look back, but she knew Megan was following. "Leave me alone!" she shouted at the woman.

"Don't be an idiot, Kira." Megan paused. "Listen, I can prove everything."

Kira turned around. "How?"

"Wait — follow me," Megan walked to the nearby alleyway. The homeless men were gone and they were quite alone. "Turn around."

"Why?" Kira asked.

Megan blushed. "Well, I really hate undressing in front of people..."

"That's it!" Kira said. She turned and ran out of the alley. *Weirdos*, she thought. *It's time to move from Denver.*

The street was still deserted — it was still too early for the normal traffic. Kira took a gulp of her now lukewarm latte and felt something touch her leg. She nearly shrieked as she turned and saw a wolf walking beside her.

It's okay, it's me, Megan, the wolf said.

"Oh my God!" Kira gasped. She started backing up. Another wolf! She felt the panic well up in her throat. She felt as if she was going to lose what little breakfast she had. "I'm going crazy — I know I am!"

No, you're not, the wolf said. *I know it's quite a shock, but I'm a lycanthrope too.*

"You're a werewolf?"

Yeah.

Kira blinked. "I can hear you?"

We're telepathic when talking to other lycanthropes, the wolf said. *You can understand any canine.*

Kira's head spun and she felt herself sinking to the curb. The package with the scone and the coffee cup slipped from her hands. "I'm crazy," she said out loud. "I'm certifiably nuts."

She felt a warm tongue lick her ear and instinctively she buried her head into the wolf's thick neck fur.

You're not crazy, the wolf said. *This is just a shock. I'm so sorry you had to get the news like this. If Trevor had been doing his job...*

Kira found she was crying. She snuffled once. "But why? Why is this happening?"

"Lady, you okay?"

Kira looked up bleary-eyed to see a man in a suit standing a few feet away. She rubbed her eyes and looked at the man. A typical businessman, he could have come from any of the businesses that were just outside LoDo. She forced a smile. "Yeah, I think so," she lied. How could she explain she was going crazy? "I tripped while walking my...dog," she said, glancing at the wolf. The wolf seemed to nod.

"Can you stand up?" he asked, offering his hand.

She took it and hoisted herself up, then pretended to test her ankle. "Yeah, I can. Thanks."

"Do you need help walking?"

"No, I'll be okay, thanks."

"Okay, well, be careful," he said and headed toward Uncommon Grounds.

Kira looked down at her "dog." The wolf's ears were flattened and she licked Kira's hand in a very submissive gesture.

I'd like to get my clothes, the wolf said. *Then, we go to see Alpha.*

"Alpha?"

Alpha wants to talk to you. You're the only survivor from the rogue wolf attacks.

They returned to the alleyway and the wolf asked Kira to keep watch as she changed back. Kira wanted to peek — to see the actual transformation — but she guessed that Megan was far too prudish and she respected the woman's privacy.

"Okay," said Megan, as she emerged from the alleyway. "I know this is weird. You'll get used it in time. Let's go find Alpha. He's waiting for you."

"Is... he... far away?"

"Nah, just a few blocks down Blake Street. He runs a pub there." She took a few steps and looked at Kira quizzically. "Are you coming?"

Kira sighed and looked down at the gutter where her spilled coffee and half-eaten scone lay. Her stomach rumbled, despite feeling topsy-turvy.

"You know, Felan makes a mean bacon and eggs at the pub," Megan remarked. "I might be able to coax him to whip some up for you."

Kira met the woman's gaze and nodded. "All right, I'll play your game for a bit. Lead on."

Megan nodded and headed toward 16th Street. She began

chatting with Kira like they were old friends. "I know it's tough when you first find out. Alpha says it's tougher on the Normals than the rest of the pack. It's a big enough shock growing up and changing with the moon, but to get bitten...You wouldn't believe what I thought when I first became a lycanthrope."

Kira saw some passers-by glance at them oddly as they walked. It appeared Megan was oblivious, or just didn't care. "A lycanthrope?" Kira repeated.

"Werewolf," Megan said. "You know—like a werewolf? The word comes from Latin or Greek. It means 'werewolf' but it sounds much more sophisticated to say 'lycanthrope,' don't you think so?"

Kira scrunched up her nose. Here she was having a conversation about werewolves just as casually as if she was talking about the number of processors in her new server. "So, you weren't always a... a..."

"Werewolf?" Megan finished her sentence. "Heavens no! I'm a vet."

"Vet?"

"Veterinarian. I got bit by one of my patients. Damn Charlie thought he was being cute when he nailed me good. Of course, I deserved it, trying to suture him after a dogfight without any anesthesia. Deserved what I got, he says."

"Charlie?" Kira repeated. "Another werewolf?"

"Yeah, cheap-ass wolf too," Megan smirked. "Didn't want to pay for human medical. He says he trusts veterinary care more. So, he shows up at my doorstep in wolf form looking forlorn. I must've had 'sucker' written on my forehead, 'cause I took him in, even though he's a wolf and all..."

"Owning a wolf is illegal in Denver," Kira said.

Megan grinned. "Yeah, well so is owning a Pit Bull. People do it anyway. You got to catch them. But they're not illegal in Colorado except Boulder and of course, Denver." She paused. "So, he nailed me. Wanna see my scar?"

"No," Kira said, shaking her head.

"Nah, it's not bad — not as bad as yours. Just on my wrist — see?" She pulled back her shirtsleeve to expose her wrist with two scars from puncture wounds. "Hurt like the dickens — but not as bad as yours, I suspect."

Kira stared at her. "I suspect not."

"Imagine my surprise when I changed into a wolf on the next full moon. Just absolutely stunned. But there's been an upside. I can understand my canine patients now."

Kira snorted. "That would be useful."

"It's handy for the profession," Megan confessed. "I can just ask the dogs how they're feeling." She paused. "Look, I know you don't quite believe me yet, but there are some things you should know about yourself."

"Like what?"

"You're stronger now. Really strong. Your hearing is way better and your sense of smell is beyond anything human."

"That's ridiculous!"

"Is it?" Megan asked. "Are you sure? How do you feel today? Last night was the first full moon since you were bit."

"What does that have to do with anything?"

"It has everything to do with it. See, you don't fully become lycanthrope until the first full moon after you've been bit by a werewolf. So, do you feel different?"

Kira opened her mouth to speak but then shut it again. Her eyes *had* changed color since last night. She had accidentally broken that man's arm. She had punched her landlord out. Come to think of it, she had noticed the stench of the city on her, the television playing next door, and the overpowering aroma of Uncommon Grounds.

"Uh huh," Megan said with a wry smile. "You're lycanthrope."

Kira stopped and closed her eyes. "Shit. You mean I'm going to go running around on all fours, howling, and attacking and eating people when the moon's full?"

"Well, the running around on all fours is pretty likely. Howling is up to you. And unless you're rogue, you're not likely to attack and eat people, either. Monkey is nasty meat." She chuckled as if she'd just made a joke.

"What do you mean?"

Megan grinned. "You can control this — like I can. Alpha can help you do that."

"Can Alpha also tell me who the son of a bitch was who bit me and killed my best friend?"

The woman winced. "Yeah, maybe. But Kira, there are some useful things about being lycanthrope too. You can't be killed except with silver weapons while in lycanthrope form."

"A silver bullet through the heart?"

"Yeah, something like that. Silver is poisonous to us. I had a really cool collection of Navaho jewelry I had to give away when I became lycanthrope." She paused and tugged on Kira's arm. "Come on, let's get moving." They headed to the cross street and turned onto Blake. "We're hoping you might be able to identify the wolf."

They walked a block and stopped at the entrance to a pub called *The Grey Wolf*. Kira recognized the sign from Trevor's shirt. The building was gray stone with green painted doors and lintels. The stairwell that led downstairs to the pub was only marked by the howling wolf sign above it.

Kira hesitated. "It looks closed."

"It's not," Megan said. "But before we go in there, there's something you need to know."

"What?"

"Pack rules." She stared into Kira's eyes in earnest. "This isn't a democracy, Kira. There's the Alpha Male and Alpha Female that lead the wolf pack. Every wolf has his or her place in the pack. New members are usually a cause for disruption. You'll probably have to prove to a few where your place is."

"I don't give a shit about werewolf politics," Kira remarked. "I want to know who the bastard is who killed my friend."

Megan withdrew slightly. A glimmer of something — respect? — shone in her eyes. "Okay, I know that. Listen,

Alpha's name is Alaric Kerr. He's a good pack leader, as pack leaders go. He also wants to find out who killed your friend and bring him to justice. Pack justice."

"You said there were two Alphas — a male and a female."

"The Denver pack doesn't have a female Alpha. Not yet." Megan gave Kira an odd look before walking down the steps.

11

Kira followed Megan down the steps and felt as though she had been transported back in time. The pub looked like something Kira would have expected to see somewhere around the 1880s. The walls, floor, and furniture were all made from well-oiled white oak and pine. The bar had an ebony top and brass foot rails and the ceiling was real tin. It was dark and smoky here from pipes, cigars and cigarettes. She looked at the walls and saw that game trophies were mounted on the walls: elk, bison, deer and moose.

But more interesting was the clientele. Although it was morning, a large number of patrons had already gathered. An eclectic mix filled the room. Some, Kira guessed, were bikers but many more looked as though they held day jobs. Many were computer hacks, but some were students, business people and workers from various classes.

As Kira followed Megan in, she became self-conscious as she realized all eyes had turned on her. Gold eyes, brass eyes, yellow eyes — all glinted in the dim faux candle light.

"Heya, Meg!" said the bartender behind the counter. He was a large man who could have doubled as a bouncer. His sandy hair was long and tied back in a ponytail and he wore a white apron over his t-shirt and jeans. His forearms sported tattoos with wolves on them. "Found a new whelp?"

"Whelp?" said Kira. The term didn't sit right with her and she suspected she was being insulted.

"Easy, Felan," said Megan. "This is Kira."

"Kira Walker?" Felan asked, his gold eyes focusing on Kira. "The girl the rogue bit?"

"Yeah, the same," Megan said.

A low rumble issued from the throat of one of the blond biker men. He had been sitting at the bar drinking what looked like a Pina Colada. *A little early in the day*, Kira thought.

But the fancy drink was the only thing frilly about him. He looked like something out of a barbarian raid, with long blond hair, braided into unruly locks, wearing black leather that Kira suspected cost a small fortune. He was a big man and his smile was cold; he flashed his canines at them. "You know the rules for bringing in a monkey."

"Bite me, Cathal," Megan snapped. "She's one of us now."

"Perhaps," said Cathal as he stood up and loomed over the two women. The smell of the alcohol on his breath was overpowering. "But I'm not particularly fond of wolf-bait." He smiled again, showing his canines.

Kira was both frightened and angry. She could see Megan stiffening at the words. Kira wasn't quite sure was the epithets meant, but she could guess. A big brute like Cathal could easily smash her face in with one meaty paw. "You're an asshole," she snarled at him, "and I don't like your tone. Didn't your bitch of a mother ever teach you manners?"

One of the werewolves at the bar stood up and glared at Cathal. He was a big man with a mustache and goatee and short cropped hair who loomed over the other werewolf. Much to Kira's surprise, he wore a kilt. "Ladies, you've got a problem?"

"Easy, Mike," Megan muttered. "We don't want trouble."

Cathal's eyes glowed in anger for a brief moment, and then he laughed. The tension broke and the other werewolves laughed, too — a harsh, grating noise that gave Kira no comfort. Kira glanced at Megan, who visibly relaxed.

"She's a feisty bitch, Meg," he said. "You better take her on back to see Alpha. He's been waiting for her."

Megan nodded and turned to Felan. "After we get done with Alpha, can you whip us up some eggs and sausage, Fel? Neither of us had any breakfast."

Felan nodded and Megan grasped Kira's hand. "Come on, we're going to Alaric before any of these thugs decide to pick on you further," she whispered.

"Who was the guy that stood up for us?" Kira said, glancing behind.

"That was Mike Fowlkes, he's sort of a cousin of mine from Missoula visiting."

"Cousin? I thought you were bit..."

"We were bit by the same werewolf." Megan pulled her along.

Kira stared at the biker bitches in the corner, who displayed their teeth at her. Did all the werewolves have tattoos? Even the geeks seemed to. "Tough crowd," she muttered.

"Yeah, stay away from Cathal Murphy — he'll rip your throat out," Megan said.

Kira glanced back at the blond biker. She didn't think Megan was joking for a moment. "Who is he?" she whispered.

"Alaric's second-in-command," Megan said, leading her through the crowded hall and toward a back room. "He's leader of the Commerce City pack, but they're all under the Denver pack leader. It's no secret he wants Alaric's position."

"I'll remember that," Kira said.

Megan led her down the hall and stopped at the door. "Before we go in, you better know something about Alpha..."

"What?" Kira asked, her eyes narrowed. So far, she was becoming less and less impressed with this little community and her stomach was grumbling from lack of food. Perhaps at one time, she might have been nervous to stand toe-to-toe with a biker like Cathal, but she was getting tired of it all rapidly.

Getting mauled by a wolf, getting fired, waking up naked outside, breaking some guy's arm, and now being told she was a werewolf could have that effect on a person, she supposed. "Is there some sort of secret handshake or something? Do we howl at the moon, sniff butts, or what?"

Megan hesitated. "Well, maybe you just need to meet him." She pushed open the door and waited. "That's Alpha."

Kira walked in. In the back room, there was a pool table where a couple of men and a woman were playing billiards. One of the men was short and a bit stocky with short brown hair and glasses. She guessed him to be in his early twenties. He was lining up the cue ball behind the six ball and aiming it for the side pocket. The woman was blonde and about the same age. She was slightly overweight and a bit dumpy, in a dress that was a few seasons out of fashion.

But what made Kira halt in her tracks was the only man whom she could imagine deserving the name "Alpha." Alaric Kerr was the most handsome man Kira had ever met.

If a man was born to be king, Alaric Kerr had to be such a person, Kira thought. Tall, lean, and muscular, Alaric looked as though he had stepped from some earlier time — an anachronism that didn't quite mesh with the twenty-first century. Dark hair with a hint of gray along the temples, a strong jaw line, and chiseled features, Kira wondered if there was something to this lycanthrope thing. She had been working too long among geeks. He met her stare with his own steady brass gaze.

The other two lycanthropes stopped the game and looked up to see Kira standing in the doorway agape. Megan coughed nervously, but Kira ignored her. "So, you're Alpha?" Kira said when she finally found her voice.

"I am," Alaric said in a clear baritone that nearly melted her. He glanced at Megan and Kira followed his gaze to note that Megan immediately looked down when he looked at her. "Thank you for bringing her; you're dismissed."

The other two lycanthropes glanced at each other, put down their cues, and followed Megan out, leaving Alaric alone with Kira. "You're wondering why I summoned you."

"You didn't summon me," Kira snapped. "I came because I've had a lot of strange things happen to me lately..."

"One which involves turning into a wolf."

"One which involves *a dream* where I turned into a wolf," Kira corrected.

"Still in denial?" Alaric asked. "That's very dangerous, especially when the wolf who bit you is still at large."

Kira shivered slightly, but still met his gaze. "All right then, what is happening to me?"

A slight smile played across Alaric's lips. "You are a bold one — as bold in human form as you are in wolf."

"What's that supposed to mean?"

"Nothing," said Alaric, but the smile did not dim as he walked over to the bar and strode behind it. "Something to drink?"

"Not this early — unless it's coffee." Kira eyed him warily as he pulled a carafe and two mugs from the bar and poured some steaming hot liquid in them. Kira's nose twitched involuntarily. Coffee — and from what she could tell, of a South American blend — maybe Columbian.

"Hot coffee — you take cream or sugar?" he asked as he brought the mug over. Kira shook her head and hesitated as she took the mug from him. "Sit down," he said, gesturing to a table. "Don't worry, my dear, it's not poisonous. If I had wanted to harm you, don't you think I already would have?"

Kira considered his words and tasted the coffee. She sat at the small table across from him and looked into those inscrutable gold eyes. "Dark, rich roast. Columbian?"

"Your nose probably told you that already," Alaric said, taking a sip of his own. "But I suspect that you've already noticed your senses have sharpened. That happens when you go *were* — or so I've been told."

"You've been told? You mean you don't know what it's like?" Kira looked into those brass eyes again. "But you're a werewolf."

"Yes, I was born this way from werewolf parents. I've never been a... Normal."

"You mean a 'monkey.'"

Alaric raised an eyebrow. "So, you've heard that term already."

"Cathal was kind enough to introduce it to me."

His eyes narrowed. "I'll have a talk with him. He knows better."

"I don't think he does and I don't think he cares," Kira remarked. "I'd be more careful whom I chose for second-in-command. That one will bite you."

Alaric chuckled. "I suppose that's true. But you're not here to talk about my choice in officers, are you?"

"No, I'm here to find out what I can do about this."

"About what?"

"Turning into a wolf— assuming I can."

Alaric cocked his head.

Was this guy dense? Kira wondered. "How do I stop being a werewolf?"

Alaric chuckled. "You don't."

"I don't?"

"No, once you're a werewolf, you're a werewolf forever," he said. "You can't simply take a potion and cure the lycanthropy."

"I don't believe that," said Kira. "It's like a disease."

"A disease with no known cure." Alaric paused and took another gulp of coffee. "But that's not why I brought you here..."

"That's why I *am* here," she snapped. "Otherwise this is pointless." She stood up to leave, but something in Alaric's eyes made her sit down again. Something urgent. "Okay, I'll listen to what you have to say and then I've got to go."

"Fair enough," Alaric said. "The wolf who bit you is still at large. He knows you're alive and you're the only one who can identify him."

She snorted. "He looked like a wolf. Big and gray with yellow eyes."

"A gray wolf, male," Alaric said. "Big?"

Kira thought back. The flash of teeth; the yellow eyes. "I don't know — it looked big in the alleyway." She paused. "It was dark."

"As big as a German Shepherd?"

"Bigger — I think."

Alaric sighed.

"Look, I'm just guessing. It happened so fast." She set the mug down. "Why? What is all this about? Why do they care about me?"

"Because the rogue wolves mean to start a war between lycanthrope and Normals — and they've chosen Denver to make their stand," Alaric said. "If you can identify one of them, it might expose them."

"A war?" Kira snorted. "But most of the Normals don't even know you guys exist, much less care about you. Werewolves are something you watch on the old movie channels with hokey makeup and bad special effects — they're not real to most of the people in Denver."

"I know — and the rogue pack is suicidal if they think that they can take on the Normals. But there's been one rogue wolf — or maybe several — who thinks that maybe if he shows the others that the Normals can be killed and the Normals don't do anything, that it will bring all the lycanthropes into the war."

"That's insane."

Alaric nodded. "That's why I've tried to keep the enclave here in Denver a secret. Werewolves have had a hard time of it in the past. If people find out about us, we could be persecuted again."

Kira finished her coffee and stood up. "Well, it sounds like you have your hands full."

Alaric stood up, too. "You're leaving?" His voice betrayed his puzzlement and dismay.

"Yeah, I'm leaving," Kira said. "This is too weird, even for me."

"You're lycanthrope now. You can't just leave," Alaric said.

"Yeah? Well, just watch me," she said. She halted as Alaric grasped her arm. "Let go. I want no part of this," she said, her voice lowering to a sinister growl as she met Alaric's gaze.

"No, Kira. You're part of this, whether or not you want to be. You became part of this after a lycanthrope bit you, like it or not."

Kira stared into his gold eyes and tried to suppress the shiver running down her spine. "I don't care."

"Don't you want to find out who killed your friend?"

That stung. Kira removed her arm from his grasp. "Yeah, I do. But I'll find out without *your* help."

13

S paz stood at the front desk of Intermountain Telecom. The building's lobby was typically ominous with black marble walls and chrome and black furniture. Too bad the company couldn't afford something tasteful. He was now staring at a very bored security guard.

"She's not here?" Spaz repeated.

"You deaf or something?" the guard said and went back to playing FreeCell solitaire on the computer.

"Did you check the name Kira Walker?"

"Yes." He didn't bother looking up.

"She's not an employee."

"No, she's not," the guard agreed.

"She's a contractor," Spaz said, exasperation creeping into his voice.

"Look, Buddy, we don't differentiate between employees and contractors in the list. If she's here, she's on the list. If she doesn't work here, she ain't here."

Spaz stared at the man. "Could you call IT Operations?"

The man looked up, vaguely interested. "Who in IT Operations?"

"The secretary?"

"There's no secretary." He clicked on a card and moved it to another stack.

"An administrative assistant, maybe?"

"IT doesn't have one."

Spaz stared for a moment at the guard. "Do you have someone who could tell me when she worked here?"

"If she wasn't an employee, no."

Spaz gave up. He turned around and walked out of the building and into the hot sunshine. "Fucking moron," he said.

Now he was stuck in Denver without a contact. Or rather, with a contact he didn't want to deal with. He was pretty certain Murphy had turned wolf, and that was dangerous. He couldn't risk what little link he had to the Forest to contact Murphy.

A cool breeze was blowing through downtown and he closed his eyes to feel the sun on his face. Damn it, he thought. If he didn't find Kira soon, he might have to give in to the wolves. Or worse — to the FBI stiks.

Well, there wasn't much to do now except to go back to his piss-ant job and pretend to work — at least until another idea presented itself. Spaz walked back to *Axioms*, on the corner of Welton and the 16th Street Mall. He walked into the cybercafé, moved the mouse around a bit on the computer to look like he was doing work, and ordered a latte.

It would be a shame to waste such a beautiful day on work, Spaz decided. He was in Denver, at least — maybe he might be able to find someone else who could give him access. Hell, he might get his own access if he could get them to hire him on. Spaz chuckled at that thought. If he could steal the right identity, maybe he could. Anything was possible, but at this time, it didn't seem probable.

What seemed less probable was Kira walking right up to *Axioms* and ordering a cup of very expensive coffee. That's why he couldn't believe it when he saw Kira walking down the street toward his cybercafé.

Kira walked out of *The Grey Wolf* without breakfast and without Megan tailing. Alaric had escorted her out, like a gentleman. *A gentleman who got a little hairy when the moon was full, ripped people's throats out, and howled at the moon*, she thought blandly. If she hadn't seen Megan's transformation and heard the werewolf in her head, Kira probably wouldn't have believed it. She passed by two more gold-eyed people as she rounded the corner.

Was everyone in this fucking town lycanthrope?

Her stomach growled and Kira realized she hadn't eaten anything. She wasn't far from Market Street where she could pick up the shuttle to the 16th Street Mall. She could grab something on 16th Street and get to Intermountain Telecom and pick up her stuff from Bob Marks.

The air was starting to warm up as she boarded the nearly empty shuttle at one end of the mall. She road the bus up to Welton and got off, not paying much attention to the people around her. Once on the 16th Street Mall, she looked around. Business people were scurrying here and there, most with cell phones attached to their ears. A couple of teenagers sat against the wall of the CD store with pink and green dyed hair, reminding her of Trevor. The girl wore a miniskirt and a leather dog collar; the boy wore an expensive leather jacket. They were huddled over something Kira guessed was a stolen PDA and were downloading porn. Or running up somebody's credit card bill. Hell, there were enough hot spots in this town where they might have piggybacked onto someone's transmission or pulled the credit card numbers off an unsecured feed. They could even have been using Intermountain's wireless. That jacket looked mighty expensive.

Kira sighed and headed toward *Axioms*, a small cybercafé on the corner. They were probably tapping into the cybercafé's wireless, for all she knew. But she wasn't an Internet cop, damn it, and it wasn't her place.

"Heya — Kira, is that you?"

Kira turned around. A brown-skinned man with oriental eyes

grinned at her. He wore horn-rimmed glasses (complete with cellophane tape at the nose bridge), a plaid shirt which hung loose over a slash-dot shirt and faded khaki dockers. He carried a PDA in one hand and a latte in the other.

"Will?" she said incredulously. She blinked at the programmer. "I haven't seen you since MIT!"

"Spaz," he corrected her. "That's my nick, you know. I go by Spaz now."

"Spaz?" She found herself grinning, in spite of herself. "Spaz? Isn't that a little cyberpunk?"

"Well, yeah," Spaz said. He stared at her. "What's with your eyes?"

"Medical condition. Doc says it's nothing," she lied.

"Bullshit," he said. "I've never heard of any medical condition that does that. I read WebMD, you know."

"Fuck off," Kira said laughing. "So, what brings you to this hellhole?"

He pushed a thumb toward *Axioms*. "They want a secure wireless, so they contacted a network hacker. Seems some leeches have been piggybacking on their domain." He glanced at the kids with the PDA. One looked up and stared at him defiantly before looking down at the PDA. "Makes me want to beat the snot out of those motherfuckers. They're giving us spiders a bad name."

"I'm going that way to get some breakfast," Kira said. "Join me?"

"Sure, why not? My tab," Spaz said, walking beside her. He glanced sideways. "Besides they don't charge me since I patched their main security leak."

"Cool beans," Kira remarked as they walked into *Axioms*. "When did you get here?"

"A couple of weeks ago — heard you were working for the Evil Empire."

"Intermountain? Yeah. But *were* is operative here."

"Oh shit. Cancelled your contract?"

"Let's talk about something else," Kira said, gazing at the menu above the barista. "I can order anything?"

"Yeah," he said. "Order what you like."

Kira ordered another scone and a latte. They sat down together and Spaz considered her thoughtfully. "You know, you might get something here — they could use an admin."

"What — Windows?"

"Yeah."

Kira shook her head. "Nah, I do UNIX, you know that." She started nibbling on the scone. Blueberry, and very tasty.

"What about Susie? She get knocked off or is she still with the Evil Empire?"

A lump filled Kira's throat and she nearly choked on the piece of scone in her mouth. She forced it down and looked away, blinking back the hot tears. "I should go now." Kira stood up.

"No, wait." Spaz sucked in a bit of air and laid his hand on hers. "What happened?" When she didn't answer, he continued. "Christ, Kira — we've known each other since MIT."

"Yeah, I know," Kira said. She sat back down and looked him in the eyes. "Susan's dead."

"Dead?"

"Yeah, you hear about the wolf attacks?"

"Yeah, I heard that some girls got...shit." Spaz looked down. "Christ, I didn't know it was you."

"You probably wouldn't have, since you've been here only two weeks. We got attacked a month ago."

"Shit." An uneasy silence fell between them. "And they canned you?"

"Yeah."

"Assholes."

"I want to go back to So-Cal," Kira said. "Know anyone?"

"Could ask in the IRC, but not off-hand." He ran his hand across his face and pushed the glasses back on the bridge of his nose. Another silence ensued.

"When are you getting Lasix?" Kira asked with a wry grin.

"Had it done two years ago. Glasses complete the image," he replied. "Look, I could get you something here. Maybe a webadmin."

"It wouldn't pay enough."

"Better than unemployment."

Kira shrugged. "Got to go get my stuff. See you around. Got a card?"

"Yeah," Spaz said. He fished out a crumpled card from his pocket. "Got a pen?"

Kira held up both hands in a gesture to show she didn't.

Spaz smirked. He got up, went to the counter and came back brandishing a pen. He scribbled an email address on the back of the card. "Okay, I've moved to *Axioms* address, but you can still try gmail or yahoo, or any of the others. Look for Spaz."

Kira glanced at the email addresses. There were five other addresses including addresses from throwaway accounts. "But the *Axioms* address is the one you're using now for the moment."

"Yeah, but I check the others occasionally."

"Why don't you just forward them to one POP3 server?"

"Kira, Kira, you're so unimaginative — they're my spam collectors."

"You really should put your real name on the cards."

"Why? Everyone knows me as Spaz."

"Yeah, right." Kira pocketed the card. "I'll see you around."

"Meet me on the IRC," Spaz said. "What's your nick?"

"Don't have one," Kira said. "But I'll think of something. Got to run. Thanks for the breakfast."

Spaz grinned. "Anytime."

Kira walked out of *Axioms* and stared up at the looming Intermountain Telecom building. She dreaded what she had to do next.

T<i>he Evil Empire.</i> Kira smirked as she walked toward the Intermountain office. It loomed over the Qwest building like a black nemesis beside the silver skyscraper. It was just a few years back when Intermountain had risen in the telecom world, driving several telecom companies into bankruptcy with their predatory practices. Her hacker friends, like Spaz, were horrified to learn that Susan and she had gone to work for "the enemy." Kira fully expected that the IRC would be abuzz over the news that she got canned.

Served her right, she supposed. She walked up to the black tinted glass and walked through the turnstile. Kira halted and took a breath. The black marble walls and floors were set off by chrome trim. The security guards were sitting at the desk behind black marble station, not even paying attention to her as she walked up to them. Kira knew she'd be able to get past them, but beyond that, everything was card-keyed and she knew they weren't so inept that they wouldn't have cancelled her by now.

Instead, she walked up to the desk.

The security guard didn't bother looking up from his terminal. Kira guessed he was playing solitaire. He pushed the clipboard toward her. "Sign in. Who are you seeing?" he asked in a bored tone.

Kira eyed him. Typical rent-a-cop. He was no more than twenty, by the looks of him. This was his first real job outside of fast food joints, no doubt. His hair was slicked back and he was already developing a paunch from doughnuts. His badge said Joseph Smith. "I'm here to see Bob Marks. I'm Kira Walker." She signed in and pushed the board toward him.

The security guard picked up the handset and dialed. After a few words, he looked up. "He'll be down in a bit." He gestured to the black leather chairs. "Have a seat."

Kira sat in a chair and stared at the ceiling. Funny, she never noticed the hanging art above her. She wondered how many thousands of dollars Intermountain had paid for it, when they could've paid her for a few more months instead. She had heard that the boardroom, where contractors weren't allowed, was made of rosewood and had million-dollar paintings. What little she knew of the company told her they couldn't afford it.

Kira sighed. How in the hell was she going to get back to So-Cal? Her mind wandered back to Alaric and his lycanthropes. *And his nut cases*, she corrected herself. What was she thinking? That there really *were* werewolves? That was one for the shrink — once she could afford a shrink. This was some elaborate hoax and these sick people must have been taking advantage of her vulnerable state. After all, she had been attacked by a wolf — most likely someone's illegal pet — and had her best friend die. She had been under stress lately — no work and lack of money would make anyone edgy and cause them to sleepwalk.

"Kira?"

Bob's hateful voice jolted her out of her thoughts. Kira stood up to see Bob Marks approaching, carrying a box. He moved with the confidence of a man who had gotten his way once too often, Kira noted with disgust. It was a swagger, she decided. Even carrying the box which contained her few possessions, he managed to swagger. Not that he wasn't unattractive — tall, dark brown hair, wide brown eyes, chiseled features — he looked like he worked out daily at the athletic club across the street. She caught a whiff of something familiar — a musky type of cologne.

No, he was downright handsome, Kira decided. Only his attitude made him ugly. Bob knew he had won and he was enjoying every moment.

He flashed a perfect smile, showing straight rows of white teeth. "Hi Kira! How's it going?" He set the box on the other chair.

Kira forced a smile and suspected it looked more like a wolf's snarl than an actual grin. "Fine, Bob. Glad you could take the time to bring my stuff down yourself." Her words sounded syrupy-sweet to her ears and she almost flinched as she heard them.

He took a moment to appraise how she looked, raking his eyes down her muscular build and back up to her face. "Wow, I didn't expect you to be looking so good after..."

Kira blanched and then caught herself. "After the attack?" she finished coldly. "Yeah, well, I've had time in physical therapy and I've been working out."

"Well, the time off has done good," Bob said with a slow smile. "Guess you'll be getting more of it, huh? Any job prospects?"

"Lots," Kira lied. "I've got a friend at Qwest who told me to put in a resume."

Bob straightened up. "Really, who with?"

Shit. Kira realized she made a mistake. Bob probably knew the managers at Qwest. "You wouldn't know them. They're in Dublin, Ohio."

"I might," Bob said. "I know the folks in Omaha."

A lump stuck in Kira's throat. "That's nice," she said brusquely. "Anyway, they may be looking to fill an internal position. They haven't been advertising."

"Hmm," Bob said with a half smile and Kira felt her face turn red. She turned to the box. "Is this my stuff?"

"Yeah — and I put Susan's stuff in there too. I figured you'd know where it goes," Bob said.

Bastard, she thought. *Didn't bother to contact the contract house for phone numbers or addresses.* "Thanks, I'll see to it her parents get it."

Kira bent over and scooped up the box when she felt a soft tap at her elbow. She turned to see Bob right beside her, so close that his musky cologne was almost overpowering. She almost dropped the box, but he caught it. "Let me help you with that," he said as he looked into her eyes.

Kira felt wobbly and unsure. She hated him and yet so close, she could feel her body react to him. "I'm fine," she said in a voice that was stronger than she felt.

"No, you're not," he said, his voice almost a husky whisper. "You're alone now, and frightened. I know. A lot has been going on and you need someone to depend on now."

Kira stared into his dark brown eyes and felt herself melt, as though she could fall endlessly into them. With a force of will, she blinked and forced herself to take a breath. "You have rocks in your head," she snapped and avoided his gaze.

"Do I?" he said softly. "I don't think so." He straightened up slightly and let Kira pull the box from his hands. "Go out with me?"

Kira nearly dropped the box. "What?"

"Will you go out with me?"

Kira stared at him speechlessly. She tried to shake her head. "You're kidding, right?"

"No, I'm not," Bob said. "I'm dead serious. Let's do lunch tomorrow. Maybe noon?"

"Bob, I can't," Kira said. "I have things to do then."

"Like what?" Bob asked. "More important than getting your old job back?"

Kira stared. "That's blackmail."

"It's just lunch," Bob said. "I'll buy. *Maggianos*. You like Italian, don't you?"

"Yeah, I do. But Bob, I don't..."

"Noon," he said with a half smile. He turned and walked past the guard station toward the elevators. "I'll meet you right here at noon."

He left Kira staring after him as the doors to the elevators closed.

"Asshole," Kira said.

Kira trudged out of Intermountain Telecom with the box cradled in her arms. Once or twice, she nearly threw the box, contents and all, against the walls of a building as she walked back to the 16th Street Mall. The nerve of Bob asking her out and then suggesting it was a way to get her job back!

Bob was handsome, yes. Even attractive. But she hated what was beyond the good looks. Deep down, Bob was about as misogynist as a man could get without showing outright hatred. He thought that women were best in the kitchen and not at a computer terminal. And he had been so certain that she would show up tomorrow at noon.

If she wanted her job back.

Kira clenched her teeth as a strangled groan escaped from her lips. She stopped walking and was about to hurl the box with its contents against the wall of the athletic club when two women walked out, chatting merrily. They halted as Kira glared at them.

"What are you looking at?" Kira snarled. She was almost pleased with their shocked expressions as they scuttled away. Kira looked down at the box in her arms — she was practically squeezing the box apart. Instead, she turned and walked to the bus stop along the Mall and waited.

The bus ride did nothing to cool her temper. As she sat, she found herself thinking about Alaric Kerr. Now, *he* was handsome, if a little crazy. And he wasn't an asshole like Bob Marks. She had told him that she wanted out, and he had simply escorted her out. No threats. Nothing. She could almost fall in love with a guy like that.

Kira snorted. Where in the hell had that thought come from? She had known a long time ago that being in computers meant dating geeks and social rejects and had pretty much avoided any kind of relationship after college. The job came first and had a tendency of ending any real relationships. After all, when you were a white-collar migrant worker like she was, you went where the job was. Her last relationship had been five years before with a guy named Darrell. A nice enough guy, even if he was an NT admin, but when their contracts were up, he went to Phoenix and she went to Santa Cruz. She had purposely lost his email address.

Maybe she still had his card.

"Next stop, Market Street Station," the voice on the loudspeaker intoned. Kira picked up her box from the seat beside her and jostled her way to the front. It was going to be a long, annoying walk back.

Kira stepped off the bus. On the way toward her apartment she saw an elderly woman standing at the curb. The old woman was obviously homeless, with a tattered old coat that was some color between brown and gray. She wore a faded flower bandana over her head, covering her unruly wisps of gray hair. As she leaned heavily on a cane, she held a coffee can in her right hand with coins in it.

Kira set down the box and fumbled in her pockets for money. She found only a couple of quarters. "Sorry, ma'am, I don't have more than this." She put the quarters in the can with an anemic clink.

The old woman looked into Kira's eyes and Kira was surprised at how blue they were. She smiled at Kira. "Don't deny what you have come to be," the old woman said.

Kira stared at the woman. "What do you mean?"

The old woman smiled wanly. "You know, Light Walker. You deny what you are, but in that which you have become, you will find strength."

"How do you know my name?" Kira asked sharply.

The roar of the next bus announced its approach, and Kira turned to see it coming a little too close to the sidewalk. She skittered out of the way as the bus passed dangerously close to the curb. When Kira turned back, the old woman was gone.

Kira looked down at her bedraggled box. Between the jostling and walking with it, it was looking as though it might not hold up long. She picked it up carefully. *Just to the apartment,* she told it silently.

As she walked, she felt very odd. The woman knew who she was. Maybe she had seen Kira's photo in the paper as the victim of the wolf attack, but Kira doubted it. Still, she knew Kira's last name. And that "Kira" meant light.

Kira paused at the apartment door, stepped into the airlock, and fumbled for the keys in her pocket. The old woman was no doubt just some crazy lady; Kira dismissed her words as the ramblings of a person on the street. Still, Kira couldn't get them out of her mind — did the old woman know that Kira was a lycanthrope?

Kira laughed to herself. She had let those crazy people talk her into believing she actually was a werewolf. She unlocked her apartment and opened the door, and the stench of rotting food overpowered her.

Kira almost gagged, but instead walked in. Funny, she hadn't noticed it before today. No doubt Alaric or Megan would blame her lycanthrope senses, she thought wryly as she pitched the old boxes full of rotting food into the garbage. Well, she thought, tying the garbage bag up, maybe being a werewolf would make her neater. She was sure her mom would approve.

After cleaning up the apartment, Kira dug through the freezer and found a half pound of Starbuck's Vienna Roast that had been Susan's. Before long, she was back at the computer with a hot cup of java, wondering what to do next.

She opened the odd message from wolfbane@den-wolfpack.
com and stared at it. Whoever sent her the message knew her, and
knew a wolf had bitten her. *Or a werewolf*, she conceded. Getting
her email address wasn't too terribly hard — Kira knew she could
be Googled and found through her blog or her webpage. Maybe
the sender was Alaric or Megan — they seemed the most likely
suspects, appearing out of nowhere — but something told her
that they weren't.

Instead, she surfed over to the Denver Post's website and
started to search the back issues, only to find she needed an
account and a credit card payment. Kira snorted and typed in,
BMARKS@INTERMOUNTAIN.COM as a new user, and
was rewarded with a message saying that the account existed. She
entered Bob's login and typed IMAMAN. She grinned as the
website let her in.

"You're a dickhead," she said out loud. "A predictable dickhead,
too. Stupid moron, I bet this is how the hackers figured out how
to break into Intermountain."

Kira enter the words *wolf attacks* in the search box and let it
run. The Denver Post soon brought up a list of articles with the
words highlighted. Kira pulled up each one as she sipped the
coffee. A homeless man was attacked on Market Street. A woman
was attacked on Wazee. Another woman attacked near Larimer.

She sat back and sipped the coffee. It would have tasted better
as a latte, she decided. "Christ," Kira muttered. "They're all
LoDo." All of the attacks, except hers and Susan's, had occurred
in the Lower Downtown area. She went through the articles
again to be sure.

She looked down at the card from James Walking Bear next to
her monitor and thought about calling him. Surely, he knew the
discrepancy already? Maybe that's why he had asked such nosy
questions. She looked at the card. She could call him and tell him
about Alaric and Megan.

Kira reached for the phone but stopped herself. What would

she say? That she met a bar full of werewolves? That she had been bitten by a werewolf and now she turned into a wolf when the moon was full? Kira snorted. He'd lock her up for sheer lunacy. She laughed at the pun. She didn't believe it — why would he?

She returned to the email from wolfbane@den-wolfpack.com. Looking at the headers, she could already guess it was spoofed, and ran a trace on it. She entered it into spamcop.net and frowned when the trace came back to Intermountain Telecom.

"Intermountain, eh? Could be anyone," she muttered. Intermountain was an ISP and hosted a large number of corporate websites and emails as well as Internet commerce and private users. They owned part of the Internet backbone which made tracing beyond them somewhat tricky, especially if the sender was a user of Intermountain or if they networked to the ISP.

Kira knew that forwarding to root or to the postmaster would simply garner Bob Marks's attention. She certainly didn't need that. She pulled up a window and entered the IP (network) address of the main server, Evans. At Intermountain, they had a naming scheme that used Colorado mountain names: Mount Evans, Quandary Peak, Grays, Torreys, and others. The telnet screen came up and she typed in root and the password.

Login incorrect.

Kira raised an eyebrow. Well, she hadn't expected Bob to be a complete incompetent, did she? She tried the Oracle database logins and other higher levels that would give her access to superuser shells. Nothing. The system was tight.

She had one backdoor. The computer's name was Mini. It wasn't really much of a machine at Intermountain, but it did have a backdoor Kira had installed when she got there. Its name was stupid and didn't go with any of the other naming conventions. She entered Mini's IP address and it came up.

Kira sighed and ran her Crack program from another window and began the long grind to try to break in. She set the window into background mode and pulled up Netscape again to surf the web. Pulling up Google, she entered *werewolves*. To her surprise, she saw www.den-wolfpack.com listed under the third listing.

"So there is a den-wolfpack.com," Kira muttered. She clicked on the link and watched it load a page with Denver's outline and a pack of wolves in front of it. Did the guy who emailed her actually have an account on a website with those servers? She did a whois and a traceroute and found that, too, went to Intermountain.

"All roads lead to Rome," she mused. She took another sip of coffee and found it was lukewarm. She felt helpless until the Crack program turned up something. She dug into her pocket and pulled out Spaz's card. Right below all his throwaway accounts was a hand scrawled address: spaz@axioms.com.

Kira hated asking for help, but Spaz was the best she knew. If anyone had the latest technology to track something, he did. She copied and pasted the headers of the email and sent a quick message.

Spaz —

Good seeing you. Got a mystery here. Odd message from a spoofed addy. I'm guessing Intermountain — can you verify and pinpoint it?

TIA

—Kira

Kira clicked into the website and went through the menus. As she clicked through, she found that the site was sparse. It featured basic definitions of what werewolves were, a history of werewolves, and even a werewolf shop with T-shirts and mugs (via Cafépress), but nothing really interesting. There was only a small button on the first page which said, *Members Only*.

Kira clicked on it and received a login prompt. It had already filled in the username as *guest*. Kira grinned and started another Crack program in another window. She chuckled after a minute or two when the Crack program came back with the word, *werewolf*.

"W00t! Easy, easy, easy," she said as the login completed. The webpage came up with a menu of choices: History, Blog,

Chatroom, News, Database, and others. Kira was about to click into the News section, when she decided to click into the Database instead.

Kira blinked as Oracle prompts came up. "Oracle?" she said puzzled. Oracle was high-buck. That meant that the people who were hosting this site had money or were using someone else's database. Intermountain had Oracle, but so did Qwest, MCI and a number of other companies throughout Denver. Still, they had to be big to use it. Or clever enough not to be seen using it.

She hit a question mark and stared at the prompt. *Enter a phrase or name.* What should she enter in? she wondered. A phrase or name? "Name?" she asked it. "Like a person?"

Alaric's name popped into her head. *Alaric Kerr,* she entered and hit enter.

Alaric Kerr, 35, Alpha pack member for five years. Son of John Kerr and Theresa Thompson, deceased. Born in Colorado Springs...

Kira gazed at Alaric's photo. *He was handsome,* she admitted, and she found herself more than just a little attracted to him. He was older than her, too, which probably added to the sense of protectiveness she felt from him. She stared at Alaric's face for a while until a beep interrupted her, indicating there was new mail.

Kira saved off Alaric's photo to the hard drive and clicked on the mailbox again. It was from Spaz.

A laric stared at the pool table for a moment and then set down his cue. Normally, he'd become so engrossed in a pool game, he'd forget all about a woman.

Not this one. Kira had been on his mind all morning and into the afternoon. She was Alpha — as Alpha as he was — and that surprised him. And despite himself, Alaric was quite attracted to her.

Besotted, Megan had said. He would've used the word, *smitten*, himself. She was beautiful in both forms, which made it exceedingly hard to concentrate on anything. Even a pool game.

"You okay?" Mike Fowlkes asked. "It's been your turn for the past five minutes."

"You guys play," Alaric said. He handed the cue to another werewolf named Marcus who had been watching. "I think I need a walk."

Alaric walked up the stairwell and into the bar. The eyes of thirty werewolves focused on him. He ignored them as he strode forward. As expected, the werewolves moved aside as he walked through the crowd. One lycanthrope didn't move fast enough and yipped as Alaric made eye contact. Only Cathal blocked his way.

"You going somewhere?" he asked.

"No, just for a walk," Alaric said. "Keep them in line."

Cathal grinned, showing his teeth. "As always. I've got to get back to work, though."

Alaric nodded. "Do what you have to. I'll be back in a bit."

As he walked out into the bright sunshine, he found himself blinking and pulling out his sunglasses. *Damn,* he thought. He hadn't really seen daylight in a while. Most weres tended to make the night their day, and he was no exception. He was feeling tired, staying up past noon, but the truth was he wasn't sleepy. His mind was on Kira.

She had stepped right into *his* bar, demanding that he do something about her being a werewolf. Alaric shook his head. Any other were wouldn't have had the nerve to do that. What's more, Kira had called it a disease — a disease! What in the goddess's name was she thinking? He had never met anyone who didn't like the idea of being a werewolf, once they understood they could control it.

She left the same way she had come in: angry and demanding. Any other woman would have made him angry, but instead he felt infuriated, delighted, intrigued, and everything in between. Most of all, he wanted her.

As Alpha, Alaric knew she was his match. Like it or not, she was a werewolf, and she would soon be his.

Kira stared at the email. She had read over it a few times to be sure she understood it.

Kira baby –

Roundy round, baby. Who'd ya piss off? Intermountain for sure but it's a fucking black hole. WHOIS shows the IP is registered to Intermountain as a subnet but can't ping the system because of the firewall.

You hit the security? Tight. Did you do that, you naughty girl? Will take me some time to crack this puppy. Let me see if I can send a worm in.
TTFN
—Spazalicious

Kira snickered. Spaz had hacked some of the best machines in some of the top companies. He was so good, he didn't even get caught. Once, he sent a UNIX worm to wreak havoc at some of the big telecom companies and tied up their machines for days, sending sysadmins scrambling for backups. She hit reply.

Spaz –
Don't tell me YOU can't get through. Shit, boy, I thought you could crack anything. My backdoors are hosed—and the network stiks are fucking paranoid. I know it's an Intermountain Subnet. I've never seen that subnet IP used, so it's not internal. In fact, I don't recognize it. Can you send them a worm like you did in 2005?
TIA
—K

"Went right through a security hole big enough to drive a Mack truck through," Kira said with a grin. "Go get 'em, Spazster."

But the toughness of tracking the email worried her. Spaz should've been able to track the account at least to an interior machine. He too had gotten stymied by the IP address. Kira leaned back and chewed a hangnail on her thumb. There was the server, Evans, but could she crack it? She considered Quandary, Longs, and Sneffles as possible servers to crack, but Bob had a stupid fondness for rdist — a program with distributed software across network machines — which meant that changes took place everywhere. Even stupid changes, she noted.

Kira turned her attention back to the bios of the werewolves and found Megan Olson in the database. Curious, she brought the bio up and was greeted with Megan's overly cheerful face. Her bio was mostly about her vet clinic south of town. Kira closed the window and entered a wildcard symbol. Up came a list of all the werewolves. She stared at the list. Cathal Murphy's bio caught her eye and she pulled it up.

Cathal Murphy, 32, Beta pack member for ten years. Son of Kyle Murphy and Joan Herberts. Born in Minneapolis, MN. Bachelors of Science, Computer Science, University of Colorado, Boulder...

"Whoa!" Kira said. "Biker boy is a Hell's Accountant?" She looked at the photo of Murphy and noted how closely it resembled a mugshot. "So, you're a bithead, eh? Pretty scary — I wouldn't have figured you out for a geek."

She looked further down the bio to the last line: *Cathal Murphy now works for Intermountain Telecom.*

Kira slammed the mug down; sloshing what little was left of the contents. "Intermountain? What the fuck?" Kira racked her brain trying to remember if she had seen Murphy's names on the logins. "Cmurphy," she muttered. She shook her head. "Probably NIS if he was on Evans. Damn, damn, damn." NIS was a database of users that the systems shared. Kira couldn't possibly remember all the names because there were hundreds.

Murphy wasn't with IS — Information Systems — that much she was sure of. But maybe he had been with networks. If so, she might not have had contact with him. Or maybe she did? Maybe he knew about the werewolf attacks on her. Maybe he *was* the werewolf who attacked her.

Maybe she was losing her mind. Werewolves. Kira snorted and shook her head. She got up and went to the mirror. "Well, if I'm really a werewolf, I should be able to change," she said, her voice sounding unconvinced. She stared at those golden eyes that stared back at her. What could she do to turn into a werewolf?

She closed her eyes and thought about being a wolf. A wolf. She tried to imagine being one and came up with a dog — her family's old Labrador Retriever, who had long since passed away. She grimaced. This wasn't working at all.

Kira tried concentrating on the wolf who attacked her. It haunted her dreams, so it made sense that she would remember it. It was big and gray with large yellow eyes, hot fetid breath, and huge teeth. She replayed the attack in her mind and began to tremble, feeling the terror once again.

Kira forced her eyes open again. This would not do. She walked back to the coffee pot with her mug and poured herself another cup. What was she thinking? That she could actually turn into a wolf? She shook her head. That was crazy.

She looked into the mirror again and stared at those golden eyes. Damn, they reminded her so much of that wolf. She took a sip of the coffee and stared into the eyes that peered over the rim at her. Kira seemed to get lost in them. From somewhere far away, she could hear a lone wolf howl and felt her vision blur. The mug dropped, splattering hot coffee everywhere. Suddenly she was shorter and floundering in her clothes. When she looked up, she was looking at a wolf in the mirror.

Kira tried to shout "No!" but only a whine escaped her lips. As suddenly as she changed, she changed back, her clothes half off her body. Her shoulder and arm were through the neck hole and her jeans were on her arms. She struggled out, feeling like a contortionist. She stared at the clothes for a few moments, then slowly picked them up and dressed again. Kira's mind was churning and she felt sick to her stomach. Every time she looked in the mirror, those gold eyes reminded her of the awful truth.

Kira was shaking as she sat at the computer one more time. She was a werewolf. There could be no denial now. She looked back at the computer screen. There wasn't any doubt in Kira's mind that she was looking at the profile of werewolf who had murdered Susan.

Spaz –
What do you know about Cathal Murphy?
—K

17

Spaz could feel the heat of the werewolves' breath through the interface. Don't look back, he thought as he navigated the intricacies of the Forest. In this section of the Forest, it manifested itself as strangely tangled willows and gnarled oaks. Technically, this was an older section, but older was relative. Most of the Forest had been built in just a few years.

He looked back, despite himself. He could see the werewolves' red eyes and ethereal forms as they loped after him. Spaz needed to find a pathway they couldn't track him down on. Problem was, most of the openings he found in the routers would let all traffic through — not just him. Spaz needed to find a door that he could close or that they couldn't easily get through. Otherwise, he'd have to blow the link — and Spaz didn't want to do that just yet.

An electronic howl buzzed in his head. He rounded a tree to see the Lizard crawling up it.

Still running from the wolves? the Lizard asked. He opened a private chat room. Spaz did a quick traceroute and found he was using an odd address. It was worth a shot to see if the wolves could follow him.

Yeah, said Spaz. He wasn't out of breath, but the energy to maintain this run was taxing him. He'd have to rest soon...

Watch your back, man, Danni's dead.

Spaz stared at the message from Lizard in the private chat window. He wasn't sure if he read it right. He tried again. The words still lingered in his consciousness.

"Fuck," he said. Spaz's heart began to palpitate and his mouth became dry. He took a swig of vanilla Coke and stared at the words as they formed and reformed in the window.

Danni? You sure?

Yeah, bullet through the brain. Wolves, if you believe the rumor...

"Shit," Spaz said and ripped off the interface. His neurons screamed from the sudden unplugging but he didn't care. Danni dead? It seemed impossible. Tom had disappeared. Randy had sold out. Who else was there besides himself?

Spaz didn't like the answer. He stood up and stretched slowly, feeling each of his joints pop. It never used to be this way, he reminded himself. He was getting old and the stress was beginning to take its toll. Already his forefinger and thumb were numb again. The carpal tunnel was coming back.

The room was dark, save for the flicker of computer screens. He liked being surrounded by darkness; it comforted him and made him feel alone. That was something he missed when he worked day jobs. There was too much light and not enough darkness. In the dark, he could concentrate.

There wasn't really much to the room he rented. The Garcia family who had rented it to him in north Denver were Hispanic and spoke little English. They were hardly there — probably holding down two or three jobs to make ends meet. For all its cow-town-like attitude, Denver was expensive, and those who lived there had to hustle or move out. Spaz had chosen this rental because it wasn't on anyone's radar screen. Cash only and week-to-week, his landlords didn't ask questions and didn't care. He suspected they were what was euphemistically called "undocumented workers" — people who had most likely entered the country illegally, and didn't want to call attention to themselves.

That suited Spaz just fine. As long as they all behaved, everyone's secrets would remain secrets and nobody was the worse for wear.

He put the interface back on and called up Gregorian chants. The solemn strains of *Preces Deus Miserere* began and the monks' voices reverberated in his brain. He envisioned a wall of flames shooting up twelve feet around him and shut off the links into the Enchanted Forest and the Internet. The firewall was quite effective and he knew he would need some quiet privacy to think about what to do next.

The wolves were dangerous. They'd always been, but now Spaz worried that they had taken their predatory behavior to the real world. He could deal with their attack programs, Trojan horses, worms, and viruses, but bullets were another thing entirely.

He felt another presence as he sat and pondered his predicament. A door opened in the wall of flames and a small red gnome-like creature walked through the door and shut it. Its face was expressionless and all business-like as it waited for him. It carried a mailbag that it had slung across its red body. It had red horns and a pointed tail, but in a strange way looked almost childlike.

Impish, Spaz thought. *Maybe I should make it look like a dog.* It was the sendmail daemon and it carried a few emails. He stared for a few moments at the Imp and concentrated, opening up the C code that programmed it. All he had to do was change it to another animated gif.

The Imp changed to a blue dog with floppy ears carrying letters in its mouth and wagging its tail furiously. Spaz looked at his surroundings. The firewall was good, but a trifle ominous. He began opening the programs and modifying them. As he did, the fire turned gray and solidified. The grassy ground beneath his feet became stone and then carpet. A chair grew out of the floor and he sat in it as he put in the finishing touches: bookshelves and a nice sturdy desk on the other side of the room. He floated a few rendering light sources above so that his cyber-eyes had some natural light. Unlike a normal room, this one had no door.

"There we go, much more friendly," Spaz said. And just as secure. Only his daemons could get in. He glanced at the first email; it was from Kira —that could wait. The next message was from Lizard.

Spaz Boy—
Murphy is looking for you. GTG
—Lizard

Spaz shivered at the news. Did Murphy already know Spaz was in Denver? If he did, it could get touchy. Murphy was one of the wolves. Although technically Murphy had no criminal record, it was common knowledge he had killed at least one man — maybe more. He was no angel, unless it was the fallen type associated with hell.

He closed his eyes. *Read the rest,* he told the dog.

The dog's voice was tinny as it began to read the email. It was one of those attempts at trying for a humanistic voice but the flatness and lack of expression made it sound even more alien.

Return-Path: <sentto-2698234-40488-1115930040
spaz@axioms.com@returns.intermountain.com>

Skip header, Spaz ordered.

The dog continued speaking without hesitation.

Spaz –
I know you're in Denver. It's a matter of time. You can see me or I can find you.
— Cathal

18

Spaz stared at Cathal Murphy's letter. How in the fuck had he found out Spaz was in Denver? Spaz could feel the sweat running down his face as he stared at the ridiculous blue dog that still wagged its tail furiously at him.

Read sent-to address, Spaz said.

Sent-to spaz@axioms.com

Shit.

Excuse me? The dog's tail wagged more furiously.

Not you, he snapped. *Go away.*

The blue daemon faded away. Spaz began to pace. Cathal knew where he worked, which was bad. Spaz wasn't done with his work at *Axioms*, but he couldn't afford to show up there again. He needed to get out and get out soon. He called up Travelocity and entered the Bahamas as his next destination. He'd feel better on a sandy beach, drinking a Mai Tai and sunbathing.

He had just finished his travel plans when the blue dog appeared again, this time carrying another email.

Who's it from? he asked.

Excuse me? The dog wagged its tail furiously.

Spaz smiled in chagrin. He forgot that sometimes he still had to give it commands. *Alias "read send-to" with "who's it from"*

Okay, the daemon said.

Now, who's it from?

kwalker@gmail.com, the daemon replied.

Read it to me, Spaz said. He turned pale as he listened to Kira's message.

Kira hadn't expected a quick answer from Spaz when she sent the email off, but by the time she cleaned up the spilt coffee the best she could — unlikely to get her damage deposit back at this rate — and poured another cup, the new message light was already blinking on the monitor.

Shit. What have you gotten yourself into? Use the phone and call me at 303-758-8896.

– S

Kira noted that the message was from one of Spaz's throwaway accounts listed on the card. *Odd,* she thought. *It was almost as if Spaz was scared. Spaz wasn't scared of anyone.* She checked the phone number and dialed.

"Kira?" came Spaz's voice over the computer. "Damn it, girl! I said use the phone! Get your ass outside in a half hour. See you in a few."

The line went dead before Kira had a chance to speak. She stared at the Sun in puzzlement. She always used Voice-Over-IP but she hadn't thought anyone would track it. Why was Spaz tracking the origins of phone calls?

Kira changed into clothes that weren't coffee stained and left the apartment. This was all very strange. When she walked out of her front door, Spaz was already there.

"What's going on? Do you know Murphy?" Kira asked.

Spaz's dark eyebrows drew together and he chewed his lips. He glanced around suspiciously. "Not here," he said. "Let's walk."

"Where to?" Kira glanced around. "What's this all about?"

"Let's walk, first," Spaz said. He took off briskly, and for the first time, Kira had trouble catching up.

They walked for a while, until Kira noticed they were heading toward Commons Park. They walked across the bridge to the bright green grass and walked down the concrete walkways dotted with trees and old fashioned street lamps. Some people were playing Frisbee on the grass and Kira could see some bicyclists riding away from them down the path. "What's this all about?" Kira demanded.

Spaz wheeled around on her. "What do you know about the Enchanted Forest?"

"The what?" Kira began to laugh. "You mean with Elves and stuff? Or are we talking Disneyland here?"

"No, no, cyberspace-wise," Spaz said. "Surely you've heard something."

Kira hesitated. "Wasn't it something that you mentioned in that old graduate paper you did at MIT?" She noticed Spaz was watching her closely. "Something about a net within the Net."

"Good girl, you do read my stuff," he said. "You check out Slash Dot or Wired recently?"

"Haven't really had the time. Look, the cyber culture is passé. I've got more important things to do."

"More important than knowing who is hacking your networks?" He waggled his eyebrows. "Kira, Kira, you are such a stik."

"Watch your mouth, asshole, or I'll send a denial of service to your machine so fast you won't have time to catch up," Kira snorted.

"Denial ain't just a river in Egypt," Spaz laughed. "Okay, you're not a stik, but baby, baby, what are you doing sniffing up Murphy's butt? He'll slap you down hard. He's a big spider, Kira. He's about the size of Shelob, and he's a nasty one. "

"Spiders can be squished."

"Not this one." Spaz shook his head. "Net within a Net. I started doing something like it at MIT. So did the other spiders. We realized that things would get locked down tight with IP6 so we decided to take matters into our own hands. So, we began to build a network within the Net. We sent worms out to various machines to rewrite routing software where we could. A few went awry — like the worms you'd see in the news — but most were covert and went undetected. We knew we'd have to use the IP4 machines because IP6 didn't let us spoof."

"Piggybacked onto IP4," Kira said. "Shit."

"That's when someone got the great idea to have IP6 and IP4. After all, there were lots of legacy machines. The network spread from Berkley to Boston and there were enough spiders looking to fix our basic problem: allowing us access into the Net without people knowing we were there. We'd add our subnets into the routers — usually with inside help. This net within the Net grew and grew. No one knew what to call it, but some jokester came up with the Enchanted Forest. Sometimes just the Forest or the Woods. Taking a walk in the Woods, as it were."

"So what does Murphy have to do with all this?"

"Baby, he set up the Forest at the Evil Empire. It's Murphy's Law there."

"And they've got werewolves in the Forest," muttered Kira.

Spaz raised an eyebrow. "You know about them?"

"I'm one of them."

Spaz looked at her oddly. "I thought you didn't know about the Forest."

"I didn't."

He shook his head. "Well anyway, the Denver Wolfpack, as they call themselves, are a bunch of tough spiders."

"They're not spiders," said Kira. "They're werewolves."

"Whatever," Spaz said dismissively. "Look, when you sent me the IP subnets, I knew you had probably stumbled onto the Forest, but I figured I'd just play dumb and act like I didn't know. But when you mentioned Murphy, I knew something was on. What'dya do, Kira? Stumble on Murphy's edge of the Forest?"

Kira paused. "What do you know about werewolves?"

"They send code to maraud the Forest. Usually tear up anyone in their path."

"No, I mean *real* werewolves," Kira said. "Not cyberwolves."

Spaz laughed and Kira felt her face turn red. "You get knocked in the head, girl? Ain't no such thing."

"No," she said softly. "Just a wolf loose in Denver who killed Susan and a few others."

Spaz looked at her curiously. "You think someone is siccing *real* wolves on people?"

"There've been four attacks," Kira said. *He doesn't believe that werewolves are real.* "So, is there a way for me to get into the Forest?"

"Yeah," said Spaz. "Just follow the yellow brick road."

"Could you be more specific?"

"What are you going to do?"

"Snoop around," Kira said, crossing her arms. "Why?"

"You asked about Murphy."

"So?"

"Murphy is bad news, Kira," Spaz said. "Don't cross him or you'll be dead."

"I'm just snooping a bit, that's all," she said. "What do you care?"

Spaz shook his head. "I don't want to see you hurt."

"Too late," she said. "What do you mean by the yellow brick road?"

He shook his head. "Go to Oz, Kira. But be really careful. These people are rough." The PDA at his side beeped and he flipped it open. "Crap, got to run — work calls. Later?" He snapped it shut. "Wait a sec." He fished out a headset from his pocket and pressed it into her hands. "You'll need this when you get there. Call me. Don't talk about the Forest and don't show anyone the headset." He turned and left her standing in the middle of Commons Park, puzzled and even more confused.

F ollow the yellow brick road," said the munchkin.
"Follow the yellow brick road," Spaz had said.
"Follow, follow, follow, follow..."
"I'm afraid we're not in Kansas anymore, Toto," Kira
said to herself as she walked out of Commons Park. *Not unless
Kansas had werewolves, too.*

The Enchanted Forest. It was the stuff of legends, among
spiders and sysadmins alike. Kira had seen vague references to it
over the years and had even tried to track it down, but nothing
had ever come of it. There had been a lot of talk and speculation,
but no one had actually seen the Enchanted Forest. The net
within the Net. It was off the map.

Here there be monsters, the old map makers wrote. Monsters
indeed. Werewolves.

And the cyber-community knew about them. Or *thought* they
knew about them. So, rogue spiders were called werewolves?
Or wolf spiders? she thought wryly. Regardless, there were
werewolves in cyberspace and in real life. She might be hunting
the same ones.

She started humming the song from the Wizard of Oz as
she walked back toward her apartment, ignoring the looks of

passersby. At least she wasn't skipping, she thought wryly.

But what in the hell did Spaz mean when he said to go to Oz? And what was the headset? She looked at it. It wasn't much — it just looked like something that you'd plug an iPod into. She put it on. Again, nothing. Taking it off again, she folded it and put it in her pocket. Was this some kind of a joke?

The sun was already low enough to throw long shadows across the streets, sending the afternoon into premature twilight. The moon would be up again soon — Kira wondered if she would turn back into a werewolf or if she could control it. But then, last night had been the full moon — it wouldn't be tonight, although she suspected that an almost full moon was nearly as powerful.

She tried to think of what she had heard about werewolves. They could only be killed with a silver bullet through the heart. Megan had said silver weapons. Something about wolfsbane — didn't it repel werewolves? And what else? She didn't really know. It made almost as much sense as what Spaz said.

Follow the yellow brick road.

The words continued to nag her as she entered her apartment building and walked back to her second floor apartment. She opened the door, walked in, and stared at the computer screen. Was this an old spider term? She tried to think back to her MIT days. Usually anything called a "yellow brick road" was a path that anyone could see and follow. And Oz. What in the hell was that about?

Kira pulled the headset out of her pocket and tossed it on the desk. The headset was worthless and she wondered why Spaz had bothered putting one in her hands.

Kira sat down at the computer and pulled up Google. She quickly entered "Yellow Brick Road" and Oz. The lists of websites showed her references to *The Wizard of Oz* — both the book and the movie — and not much else. Kira sighed and shook her head. Did she really think she could find a secret entrance through Google? And yet, sometimes the most obscure things were hidden in plain sight. She felt like she was missing something.

Something important.

She glanced at the clock on her Sun's monitor. It was 6:30 already. She was hungry again. Kira surfed over to a local delivery pizzeria's website, ordered pizza and opened a window to write some code. She stared at the blank screen for a while and then began to write C code.

It was simple really. If Spaz wasn't lying, her best bet was to start with the open nodes and go from there. But there were thousands, if not millions, of open nodes in the Internet. Where would she start?

Go to Oz.

Kira stared at the code. She wasn't getting something — something important. She decided to write a threaded subroutine that would open ports in the routers, knock, and see what opened. As she did, she pulled off the current list of black hole routers. There were some in the US. But many were overseas.

Oz...

The intercom buzzed. Kira glanced at the time — it was 7:00. Damn. She walked over to the intercom. "Yeah?"

"Pizza," the voice said.

"I'll be right down." She released the button and stared at the screen again. Kira knew there was something she was forgetting. As she fished the cash from her jeans, she stared again at the database in the separate window, glancing down the list of URLs. Several ended in .au.

Aussies.

Oz.

Go to Oz. She began laughing. The Aussie regularly referred to the land downunder as Oz. Kira was elated as she bounded out the door, nearly forgetting her keys, before taking two steps at a time downstairs.

How could she have forgotten that Australia was Oz? She chuckled as she opened the front door.

"This yours?" said the delivery guy, holding out a pizza box and a bottle of Dr Pepper. Kira grinned at the teen, snatched up the food, and handed him a twenty, telling him to keep the change. She dashed upstairs and was in the apartment before she realized she hadn't ordered the soda pop.

"Oh well," she said, pouring the Dr Pepper. If it was good enough for an American werewolf, it was good enough for her. She set the routine to search the Australian nodes and ate her pizza, feeling pretty smug. Now all she had to do was wait.

An hour passed and then another. Kira glanced out the windows and saw that it had grown dark and an imperceptibly less than full moon was rising in the east. The moon was blood red as it crested the horizon and peered through the Denver high-rises. Even as she looked at the moon, she felt a strange pull. A tug within her that told her it was time.

"No," she said aloud, turning back to her computer. "I won't let you win."

She stared at the program as it ran. It would probably take a while to search through the Australian nodes. Still...

A lone wolf howled somewhere...

Kira got up and pulled out a lukewarm piece of pizza. She took a bite and turned and stared at the moon as it glowed through her window. What harm would it do if she decided to become a wolf? Unlike the werewolves of horror movies, she knew she'd keep her intelligence. What harm could it do?

Kira could feel the pull deep inside her. Something akin to an itch that needed scratching. It started deep within her chest, tightening her muscles. She stared at the half-eaten pizza and tossed it back into the box. She picked up the box and began carrying it toward the refrigerator.

She nearly dropped the box when she saw her fingers try to shorten. Kira stared at her hands and they returned to their normal size. She opened the refrigerator and a growl issued from her throat as the light flickered on. She fought the growl and tossed the pizza in before shutting the door.

She walked back to her computer and paused to look at herself in the mirror. She looked normal so far, but she wondered how long she could fight the transformation. While she was awake, she could. But what could she do when she was asleep?

Kira sat back and closed her eyes. The pull to transform was becoming stronger. She could hear the wolves' call in her mind. It was growing louder.

"Okay, you win," she said aloud. "But we do it my way."

She grasped her keys and headed out the door.

20

Spaz's gut roiled as he walked away from Kira. He wanted to throw up. He put on the headset and once again was in his firewalled enclosure. The blue sendmail dog was there holding his email. The message blinked softly at him: *From: cmurphy@intermountain.com.* Shit.

Spaz wanted to kick himself for not catching onto Murphy sooner. Murphy was a wolf and a big one, but Spaz had always thought that Murphy wasn't quite as smart as he pretended. Network engineers — "nets" as they were often called — were clever, but usually fell into the position either on their way up or as a lateral. Spaz had known a lot of burnt out programmers who became nets and known quite a few telephony types who took a Net job because no one else wanted it. Cathal was probably the latter. Spaz had let his prejudice get the better of him and had not seen Murphy for the danger he really was.

How did Kira know Cathal Murphy? Maybe she knew him from Intermountain, Spaz thought. But Kira was no net — she was an admin, which made her clueless about the net-in-Net thing. Kira may have called herself a werewolf, but she wasn't a player in the Enchanted Forest — that, Spaz was sure of.

The work on linking the Enchanted Forest was going slower

than he had expected. Of course, part of the problem had been the lack of someone on the inside. Kira, for all her coolness, was pretty much a stik. She had sold out to the establishment long ago and hadn't even known it. Oh, she *knew* about the Enchanted Forest on some level. But she was still thinking too far within the box to make her a player. Which was too bad, because she really did have talent.

Spaz decided not to read the message, but instead pocketed the headset and kept walking. The werewolves had gotten to Lizard, who had switched over. Danni was dead. Randy had disappeared. He wondered if it was safe to go back to the Garcia's residence. He had left an interface there, but not much else. A talented spider would have problems cracking the encryption — assuming the wolves or the stiks at the FBI figured out what it was; they were unlikely to crack it. No, it was better to get out now and worry about the interface later. He could get into the interface and wipe the memory once he was in the Bahamas drinking his Mai Tai.

Spaz had enough fake ID with him to bug out now. He had become Tom Smith — a nice simple name on a passport and credit cards. He had bought the ticket to Bermuda with Smith's credit card number. Flight left tonight at 5:30. Spaz hated taking late flights.

He rounded the corner toward Market Street when he paused. He could see the bus terminal ahead. There weren't many cabs in this area, so he'd have to catch the bus to Denver International Airport. He wasn't fond of public transportation but he really didn't have much of a choice. He could call a cab and wait, though.

He slipped on the interface and called up the yellow pages to look up cabs. He didn't notice the shadow in the alleyway he passed.

Suddenly, he was knocked off his feet; his headset torn off. Spaz screamed as he felt the hot breath and teeth sink into him.

Kira wandered down the street, gazing upwards at the moon as it cast its pale glow through the city. It was bright enough to see by — even if she hadn't had her vision augmented by her werewolf senses. The cold orb reflected in the mirrored windows of the high-rises around her. As Kira walked, she wondered where she could change into a wolf without anyone seeing her and where she should stash her clothing. She didn't want someone to find her things and steal them.

She made her way through the alleys until she came to a small alleyway where she doubted even the vagrants went. There was a Dumpster and not much else. She sniffed the air, catching only the scent of garbage and dirt — no one had entered this alley in some time. She slipped into the alleyway and rummaged through the Dumpster until she found a box that had contained copier paper. Kira quickly undressed, stashed her clothing and keys in it and fitted the lid onto it. She slid the box behind the Dumpster and hoped that no one would come by to inspect what was behind it.

Standing naked in the cool night's air, she shivered as goose bumps prickled her skin. She had turned into a wolf the night before, but now she was suddenly apprehensive. Was it painful like in the old movies? Did she feel everything as it happened, as some bones grew longer and others shorter? She hadn't felt it when she turned into a wolf in front of the mirror, but that had only been for a few seconds. Would she really retain her human intelligence or would she become a wolf without sense of what she was? Kira hesitated. Maybe this was a bad idea.

She thought about going back now. Maybe there was a cure for lycanthropy. Maybe someone already knew of it and she just need to talk to the right doctor — one who wouldn't think she was a nutcase. Maybe she could get help in controlling this.

And maybe she was kidding herself. The howl of the wolf rang in her ears. She felt the tug even though the moon was slightly less full tonight. She knew she could either transmute on her own terms or on its. Wouldn't it be better to control it?

Kira closed her eyes and focused on the call of the wolf. She felt woozy and her gut twisted as she felt her skin itch all over. The itching became burning and she felt herself drop to her hands and knees — but they were no longer human hands and feet. She shuddered and wanted to scream but instead a howl escaped her lips. As the disorientation lifted, she found herself looking from a much shorter height.

She sat back on her haunches to wait for her head to stop spinning. The transformation *was* unpleasant, and she had wished that she had been asleep when she changed. Still, then she wouldn't have had the control over it.

So, now what, Kira? she asked herself. She really hadn't planned this out, but then again, she hadn't really expected to be a werewolf. She snuffed the night's air. Mixed with the overwhelming smells of the city was a scent of something she couldn't quite place but that made the hair on the back of her neck and shoulders rise. Something that called to her.

The scent of others like her. The scent of other werewolves.

She shook her head and stood up. Kira knew that she could probably hold her own as a werewolf against another, but it would be dangerous to run into a pack of them. Maybe she should look for Megan? Or maybe that handsome black wolf she had seen in what she now knew had been no dream.

Kira looked both ways before exiting the alley. The streetlights cast shadows all around, but in this section of LoDo, nothing moved. And yet, the night wind called to her. The scent drew her forward and she padded quietly across the street and through the alleyway as she made her way toward Union Station.

The wind ruffled through her fur, but she was no longer cold with her thick double coat. She trotted effortlessly down the empty streets, ducking occasionally into the shadows when a car or human came into view.

As Kira continued to trot away from the bars and restaurants, her mind went back to the Enchanted Forest. *Where was the gateway?* she wondered. Somewhere in Oz, most likely, but where? And how was this connected to her and Susan?

A scream pierced the night, raising the hackles along Kira's back and jolting her out of her reverie. The screams were followed by the throaty growls of a predator as it savaged its prey. A low growl issued from Kira's throat and without thinking, she turned and ran down the alley toward the noise.

Suddenly she stopped. At the end of an alleyway stood a large gray wolf looming over something lying on the ground. Her wolf senses told her that it was a homeless man who had been brutally savaged. His blood stank in her nostrils and she stared at the scene in horror. The wolf was tearing into the man's throat as it looked up. In the dim light, those malevolent yellow eyes seemed to glow red. A growl issued from the creature's throat.

Kira knew she had made a mistake. The wolf was nearly twice her size and by the look in its eyes, she knew it was in no mood for company. She fought the trembling. It was the wolf who had killed Susan a month ago.

It leapt at her, bloody jaws snapping. Kira turned and fled, barely avoiding those large teeth as the creature bore down on her. She ran as fast as she could out of the alley and down the street with the killer in pursuit.

Kira was terrified. She fought the urge to transmute back to human form, lest the wolf catch her. She also knew not to look backwards. *Look backwards and you will die,* she told herself. She ran, not caring now if anyone saw her.

She crossed the street. A car screeched to a stop, barely avoiding her, and still she ran on. The click of nails and the pad of the pursuing wolf's paws were terrifying. She could hear the creature panting as it ran behind her. Kira found herself on the north end of the mall and ran past humans as she tried to flee. She heard people screaming and the panting become louder in her ears — or was that the blood pounding in them? She didn't know and didn't care.

She turned down another alleyway and stopped short. There were three wolves working on scraps of garbage. They looked up and one lifted its lip. Kira glanced behind to find two other wolves there. She was trapped.

21

Five to one. Kira stared at the wolves and felt her paws grow numb. She shivered as the hackles rose along her back and she fought the whine that burbled in her throat. The panic numbed her mind, slowing her thoughts and reactions. She wanted to run, but where to? There was no way out.

Five to one.

Kira had never been in a situation like this. It was like every action movie Susan had dragged her to. At some point, the good guy was surrounded by villains. It was time for Arnold to pull out a gun and start blasting. Her sluggish mind groped for something — anything — that she might be able to use. In most of the films they had seen, the heroes used guns or blasters. *Star Wars. Terminator. Indiana Jones. The Mummy...*

Jackie Chan. What would Jackie Chan do?

Jackie Chan wasn't here, and she couldn't remember any time he had been surrounded by five pissed-off werewolves. She looked from wolf to wolf. They were big. Really big. Their teeth gleamed white and their yellow eyes glowed in the dim light. They were shaggy creatures with dark gray fur, hackles raised, and saliva dripping from their teeth.

Kira felt like little Red Riding Hood: *My, what big teeth you have! The better to eat you with, my dear.*

She winced and felt her head tilt slowly. It was an involuntary reaction — something her body knew to do, even if she didn't. She lowered her head and allowed the whimper to escape from her lips. Her hackles lowered with her body posture. Her wolf body knew to go submissive even if she didn't.

How embarrassing, she thought. As she looked into those yellow eyes, Kira knew this was her only chance. *Listen to the damn werewolf*, a part of her mind told her. *She'll save you if she can.*

The three gray wolves in front of her hesitated as she lowered her stance. The biggest of the three slunk forward and started to circle around. By his demeanor and lankiness, Kira guessed his human form to be in his twenties. His coat was ratty and had loose tufts of fur from his biannual shedding. He slid around toward her flank and she turned with him, baring her white, sharp teeth as she did so.

A growl escaped her lips as he tried to sniff her, and he hesitated. Then, his eyes hardened. White, sharp teeth flashed as he leapt at her and grasped a mouthful of the fur and skin on Kira's back. She snapped and turned, trying to shake the big wolf as he leapt up on her back to mount her.

Kira was horrified. He was trying to rape her and by the looks of it, would succeed. She redoubled her efforts to escape. The other wolves jumped into the fray and somehow she found herself rolled over on her back. At that moment, she saw the wolf standing above her getting into position. She snapped and her teeth bit hard. Blood gushed into her mouth and she pulled back, tearing skin and fur.

The wolf screamed in pain and leapt off her. Kira jumped up and leapt over the stricken wolf, spitting out the wolf's testicles. The two wolves who had blocked her exit attacked now. Their teeth sunk into her hide and she screamed.

Suddenly, Kira was knocked off her feet by a dark shadow that passed between her and the other wolves. She heard the other wolves screaming as the shadow attacked them. Then, she realized that she was seeing another wolf. A black wolf.

The black wolf bowled over the ringleader of the wolves and was tearing pieces of skin and fur out of him. The screaming was pitiful and Kira slowly stood up, dazed. The black wolf's violence was something she had never seen before. The other wolves had scattered and fled, leaving their hapless leader to his fate. She watched in a kind of fascinated horror as the black wolf continued to tear into the leader, ripping flesh from his throat.

When satisfied with the damage, the black wolf left the dying wolf and strode over to Kira. Kira stared at the black wolf, at the blood still dripping from his maw. *Out of the frying pan and into the fire,* she thought. Her heart raced as she tried to think of a way to escape. He was huge — twice the size of those smaller werewolves. She was sure there was no way she could outrun him. She was now at his mercy.

22

Kira, are you all right? the wolf asked.

Kira blinked. He knew her name? She stared at him.

Did they...touch you? the wolf asked. His mind-voice was reticent.

No, Kira said and then hesitated. Why did he care about her?

Good, he said, and nuzzled her.

The nuzzle was not sexual in any way, but comforting. *As one might hug a small child*, she thought. His touch was remarkably gentle considering that a few moments before, he had been ripping into another werewolf.

Who are you? Kira asked.

A gleam entered the black wolf's eyes. *You don't recognize me?*

The wolf looked familiar. He was remarkably like the wolf in her dreams, and yet Kira knew she had met him in human form. A name came unbidden to her mind. *Alaric?*

The black wolf flashed a toothy grin. *I would give you more proof, but I'd get arrested for indecent exposure.*

Kira laughed. It came out as a coughing sound. *Indecent? I doubt that's what I would call it.*

If a wolf could blush, he nearly did. Alaric glanced at the alleyway's entrance. *You need to be more careful,* he said, changing the subject. *I had Trevor tailing you tonight but he came back whimpering — you both ran into the rogue wolves.*

There was only one wolf, Kira said. *And he attacked another person.*

Alaric's golden eyes glowed with concern. *Trevor wasn't tailing you?*

Kira cocked her head. *I think I'd know if someone was following me. It's not as if I'm human anymore.* She closed her eyes and turned away. A lump was in her throat.

Kira, I...

Damn it, Alaric! Can't you control your people? It was the same wolf who killed Susan and who attacked me! A snarl issued from her throat.

Are you sure?

She met his gaze. *Don't you think I would know the wolf who nearly killed me?*

Alaric sucked in a breath. *Kira, I am so sorry, but I didn't think.*

Kira looked at him. Next to her he was huge, and yet he was putting up with her tirade. He could kill her with a single bite of those massive jaws. She trembled. *I'm sorry,* she said. *It's been a rough night already and I shouldn't have taken it out on you, my defender.*

Alaric smiled a wolfy smile. *It looked like you were handling the situation until those other wolves jumped you. You have a way of getting a male's undivided attention.*

Now it was Kira's turn to nearly blush. *I'm afraid I didn't mean to bite there. It was just a handy target. I don't think I could have held them all off. You came in the nick of time.*

I am honored to be your defender, milady. Was the wolf who attacked you a month ago one of the ones who attacked you now?

Kira thought back to the young wolves. *No,* she said. *The one who attacked me was older and bigger. Almost your size.*

Hmmm. Alaric fell silent as if lost in thought.

Kira glanced at the mauled wolf on the ground. *Is he dead?*

Not yet, but he will be, Alaric said. *I'll have Murphy clean him up so no one finds his body.*

Now Kira really trembled. *You'll kill him in cold blood?*

He's a rogue wolf, Kira, he said. *He nearly raped you. Anyway, there's not much point to his life anymore now that you've done a field neuter.*

There are laws and prisons, she said.

Not for us, Alaric said. *What kind of jail would hold a werewolf? And if they managed to, the moment a full moon rose, we would be discovered.*

Kira blinked. *Then, there is nothing you can do?*

We kill him and cremate the body. Look, he's already changing back.

Kira looked to see the faint glow of the transmutation. The wolf features began to slowly give way to human features. As she watched, she saw a pocked-faced boy with sandy hair and glassy gold eyes stare blankly ahead. *He's barely nineteen.*

He's eighteen.

She turned back to Alaric. *You know him?*

Cindy Jones' kid. Running with the wrong pack. He paused. *Don't tell me you feel sorry for him. He nearly raped you.*

I don't feel sorry, she said. *I just didn't expect him to be so young.*

Alaric shrugged. *I'll have Murphy come clean him up.*

Not Murphy, she said. *I don't trust him.*

He grinned. *I don't trust him either. He knows I don't and therefore is trustworthy — to a point.* He paused. *Let's get you home. I think you've had enough excitement for one night.*

We've got to get my clothes, she said.

A glint entered his eyes, but he turned away. *I'll escort you.*

━━━ ⌇K

Spaz awoke to darkness. Blindfolded and gagged, his arms behind his back hurt terribly and he was terribly thirsty. Where was he? What was going on?

It wasn't the cops or the FBI. Those stiks didn't do this to you unless you were a terrorist. While Spaz had been called many things, terrorist wasn't among them. He lay for a while listening to his heart pound in his ears. Something had hit him, knocked him down and bit him hard. His arm felt swollen and bruised from the bite. It could've been Cathal, but he didn't know if Cathal had a big dog.

Spaz replayed the attack in his mind. He didn't remember much of it; he'd been knocked unconscious when he hit the ground. His headset was gone and his palm top was probably smashed into thousands of pieces. He had to get into the Enchanted Forest and get help — even if it meant revealing its secrets. He had to get a message to Kira...

He heard noises and then the sound of a door opening. Two men were talking; one sounded vaguely familiar. Someone grabbed him and hauled him up so that he was sitting at the edge of something — a table? The gag was pulled out of his mouth.

"We want the encryption codes for the Forest," the familiar voice said without preamble.

"Bite me," Spaz said. "Don't know what you're talking about."

"The Enchanted Forest — you wrote the code." The other voice was deeper and rough.

"Sorry, you got the wrong one."

"Bullshit, Spaz," said the familiar voice.

"Randy?"

"Yeah, now give us the code."

"Bite me." Spaz spat. "You got some water?"

"They ain't playing games, Spaz-boy. And I'd be careful who you tell to bite you."

Spaz heard growling. The two men grabbed him and cut the duct tape bonds. "Hold him tight!" Randy said.

He struggled to no avail. They pulled his right hand out and for a split second, he felt hot breath on his arm before the jaws clamped down.

23

They set out of the alleyway toward LoDo, not far from Kira's apartment. Kira tried to recall the exact alleyway, delaying them with two false alarms. Alaric didn't seem annoyed or angry with the delay; he seemed to be enjoying her company. Despite herself, Kira felt as attracted to Alaric in his wolf form as she had in his human form. There was something charismatic about him that made her wonder. He seemed at ease as a leader — whether in charge of the Denver wolfpack or as a CEO.

Not a CEO, she told herself. *A king.*

Here in Denver, Colorado, trotting beside a werewolf, Kira could still envision Alaric Kerr in his human form, looking like the long-lost heir to some medieval kingdom. In her mind's eye, she envisioned him in chainmail, riding a warhorse and leading knights into battle. She grinned at the thought.

What's so funny? asked Alaric, interrupting her reverie.

Nothing, she said. *Just thinking how odd it is to have a werewolf escort.*

Before he could respond, she halted at the alleyway and squinted. She could just make out a cardboard box behind the Dumpster. *This is it. Hang on a moment, my clothes are there,* she said.

Are you sure now? he asked.

Pretty sure, she said. She trotted in and noted that he waited at the entrance, turning around to give her some privacy. She slipped behind the dumpster and nosed the box. Her clothes were in it. Quickly, she transformed back into a human and slid her clothing on.

She noted that he hadn't turned around, and she chuckled. She had half expected him to look, after all. *Well, well,* she thought, *you are a gentleman.*

"I'm dressed," she said, not loudly, because she knew he could hear her.

Good. Let's get going, Alaric said. *I'll get you home safely, but promise me that you won't come out again without contacting me first.*

"Why?" Kira whispered.

Because whomever attacked you is still around and is looking to finish what he started, Alaric said gravely. *I suspect he knows you recognize him. Don't go out at night without me.*

Kira stared. "But I have a life."

Yes, but until I find him, promise me that you will call me before you go out at night. Kira, I don't want you hurt.

He licked her hand and she knelt down to look into his gold eyes. They nearly melted her. "All right," she said. "I will."

Good, he said. *Let's get you home.*

They started walking toward Kira's apartment. Kira was silent, contemplating. In one night as a werewolf, she had seen a man murdered, and had been chased by Susan's murderer, had been attacked by five werewolves, was nearly raped, had seen a young werewolf's throat torn out, and had been saved by a very enigmatic man. *No... werewolf,* she reminded herself. Alaric was as much a werewolf as the creatures who attacked her. She shivered.

Alaric looked up at her as they walked, studying her with his gold eyes. If he noticed her trembling, he didn't say anything. *It's probably best,* she thought. She didn't want him to know just how confused she really was.

At last, they arrived at her apartment. They stood for a long time in silence; the only light was from the nearly full moon and the streetlamps. Even as a human, she found herself strangely attracted to Alaric. He was handsome in both human and wolf forms. Maybe it was because they were both werewolves. Maybe she was crazy...

"I'm very tired," she said lamely.

I know, Alaric said. *Go inside, pretty one. Call me tomorrow.*

"I don't have your number."

You can reach me at The Grey Wolf.

Kira hesitated and then knelt beside him. He licked her face and she kissed him on the muzzle. "Thank you," she whispered as she buried her head into his black fur.

Go, my Kira, he said. *I will see you tomorrow.*

Kira nodded and stood up. She entered her apartment and unlocked the door. Before she walked inside, she glanced back toward where Alaric had been. The large black wolf had vanished into the night.

Kira stumbled into her apartment. She sagged into her computer chair and stared at the scrolling numbers that flashed on the screen. She knew they were IP addresses, but her exhausted mind didn't comprehend them. They'd have to wait until morning, she decided. She pulled herself up, made sure the door was locked, and stumbled into bed.

Kira lay in bed for a while, too tired to move but too exhausted to sleep. Instead, her mind replayed the night's events. She trembled as she replayed the rogue wolves' brutal attack. Chances were, she would've been raped, killed, or both, had Alaric not appeared. She was too tired to be terrified at the night's events — she reserved that emotion for the morning, when she would be lucid. Right now, she was still under the throes of the lycanthropy even though she was no longer a wolf.

Kira stared up at the ceiling, watching the moonlight play through the mini-blinds. The call of the moon was still there, but was waning. She could control the urge to turn into a wolf now, but her mind was still part wolf. Being a werewolf wasn't just a nuisance, it was downright dangerous — and she knew she couldn't rely on Alaric to protect her forever. She had to figure out a way to control it, or risk another episode like what happened tonight.

Despite her horror at seeing Alaric kill the rogue wolf, there had been a sense of justice served. Alaric was right — how could the werewolves hide their own once one ended up in prison? They were likely to be noticed among the normal human population again — and not kindly. Perhaps people were more tolerant of other minorities, but how tolerant would people be of werewolves?

Kira wondered what her own reaction would've been before she had become a werewolf. Having a neighbor who could afflict you with lycanthropy with a nibble didn't make her feel all that charitable. She didn't think that she would be sympathetic to anyone who moved in once her neighbor's pets — or kids — started disappearing after dark. *On the other hand, the stock for flea and tick collars would go up,* she thought wryly. She'd invest in some pet company's stock, make a million, and retire.

Her addled mind turned back to Alaric. If there were one thing that would keep her lycanthropic, it had to be him. He was charismatic both as a man and a wolf. He awoke feelings within her that Kira had thought long since buried. If she had to pick the perfect man, Alaric would come close. With one exception: he was a werewolf.

You're a werewolf too, the wolf part of her reminded herself.

I wasn't born to this, Kira replied to the wolf. *Not like Alaric. I was bitten, remember?*

It doesn't matter, the wolf said. *You are now a werewolf.*

Kira was too tired to argue. She fell asleep.

24

The phone rang and jolted Kira awake. She groaned as it rang a couple more times, and then the computer picked it up, silencing it. She groaned again and covered her head with her pillow, trying to squeeze the daylight out.. *Damn telephones,* she thought. *I should set it to pick up on the first ring instead of the third.*

As she woke slowly, her mind went back to the events of the night before. She had nearly been raped — in wolf form, to be sure — but nearly raped. She was puzzled by her lack of response to it. As a human, she'd be in need of some serious counseling that her COBRA insurance wouldn't cover — no doubt — and she'd be a mental wreck. Instead, the werewolf part of her was slowly changing her response. Okay, so she was nearly raped, but Alaric was there and got her out of it. No problem. It might have been a problem if he hadn't been there, but she'd bitten off the wolf's testicles.

Again, no response. It was like she had seen a movie about it, or dreamt it; she wasn't feeling the way she should. Kira puzzled over it for a while. The wolf was changing her; making her less vulnerable — and less human. She knew she should be horrified by this, but she wasn't. Everything was as it should be. Only it wasn't.

Instead of pondering this new experience further, Kira's mind went to work on the algorithm for setting up the phone to ring only once between the hours of midnight and ten AM. It was a simple algorithm, really, and she was surprised why she hadn't done it before. All it took was getting the time function from the system clock and setting a loop to pick up on the first ring or the third ring.

"Oh hell," she muttered, tossing the pillow aside and pulling herself out of bed. She slid into the jeans she had worn for three days straight and a Star Trek t-shirt. "Resistance is futile," she repeated. "I have already been assimilated — but not before coffee." Once her mind got to working on a problem, she couldn't shut it off. She walked into the kitchen, started a pot of coffee (the last of Susan's Starbucks roast) and walked to the computer.

As she sat down, she stared at a window on the computer filled with IP addresses. "What the...?" she said, and glanced at the addresses her program came up with as possible entrances to the Enchanted Forest. There were well over a hundred of them. Kira groaned. She'd have to visit each one and see — assuming the little webcrawler bot she created had done its job properly. At this point, a bot couldn't do what she needed to do — and that was figure out which were really entrances and which were traps. If she knew Spaz, he would've put traps all along the gateways.

"Damn it, Spaz, I'm not a spider," she grumbled. She was good, but she hadn't dedicated her life to the cyber equivalent of breaking and entering. Her job had always been to keep the spiders *out* — not to become one. She did that with good firewalls, tough passwords, and shutting doors where the security weaknesses were. In theory, the safest computer was one that was never hooked up to the Internet, but that just wasn't practical.

Kira typed in the address for the Denver Wolfpack and clicked on the message boards. She entered "Enchanted Forest" and "Yellow Brick Road" in the search engine (powered by Google) on the website and came up with nothing. After clicking through various webpages, it became obvious that what she was looking for wasn't there. She decided instead to check the links.

The links were as useless as the webpages. She pulled up Google and entered "Enchanted Forest." The webpages came up with the typical Disney stuff. She found a growl issuing from her throat. She got up and poured herself a mug, then sat back down at the computer, sipping the coffee. She smiled wryly and entered "Enchanted Forest" and "werewolf."

At the top of the search was "Rogue Wolf — the Website for Renegade Werewolves." Kira clicked on it and stared at the site.

What came up made her hackles rise. The site was a flash intensive and featured a movie of a werewolf mauling a human. She quickly clicked on **Skip Intro**, stood up, and walked away from the computer.

Kira paced for a while, wringing her hands. *What in the hell were these people?* she asked herself. The flash was far too reminiscent of her own attack. How could anyone be so perverse as to find *that* even interesting or enjoyable? If it had been a website on her server, she would've shut it down long ago. She sat back down and typed **whois www.roguewolf.com** at the prompt. The **whois** record showed that the website was hosted by Intermountain.

"'Curiouser and curiouser,' said Alice," Kira mused. Was Spaz wrong about Oz or was there something else she wasn't getting? She clicked on the message boards and scrolled through them. One user's post caught her eye.

Subject: KILL ALL THE MONKEYS!
Author: Wolfbane

"Wolfbane?" she mused. Was that the Wolfbane who'd sent her the email message that had ended up in the Intermountain Telecom black hole? She opened the message and stared at the words in horror.

For too long we've been the victims of the monkeys. It's about time we make the monkeys the victims. Too bad we didn't kill the last one — the bitch is one of us now. See you on the yellow brick road.
— Wolfbane

Kira stared at the post for a while and then scrolled through the responses.

Subject: Re: KILL ALL THE MONKEYS!
Author: Fangtooth
Yeah, Wolfbane! Kill em all!

Subject: Re: KILL ALL THE MONKEYS!
Author: GreyWolf
Weres rock! Down with Monkeys!

Subject: Re: KILL ALL THE MONKEYS!
Author: Southpaw
Let's kill them all. Freedom is at paw.

Kira scrolled through the postings. They were mostly "me-too" postings and anti-human blather. The reference to her survival frightened her — this Wolfbane must have been the same one who had written her a few days ago. Somehow, Wolfbane knew Kira — and had something to do with the attack on her and Susan. He might have even been the wolf who had attacked them. Kira thought about it a while. Maybe Alaric would recognize the name.

Thank goodness Alaric is in charge of the Denver Wolfpack, she thought. Otherwise, there might be an all-out war between humans and werewolves. She leaned back in her chair and took a sip of the coffee. The werewolves would lose, of course; there weren't as many werewolves as there were Normals. She wondered what would happen then. Persecution of werewolves again, just as there had been in the Dark Ages? She shivered. No, Alaric was right to hide his people from the Normals.

But what she found curious was Wolfbane's reference to the yellow brick road.

Yellow brick road. What in the hell is that? she thought. She typed out a message to Spaz:

S –
We've got to talk. What'cha say today? What does your PDA look like?
— K

Kira sent the message and sat back in her chair for a bit, then remembered the phone call. She glanced at the time on the monitor and realized it was later than she thought. Ten o'clock. She grimaced. The phone call had come at nine. She clicked the voicemail message.

"Hello, Ms. Walker? This is Officer Walking Bear. We found a wolf prowling around not far from your apartment. I need you to come down to Animal Control and identify the animal."

Kira felt shaky as she listened to the message. Could the police have caught the rogue wolf — or one of the rogue wolves who attacked her?

"I was also wondering if you'd like to have lunch with me," James Walking Bear's message continued.

Kira grinned as she wrote down the phone number and called him back. They agreed to meet by 11:00 — plenty of time for lunch. She'd identify the wolf and the police would do the rest. It would be so simple. She jotted down the address and frowned. Animal Control was on Jason Street, south of Denver proper. Kira frowned — she didn't have a car. She went to the mass transit website to see when RTD ran their buses.

She frowned again. She'd have to take a cab to meet him. It would be a lot easier to turn into a wolf and run down there, but she had no way to carry her clothes once she got there. Kira remembered having seen some dog hiking packs in the local REI. Well, they wouldn't help her now — and anyway, assuming she could figure out how to slip one on without opposable thumbs, a wolf with a pack would certainly draw attention.

Kira glanced at her email messages. There were none from Spaz, which was rather unusual. The man lived on his computers.

She sent a quick email to Spaz's gmail account in case he hadn't been checking his business email, and frowned. It was very unlike Spaz. Maybe the network was down?

She glanced at the time — she couldn't do anything about this now. Walking Bear would show her the attacker; she would identify him, and then what? She hesitated. Would they euthanize the animal? What if he turned into a human? With these disturbing thoughts in her mind, she called the cab. Maybe it wasn't as simple as she first thought. The wolf who killed Susan certainly deserved the death penalty, but didn't he deserve a trial first?

Kira pondered this as she rode in the cab toward Animal Control. She wanted to see the bastard pay for his crime. A lethal injection was just fine by her. The cab stopped off at the holding facility. A squat building, she would've hardly guessed it to be a place where dogs were held.

No sooner had she opened the cab door than James Walking Bear came out of the building. Kira handed the cab driver the fare and a tip before turning to the detective. She felt very sullen now — the fare had taken her last ten in her pocket.

"I didn't know you didn't have a car," he said. "I would've picked you up if I had known."

"No problem," Kira muttered.

"How much was it?" he asked.

She shrugged.

"Look, let me pay for it. I'll have the department reimburse me."

Kira stared at him. "Are you sure?" She had never heard of such a thing.

"Yeah, I'm sure." He took the receipt out of her hands before she could protest, opened his wallet, and handed her ten dollars. "That's with tip, right?"

Kira stared at the ten dollars he had shoved in her hand. She stared at it for a few moments before folding it and putting it in her jeans. "Thanks. But you didn't have to."

He met her gaze. "Yes, I did," he said. "Come on, let's see this wolf."

She walked in with him and noted that the building was

almost as plain on the inside. Once inside, Kira's werewolf senses prickled. Dogs were barking loudly here and the smell of bleach and cleaner assailed her. But the overwhelming scent was of fear. The dogs knew this was a holding place — quite possibly the last place they would ever be. Kira nearly gagged, wanting to run away. It frightened her, and took everything within her human mind to control the wolf she had now become.

"You okay?" Walking Bear asked.

"What a terrible place!" she whispered.

"It's not so bad," he said. "They care for the animals well here."

"I don't care," she said, shivering as she heard the frightened barks. "I don't want to be here." She turned around to leave and felt Walking Bear's hand on her shoulder.

"I know this is tough, Kira, but you have to see this wolf. You have to identify it."

Something about the touch of his hand made her stop. It was warm, and her acute sense of smell picked up his scent. Warm, too, and earthy. A pleasing scent, even to a werewolf. It seemed to relax her.

"Very well," she said.

"Good. We won't take any more time here than we have to." He led her back through the runs and cages filled with dogs. Kira didn't look at any of them. The dogs saw her and fell silent — some whimpered in fear as she passed. She heard their hushed voices as they recognized what she was.

Werewolf.

Her heart went out to them. They were the neglected, the abandoned, and even the abused. Most were mixes — nondescript brown dogs of medium size with floppy ears and short coats. They looked up at her with soulful eyes, each one hoping she could help them find a loving home.

There's some sort of mistake, she heard a puppy say to her. Kira paused and stared at the puppy. A purebred Labrador Retriever, it couldn't have been more than six months by Kira's reckoning. She looked up at Kira with soulful eyes. *My human came by and dropped me off. They tell me here I am awaiting my death. Please help me find my human — he would never do this to me.*

Kira jerked her gaze away from the puppy and swallowed hard. She could feel tears welling in her eyes. She looked straight ahead as she followed James to the back door. A largish woman opened the door and came out. She had graying brown hair and hazel eyes, and wore a work jumpsuit that said Denver Animal Control.

"You here for the wolf, Detective?" she asked.

"Yes, Martha," James replied. "This is Kira Walker, the woman who is here to identify it."

"Good," Martha said. "That wolf gives me the creeps. It's nasty — you can't get near it to feed or water it."

"Well, I'm sure you won't have it much longer," he said.

"Hi," Kira said weakly.

Martha eyed Kira appraisingly. "I hope it's your wolf. We don't need to worry about wolf attacks here." She paused. "Please excuse me. I have to clean some kennels."

"Excuse me a second," Kira said. "You know that puppy in the cage over there?"

The woman hesitated. "The Lab? Yeah."

"What will happen to her?"

The woman smiled. "That one's lucky — she's young. Labrador Rescue is coming by to pick her up."

Oh thank God, Kira thought.

"But others aren't so lucky," Martha added. "We had to put down a whole litter of mixed breed puppies the other day to make room." She shook her head. "It's a nasty business." She walked to the sink and began filling up the buckets for cleaning.

Kira felt sick as James led her back to the holding cages. Her gaze went immediately to the middle of the room. There, in a cage, was Alaric.

Ala..." Kira began and stopped herself. Seeing her rescuer and champion behind bars was horrifying. "Oh my God!" she gasped, covering her face with her hands. Alaric rocked the cage and grasped one of the bars with his jaws, tugging at it with all his might. She noted the cage was locked with a chain and padlock. "Oh God, not this!"

"It's okay, Kira. It can't hurt you," Walking Bear said, putting his arm around her shoulder. That seemed to incense the wolf further, and it snarled and lashed out at the bars with renewed fervor.

Her stomach was churning now, and she felt like she was going to throw up. She steeled herself. "Damn it, James! This isn't the wolf."

He looked at her. "It isn't? Are you sure?"

"Yes, I'm positive!" She looked at Alaric.

Get me out, Kira, Alaric said. *I'm doomed if you leave me in here.*

Kira wanted to run but something deep inside seemed to take control of her. "Yes, I will," she heard herself say to Alaric. "But how?"

"How are you sure?" James asked, confused. "I don't know — you tell me."

Kira turned back to the detective. "I'm sorry, I'm just confused. I don't know — I just know. This isn't the wolf."

"Well, I'm sorry to have brought you down here," he said.

"Maybe I can make it up to you."

Like hell you can! Alaric shouted telepathically. *Kira, get Cathal and get me out of here! Stay away from him!*

"That's some nerve," she muttered.

"What?" Walking Bear asked.

Speak in telepathy, Alaric said.

"I'm feeling sick," Kira said.

"Let me help you out," James said. He put a comforting arm around her and led her from the room.

The black wolf threw himself at the bars. *Kira! Kira! Help me! Don't leave me!*

Kira glanced behind her. *I will,* she said sounding far braver than she felt. *I'll get help.*

Alaric stopped throwing himself against the bars. She didn't dare look behind for fear she would see those golden eyes.

Once outside, Walking Bear turned to her. "Are you sure that wasn't the right wolf?"

"Yes," said Kira. "The wolf that attacked us was gray — this one is black."

James nodded. "Well, we'll find that wolf. Let me give you a lift back."

"Okay," she said.

"And lunch?" he asked.

Kira frowned. There was something nagging her, but she couldn't remember. "Okay. Lunch, then." She walked with him to his car, a red mid-eighties Corvette. "Wow! Is this yours? They must pay you a lot."

He laughed. "This thing? I got it at auction. One of the benefits of being a cop."

She opened the door and settled into the tan leather seat. "It's nice."

"Yeah, I like it," he said. He climbed in. "You okay?"

"Yeah," she said. "Detective?"

"Jim."

"Jim." She tried the name out. "Jim, what'll happen to that wolf?"

He shrugged. "I don't know. It's up to the city. I've heard that it might get relocated in a wolf preserve or something if it isn't the one that hurt you."

"When will they decide?"

He started the car. "I don't know. Maybe a few days. You know how government moves."

Kira sat back. That gave her a little time. She could contact Cathal by then and get him to rescue Alaric. "You'll let me know what they do with it before they do?"

Jim gave her an odd look. "Yeah, I suppose so." He put the car in reverse and backed out of the space. "Why the interest?"

"No reason," she said, looking out the window.

"I would think you'd like to see all wolves killed after what happened to you."

A shiver ran through Kira. "Yeah, well let me just say I don't want to see an innocent animal killed."

"Innocent?" He raised an eyebrow. "That creature was ready to rip our throats out if there hadn't been bars between us."

"It was frightened."

"It was pissed." Jim glanced at her as they drove back toward LoDo. "I grew up on a reservation — I know when an animal is pissed at me. That wolf would've killed us."

"I wouldn't want to see it killed."

He shrugged. He glanced at the Intermountain high-rise as they drove toward it. "Ugly building — it's a total blight." They approached a red light at an intersection and the car stopped.

"I used to work there..." Kira began. "Shit!" Bob had said if she wanted her old job back she had to meet him for lunch. She glanced at the old F&D tower. It was ten after twelve. "Shit! Shit! Shit!"

"What?" he asked, but Kira was already opening the door.

"I forgot — can I get a rain check for lunch?" she said.

"Yeah, but..." Jim began. The light turned green and the cars behind him began honking.

"Call me!" Kira shouted as he drove off. She ran into the Intermountain lobby.

Bob was standing there. "You're late."

Who was that, a boyfriend?" Bob asked. He stood with his arms crossed; his brown eyes slightly mocking. Kira could feel her hackles rise along her neck as she looked at him. Always handsome — and always smug — Kira was sure that Bob practiced the attitude in front of a mirror.

Kira grimaced. "A friend."

"Lose him. Anyone who drives an 85 'vette is a total loser," he said.

Like you would know? Kira thought. She said nothing. *I'm here to get my job back — not argue with Bob.*

"I would've thought you would've dressed better," Bob remarked, eyeing her jeans and shirt. "Or have you spent all your contractor money?"

"Yeah, on medical bills," she said. "I didn't realize we were going to a fancy restaurant."

"We're not," Bob said. "But most restaurants have some sort of standard."

What, McDonalds? That'd be not quite in your budget. Kira gritted her teeth. She could see Bob was enjoying her predicament. "Where to?"

"I was thinking *Maggianos* but they're crowded now, so how

about *Axioms*?" Bob said. Kira held her breath, not believing her good luck. She could see if Spaz was around and why he wasn't answering his emails. "I hear they're good — if new. They're got good wireless and decent sandwiches..." He paused. "Are you listening to me?"

"Yeah," Kira said, a little too abruptly. "That's sounds fine. I had breakfast over there not long ago."

"Okay," Bob said. They walked out of Intermountain toward *Axioms*. Bob began blathering in his self-absorbed way, so Kira had some time to reflect on the day. Last night she had been attacked by werewolves and nearly raped, and now her champion was incarcerated in animal control; she had ditched a very nice man who was willing to buy her lunch, and was now having lunch with the man she most despised. Kira tried to imagine the letter she'd send to her parents:

Dear Mom and Dad –

Turned into a werewolf last night. No worries, it's really okay. Was rescued by this really cool werewolf but he got locked up. Got to figure out a way to rescue him...

"Kira?" Bob asked, snapping her out of her reverie. "Are you listening?"

"Yeah," Kira said distractedly.

"Well?"

"Well, what?" she replied. She could tell by the way he scrunched up his face that he knew she wasn't really listening, and she didn't give a damn.

"What do you think about the new routers?"

"I haven't seen them, so I wouldn't know."

Bob frowned. "They're IP6 only."

"You'll have to switch them to dual mode."

"Can't be done."

"Then, they're a piece of junk if they won't work off legacy," Kira replied. "Did you buy them already?"

"Yeah."

Kira fell silent. They stood at the door to *Axioms* and stared at each other for a long moment. The door opened and as a patron walked out, Kira ducked in. The conversation had taken several wrong turns so far, and she couldn't see how she could get them back on track.

Kira looked up at the menu in *Axioms*. It was written on a blackboard that hung from the ceiling. She wondered how long it would take Spaz to change it over to flat panel display.

"Well it'd be just like you to suggest that," Bob said, slipping behind her. "Being a hacker and all."

"Spider," she corrected him. "And I'm not."

"Oh? Why hang onto legacy stuff when it enables your — spiders — to gain access?"

"Why support anything older than two years old?" she countered. "You can shut the door on spiders through your routers, but your networks are wide open and anyone can spoof."

"Are you saying I don't handle my security well?"

"The SNMP passwords on your system were defaults."

Bob glared at her. "Like DEADB0B was creative?"

Kira turned back to the counter. The barista was waiting patiently and enjoying the conversation. He looked to be in his twenties, with an earring and a tattoo of a dragon on his neck. He wore a white apron over a t-shirt and jeans. "Are you ready, Miss?"

"Yeah. I'd like a chicken salad sandwich and an ice tea." She glanced at Bob. "You buying?" His glare told her no. She shrugged and slapped her ten dollar bill down. "Look, Bob, we may not see eye to eye, but come on, you can take a little joke." She looked at him. "I mean, 1MAMAN? What kind of password is that?"

"Obviously not secure enough."

Kira took her tray and change and left the counter, finding an out of the way table. As she bit into the sandwich, she looked around. She half expected to see Spaz pop out from some server behind the counter and offer to refund her money. The food was tasty, but she knew she couldn't afford to consistently spend so much on lunch. Her mind wandered back to Jim Walking

Bear. Perhaps she was a bit hasty to have left him. She *liked* his Corvette, even if it was old. He made her feel comfortable — not the way Bob was making her feel now.

Bob sat down next to her carrying a club sandwich and chips. "You know," he said with a full mouth. "You could be nice to me."

"Uh huh," Kira said, wondering where this was going. She finished half of the sandwich.

"That was a cruel joke."

"Sorry," Kira said. "We were just blowing off some steam."

He smiled and Kira shivered involuntarily. There was something in that smile that told her he wanted something else. "You know, steam isn't the only thing you could blow."

"I could blow a whistle."

"Yeah, you could, but it won't get your job back." He paused. "However, if you were nice to me, I might consider bringing you back on board."

She stared at him. "You're joking."

"No, I'm not. After all, sweetie, you've only got so many good years left. You might as well use it while you can. You'll get further that way."

"Bite me," Kira snapped. She picked up her sandwich and drink. "Try that with someone stupid — don't waste my time." She walked over to the counter. "Can I get a box for this and a to-go cup?"

"Sure," said the barista. "The food no good?"

"No, the food's good — the company isn't," Kira said. She didn't bother to glance at Bob. "Say, have you seen Spaz, your computer guy?"

"Skinny guy with glasses? Japanese with dark skin?"

"Yeah."

"He was supposed to come in today," he said. "He didn't show up."

Kira frowned. "Odd. That's not like Spaz."

The barista shrugged. "Maybe he called in." He handed her the to-go items.

And maybe he didn't, thought Kira. Spaz had acted awfully nervous about the Enchanted Forest. She poured the tea in the cup and boxed the sandwich. Without a glance behind, she walked out of *Axioms* and down the street toward home, wondering what she was going to do about Alaric.

28

The message light on the computer was blinking when she returned home. Kira shut the door, set down the food, and clicked on the messages.

"Kira, this is Jim. I'm so sorry I upset you by showing you that wolf — can I make it up to you and take you out to dinner?"

Kira hit pause and shook her head. Even when she behaved badly, he still wanted to go out with her. A nice guy, if there ever was one. Too bad he'd dump her if he found out what she was.

She sat down and stared at the screen. So much for her getting her old job back. Not that Bob had really been ready to give it back anytime soon. He'd have used her and then laughed at her when she asked for a job. Asshole. But now Kira had more pressing problems.

Her first problem was Alaric. How in the hell was she going to get him out of the pound? He had said to contact Cathal, but she had her doubts about him. Alaric might trust him, but she surely didn't.

Her second problem was Spaz. Although he was a spider and a bit unreliable, she knew that if he was working it was because he needed the money, and he wouldn't have just disappeared. It was totally not in character. She pulled out his card and entered his name in the white pages on the Internet. It didn't turn up.

She frowned. "Okay, let's find you via your website." Kira Googled him and the search engine came up with Spaz's Home Page.

Spaz's Home Page.

Only my mom calls me William. Welcome to my website. I'm just your itsy-bitsy spider in the corner doing no harm, unless you're Little Miss Muffet.

Beneath the intro there were a number of links. One stared back at her: **The Yellow Brick Road.**

"Oh Spaz, Spaz, Spaz!" she grumbled and clicked on it. "Why couldn't you have been clearer?"

The link brought her into a rather staid looking site for an Australian Bed and Breakfast called, aptly *The Ruby Slippers*, www.therubyslippers.co.au. So far, so good, Kira thought. She had gone to Oz and had found the ruby slippers. Now to get them to work. Only she didn't want to return to Kansas — or Colorado, for that matter. She began clicking on links on the website — and found nothing. There were pictures of the quaint Victorian-style Bed and Breakfast. It showed beautiful blooming flowers and rooms with quaint beds and patchwork quilts.

"Damn, why would you have this link, Spaz?" she muttered. She knew that he didn't put up businesses on his site without a purpose. Unless perhaps the site had some sort of hidden webpage that she could get to. She glanced at the link and found that it wasn't an index page, but rather www.therubyslippers. co.au/BandB.html. Kira entered the site name without the page address. Technically, it should have brought her to the index. Instead, it brought her to the root file system of the computer.

"Oh Spaz," she said. She was in the public files. There had been a script that logged her onto the site. There was one file there: followtheyellowbrickroad. She entered *type followtheyellowbrickroad* and received **permission denied**. Frowning, she then entered *pwd followtheyellowbrickroad* and found it was only executable. But it was world executable. She frowned. What in the hell would it do?

Feeling like she had crossed over the line, she entered the command. She saw some gibberish flash across the screen and then, **opening port 42000, axioms.**

"Axioms?" She stared. "All the time it was on *Axioms'* site?" Or was it? She glanced at the IP addresses and found that they were linked into Intermountain computers. "All roads lead to Rome," she said. "Damn, what a twisted bunch of pricks you are."

Welcome to the Enchanted Forest, the words scrolled onto the screen.

The phone rang. Kira grumbled and glanced at the caller id. It was the police station — probably Jim Walking Bear. The Enchanted Forest would have to wait a little longer. She sighed and picked up the handset. "Hello?"

"Hi, Kira?" Jim's voice came through. "Did you get my message?"

"About dinner? Yeah, I'm up to it," Kira said.

"Didn't you hear the rest of the message?"

"No," she said, feeling guilty now. She had put the message on hold.

"Animal control has made a decision about the wolf," he said. "They're euthanizing it tomorrow."

S hit! Shit! Shit!" Kira shouted.

"I thought you'd be pleased."

"Why don't they turn it loose in the forest or something?"

"Kira, there haven't been wild wolves in Colorado since 1935," said Jim. "The Colorado Division of Fish and Wildlife considers any wolf found in a populated area to be a job for Animal Control, not them."

"What about wolf preserves?"

"They don't want an aggressive wolf." He paused. "Look, Kira, I don't understand why you're concerned about this."

"Well," Kira said. "Well..." She fell silent. How could she explain to him that they had captured the Alpha of the Denver werewolf pack? An uncomfortable silence followed.

"Dinner tonight?" Jim asked. "We can talk about it then."

Kira held her breath and looked at the clock. It was one o'clock. Maybe she had enough time to talk to Cathal by then. "Let's say six."

"How about the Italian?"

"Are you kidding?"

"I'll make reservations," he said. "Meet you in front of your apartment?"

"Sure," Kira said. She hung up the phone.

Kira stared at the words: **Welcome to the Enchanted Forest.** The Enchanted Forest was going to have to wait if she was going to rescue Alaric.

⚏K

Kira pounded on Trevor's door. Music from Warren Zeevon was blasting inside. She pounded again, this time using her werewolf-augmented strength. Now if he'd use his werewolf hearing — assuming he wasn't already deaf...

Trevor opened the door, looking sleepy. His clothes were baggy and rumpled — Kira couldn't tell if they were pajamas or real clothes. "Yeah? Oh, it's you." He tried to shut the door. She gripped the door and held it open. He turned around and walked into his apartment. "What do you want? An extension on your rent?" He wandered over to the couch and sat down. "You know, once they become were, half of them become deadbeats. They figure I won't evict them because they'll beat me up at night. Well, I don't think so. A deadbeat is a deadbeat, that's what..."

Kira walked over and turned off the stereo.

"Hey! What'dya do that for?"

"Alaric has been captured by animal control," she said.

Trevor raised an eyebrow, causing the brow-ring to move upwards slightly. Kira winced. "Oh?"

"What do you mean, 'oh'?"

"That's interesting news," Trevor said. "Can I turn my music back on?"

"No," Kira said. "What are you going to do?"

"Well, since you woke me up, I guess I'll have breakfast."

"It's one o'clock."

"Ten past, actually." Trevor shrugged. "What do you want me to say, Kira?"

"That you'll help me get him out. They're going to euthanize him."

"No they won't," he said. "Alaric will attack and tear their throats out."

"Not if they dart and sedate him first."

"Oh, I didn't think of that." Trevor smiled. "He could become human right there. Wouldn't that surprise them?"

"Yeah and expose more than just him," Kira said. "You know, they'll find out about the werewolves. And it won't take long before they figure out that the wolf attacks were actually werewolf attacks. Now, be a nice boy and help me."

"Bitch," Trevor remarked.

"Thank you," Kira said. "You say that like it's a bad thing."

"What do you want?"

"Who do I need to talk to?"

"Cathal," Trevor said. "He's at *The Grey Wolf*."

"Okay, come with me."

"Why?"

Kira hesitated. What could she hold against him that would make any difference? She knew nothing about werewolves except that they seemed to behave according to pack politics. She paused. *Pack politics.* That was her edge. "I know you weren't tailing me last night," she said. "And you should've been. You've disobeyed orders from your Alpha."

"So?" Trevor said. Despite the bravado in his voice, Kira could see uncertainty in his eyes.

"That doesn't make a wolf popular, does it?"

"Doesn't matter," Trevor said.

"It does when you're at the bottom of the pack," Kira replied. "Oh sure, if you were one of the Betas looking to grab the Alpha spot away, that'd be one thing. But you aren't, are you?"

A growl issued from Trevor's throat.

"How low in the pack are you, Trevor?"

"None of your fucking business, bitch."

"I think it is," Kira said. "Alaric gave you a job and you failed to perform. That'd drop you right down to — what? Below bottom of the pack? They might just drum you out."

"You don't scare me. You don't have Alaric to protect you."

"No, but I have Cathal." Kira wondered how much she could bluff. "Even if Alaric doesn't get rescued, I'll tell Cathal what a worthless prick you are and how you don't obey orders."

Trevor became very pale. "You wouldn't."

Kira smiled. "Try me."

"Bitch."

"And?"

"I hope Cathal chews you up," he muttered. "Okay, you win. We'll see Cathal."

Trevor brought her back to *The Grey Wolf*. This time, Kira decided she wouldn't show fear — too much was at stake here. Cathal was brutish but she hoped he cared enough about Alaric to at least save his life. If not, than at least maybe he cared enough about keeping the werewolves hidden. Kira suspected Alaric would change into a human if he had no other choice but to face a lethal injection, and then the werewolves would be exposed, so to speak. Kira wondered how the shelter worker would react, finding a naked man in a wolf cage.

"I'll lead you to Cathal, but I'm not going to back you up," Trevor remarked as they walked through the bar with the various patrons staring at them.

"Why are they staring?" Kira whispered.

"Because you're new, and because I'm with a woman."

Kira stared at Trevor for a moment. She remembered Megan's statement. "I forgot, you're a gay werewolf."

"You've got a problem with that?"

Kira laughed and shook her head. "No, I don't. It's just so — unexpected."

"What *did* you expect?" Trevor challenged, showing his teeth.

"Save it for someone else," Kira snapped. "I don't know *what* I expected, I guess."

Somewhat mollified, Trevor turned and asked two young werewolves at the bar where Cathal was. They pointed to the pool room. Trevor glanced at her and gave her a nudge toward the back room where she had first met Alaric. Kira nodded, whispered "Thanks," and made her way through the various lycanthropes to the back room.

There were no guards, so Kira entered. Cathal was playing billiards with another werewolf with long, dirty brown hair, wearing leather. He was younger than Cathal by a few years and had fewer scars on his face and more tattoos. His gold eyes watched Kira with mistrust.

Cathal didn't bother looking up. Instead, he was studying the position of the cue ball relative to the solid balls on the table.

"Come on, Cathal, don't take all day," the other werewolf said. He glanced at Kira. "Who's the bitch?"

"Wolf-bait," Cathal said, flashing his teeth. "What are you doing here, bitch?"

"Alaric has been caught by animal control." Kira eyed them both. She doubted she could take them on in either of her forms so she figured she'd have to bluff if they became aggressive.

Cathal laughed. "So?"

"He's scheduled for euthanasia."

Cathal lined up his cue and took his shot. The white ball clinked against a blue solid and sent it ricocheting off the sides. "That's not my problem."

"You're his second-in-command."

"And?" Cathal looked up. "Look, bitch, I don't know how the monkeys do things, but the pack law is how we do things."

"Meaning?" Kira asked.

"I'm now in charge of the Denver pack." He bared his teeth. "Alaric is a monkey-lover and he deserves what he gets. He was too damn concerned about what the rogue-wolves do, but he doesn't get it, now does he?"

"His beloved monkeys are now going to give him the needle. Ironic, isn't it?" the other werewolf spoke up as he took careful aim. He hit the cue, and a striped ball went into the corner pocket.

"Yeah, it is."

"You're not going to try to rescue him?" Kira said. "He's your friend and leader."

"He ain't my friend," Cathal said. He walked over to the table where his beer sat and took a gulp. The other werewolf tried to send another ball into a side pocket and it bounced and skittered into the middle of the table. Cathal met Kira's gaze with his own. "You don't understand, do you? He made a mistake and he'll pay for it. That's pack law."

"What about loyalty?"

Cathal chuckled. "You're wasting your time, wolf-bait. Go home."

Kira frowned as he went back to playing pool. She stepped back and stalked out of the room without another word.

As she returned to the main room, she spied Trevor in the back of the bar. He was drinking beer with a man with orange hair and earrings. "Trevor!" she shouted above the music. "Trevor!"

Trevor glanced her way and then turned to his companion. Kira pushed her way through the crowd of werewolves until she made it to Trevor's table. "Trevor," she said. "Cathal didn't go for it."

"So, who's your new girlfriend?" the werewolf with orange hair asked in a falsetto voice. "I had no idea you went both ways."

"I'm not his girlfriend," Kira said flatly.

"Thank Hecate for that," said Trevor. "She's a bitch."

Kira glared. "You're some help."

"I got you in to see Cathal."

"For all the good it does," Kira said. "He won't help Alaric."

"Well, little wonder, girlfriend," said the other werewolf. "Cathal is Alpha now."

"This is Mark," Trevor said quickly to her quizzical gaze. "We're friends."

"Yeah," said Kira. "I bet."

"You know, I could really do something with that hair," Mark said. "I did Trevor's — don't you like it?"

"A little too punk for me," Kira said.

"I'm a hairstylist," Mark said. "I also do wardrobe consultations."

"Somehow, I guessed," she said blandly. "Look, Trevor, we have to do *something*."

"Like what? This is pack rules, Kira," Trevor said. "Cathal is Alpha. Get used to it."

A low growl rumbled in Kira's throat. She turned and made her way out of the bar without another word.

Despite herself, her ears picked up a snippet of Mark and Trevor's conversation. "You know, I think she has something for Alaric," Mark said.

31

Kira walked out of *The Grey Wolf*, her eyes watering from the cigarette smoke and from her own anger and frustration. What in the hell was going on? What was wrong with these people? Didn't anyone care that a man was going to die? She sat on the curb and put her head in her hands.

Pack rules. She was getting a little tired of hearing those words. Sure, they were wolves, but they were also humans. That meant that they still had the ability to rationally think and act like humans. Somehow, along the way, the werewolves had not evolved the kind of society that valued fairness, kindness, and decency toward each other. Instead, they were concerned with pack law — that is, the biggest, baddest wolf became Alpha.

She wondered if someone like Alaric could change things. Kira could see plenty of good attributes in Alaric that made him the ideal Alpha. He didn't want a race war between werewolves and normal humans. He appeared to genuinely care about his pack members. And he seemed to have the kind of human side that, as Kira was quickly learning, most werewolves had abandoned.

But what could she do to free Alaric? The Animal Control building looked impossible to get into without keys. Even if she figured out some way to break in, she still had the daunting task of getting Alaric *out*. The cage was locked and she had no idea how to free him without the key.

She needed someone inside. She needed Jim Walking Bear.

Kira frowned. Convincing him would take some doing. And even if she did prove to him that her story was true, there was a little matter of whether or not he'd help her.

Kira walked back to her apartment and checked her messages once she got in. Nothing from Spaz. Kira called *Axioms* and found out that Spaz still hadn't shown up for work, nor had he called in. Kira shook her head as she hung up the phone. This was so unlike Spaz.

She checked Jim's number and called.

"Hello?"

"Hi, Jim," she said. "This is Kira. Hey, I need a couple of favors."

"A couple of favors?" Jim said lightly. "You know, it's going to cost you."

She chuckled. "Yeah, I know. I'll owe you, big time."

"Okay, shoot. What is it?"

"Well, I have a buddy from college who came into town not too long ago."

Silence greeted her.

"No, not a boyfriend, just a good friend. His name is William Tagura. Anyway, he's pretty regular about work and all, and he hasn't shown up at his job today and hasn't called in."

"You sure he's not playing hooky?"

"Pretty sure," Kira said. "He was talking to me about something two days ago and sounded really nervous."

"What was it about?" Jim asked, his voice becoming increasingly interested.

"Well, it was about some computer stuff," Kira said. "I didn't understand it exactly. He was so cagey about it."

"What's his name again?"

Kira gave him the specifics. She could hear him typing the information in the background.

"Look," he said. "It's probably nothing. If he's a geek like you say he is, maybe he found a girl and went on a vacation or something."

"Yeah, I suppose," said Kira. "Let's hope so."

"I'm sure he's fine. I'll send a uniformed officer to check on him, okay?"

"Okay. I just wish I knew where he lived."

"We'll find him," Jim said. "Anything else?"

"Yeah, there's also something else you need to know." Kira swallowed hard.

"You're married?"

"No."

"Engaged? Have kids?"

"No and no," Kira said. "Let me finish. We've got to meet early. I need to talk to you about something. It's important."

"You're not a criminal, are you? I mean, I already ran you through the database."

Kira felt like slamming down the receiver. "Will you listen? We just need to talk."

"Is this our first argument?"

"It will be, if you keep that up," Kira said. "Meet me at my apartment at five, okay?"

"Will do."

Kira checked the time. It was three o'clock, which meant she had time to shower and change. As she stepped in the shower, she remembered that the Enchanted Forest was still waiting for her on her computer. If she had time, she'd pay a quick visit before meeting Jim for dinner.

Despite the fact that he was a cop, Kira had to admit she liked him. He had also seemed to be interested in her — something pretty unusual, since she was a geek. Normal guys didn't date geeks. Geeks dated geeks, and even that was uncommon in Kira's experience, since many of the geeks she knew didn't have the interpersonal skills to even ask someone out for a date, let alone *really* date.

As she rinsed her hair, her mind turned to Alaric. He wasn't a geek at all. In fact, if he hadn't been a werewolf, he'd be the first one she'd think about pursuing. Unfortunately, he was locked in a cage in Denver Animal Control. And now, she was going to have to try to convince Jim that Alaric *needed* to be saved.

As she got out of the shower and dried herself off, she wished she had a time machine. Her life had been so much simpler before the attack. Hell, she might have even let Susan talk her into moving back to So-Cal.

After drying her hair and getting dressed, Kira sat down at the computer once more. The link to the Enchanted Forest had timed-out, which was not unexpected. Kira retraced her way through the links until she came to the welcome message: **Welcome to the Enchanted Forest.**

"Now what, Spaz?" she said. She did a quick *ls* *–l* and found herself in */bin*. "Okay," she said. "Now what?"

She listed the files again. Something didn't look right to her. She went through the UNIX commands one by one. She was on the "E's" when she noticed the word ***Enchanted***. It was, naturally, executable.

"Okay, Spaz, you've got my attention," she said. She entered the word. Nothing. "Great, just great." At the same time, she heard a peculiar buzzing just to her right. Great, she didn't need the old computer to be on the fritz.

She was about to get up when she noticed that it wasn't the computer buzzing, but the headset. She picked it up and felt it hum beneath her fingertips. It was a very slim thing — she had no idea it even had a battery pack — but it was obvious it had some microcircuitry in it. It looked and felt like a headset she might wear with an MP3 player, but with two more ear sets. She slowly put the headset on...

Suddenly, she was no longer standing in her apartment, but in an alpine forest — the kind she'd seen in tourist ads for Colorado. She was surrounded by coniferous trees and was standing on a small path that wound its way through the darkened woods. The wind was blowing, giving her goose bumps along her arms. She gasped and raised her hands, fumbling for the headset and pulling it off.

Kira found herself in her apartment once more. Her heart was pounding so hard that she could hear it in her ears. She stared at the headset. What had happened? The headset still buzzed. She gingerly put it on.

What's happening? she wondered.

Suddenly Spaz appeared in front of her. She almost jumped back. His hair was slicked back and he actually had a suit on. *Welcome to the Enchanted Forest,* he said.

A recording? she thought.

He turned to her but there was no recognition in his gaze. *Yes, I'm a recording. I'm a comprehensive FAQ guide to the Forest.*

What is this? she asked.

Please define.

The headset. This world. Everything.

Please state your text in the form of a query.

Damn computer, Kira muttered. *Okay, what is this headset I'm using?*

Headset is MIL-SPEC 1158, manufactured by Northrop Grumman Skunk Works, serial number 00129387...

Stop! Kira nearly shouted. *This was manufactured by Northrop?*

Yes.

Shit.

I don't recognize that command.

Pause FAQ and recognition software, Kira said. She pulled the headset off and stared at it. She could just faintly see where the Northrop logo had been filed off. "Damn, Spaz, what were you doing with classified shit?" Kira had heard of the military's interest in thought readers for tactical displays for weapons — but what the hell was this? And why would Spaz have access to classified military inventions?

Resume recognition software. State applications and versions.

Spaz smiled. *Enchanted Forest, version 1.32. TPRE – Thought Pattern Recognition Software version 2.43. EPRE—Emotion Pattern Recognition Software, version 2.45. CPI – Command Parser Interface 4.7.0. Msh – M-Shell version 3.32...*

Stop, said Kira. TPRE and EPRE? Kira had heard of this code being developed, but thought it was only in the early stages.

Kira's first thought was to shut it down and go to the police. Or maybe not the police; maybe the FBI. She had never thought of Spaz as a thief, but there were a lot of things Kira was finding out about him. Ten years tended to change a person. She had become what Spaz would consider a stik, while his spider tendencies had nudged him over to shady activity.

She put the headset back on. The FBI could wait. *Resume FAQ,* she thought. The Spaz image became animated but looked out vacantly as though it did not see her. *Resume recognition software. How am I able to use this?*

Define 'this.'

How am I able to use the headset?

The headset requires wireless communications of the hi-rFreq band...

Like the Intermountain wireless?

Spaz paused and looked confused. *Define Intermountain...*

Kira frowned. The logic of the speech parser was good, but not that good. She had to remember she was dealing with a machine. *Do you take commands?*

Command mode, Spaz said. *Command?*

Break, up one level.

Okay. Command?

Query connection software.

Enchanted Forest, version 1.32. Author William Tagura. Host Enchanted, LLC layer. Headset, client. Proximity, 500 meters...

Proximity? Wait. Pause.

Okay.

Kira thought about the software. Proximity was the distance between a transmitter and the headset. 500 meters wasn't that much but was good for a city block where there would be numerous transmissions. *Proximity to headset, serial number 00129387?*

1.23 meters, Spaz said. *Okay.*

Signal strength?

Excellent. Okay.

Kira took off her headset and stared at the computer. It was a little more than a meter away. The wireless router was hooked in right behind it. "The damn thing runs off the hi-rFreq," she muttered.

She walked over to her Sun and pulled up a web browser. She wasn't willing to use the headset *just yet*. She pulled up Slashdot and went through the rFreq, TPRE and EPRE information.

"Lizard97 writes "The MIT cowboys are at it again, this time with the rFreq. Can it possibly change the way we hook into the Internet?"

Kira went through every post, looking for TPRE and EPRE without success. She was getting ready to quit when she saw a reply to a post that looked intriguing. *Interfacing the new rFreq.*

Has anyone noticed that the rFreq bands affect animals in studies?

The post was by *Anonymous Coward*. Which meant that the person hadn't signed in or had decided to *not* sign in. She typed in *rFreq* and *Animals* into Google and came up with a number of Animal Welfare and Animal Rights sites. As she paged through them, some of the statements bordered on hysterical, claiming that rFreq shrunk animals' brains or caused stillborn deaths. Most of the claims had no foundation in scientific study. But one noted unusual reactions among mice, and cited a study funded at MIT.

Kira clicked on the link and received a *404: File Not Found*. She groaned.

At that moment, the door buzzed.

Kira jumped up in surprise and glanced at the clock on the computer. Five o'clock.

"Shit!" she exclaimed. She stashed the headset and ran over to the intercom. The Enchanted Forest, no matter how intriguing, would have to wait. "Who is it?"

"It's Jim," came Jim's voice over the speaker. Kira pressed the button to let him in the front door of the apartment building and then yanked her apartment door open.

"Wow," Jim said, "you got rid of the pizza cartons." He looked good in casual clothes. He held out a bouquet of flowers.

"Very funny," she said, scooping the flowers out of his hands and smelling them. "I knew I'd have to clean off the couch at least."

"So, I see," he said. "Hopefully, not just for me?"

"No," she said. "But how about if we pretended I did?" She paused as she put the flowers in a tumbler filled with water. She had no idea where a vase was or if she even owned one.

"You're welcome," he said, sitting on the couch. "So, what's the big secret? What couldn't you say on the phone?"

"It's hard to explain," Kira said, and took a deep breath. "You know the wolf."

"Yeah?"

"It can't be put down."

"Why not?"

"What do you know about the wolf attacks?" Kira asked, looking for a hint of recognition in his eyes. There were none.

"Well, there were five attacks, almost all centered around LoDo, with the exception of yours." He paused. "Kira, why don't you tell me what's up?"

"It's bizarre," Kira said. *How do you tell a potential boyfriend you're a werewolf?* "That wolf really isn't a wolf."

"Oh? Some kind of nasty dog?"

"No." She felt her voice sink as her hopes did. "There is a sub-culture in Denver that I knew nothing about until a few days ago."

"Really? What kind of subculture?" He was looking interested.

"Lycanthropic."

"What?" Jim frowned. "You mean people who think they're werewolves?"

"No, people who *are* werewolves." Kira saw disbelief in his eyes. "Look, I know it sounds crazy..."

"Have you been drinking? Taking pain meds?"

"No and no," she said. "Susan and I were attacked by a werewolf."

Jim laughed. "Good joke, can we go eat now?"

"No," she said. "I can prove it to you."

"It's not a full moon."

"Don't be stupid," she said. "I don't need a full moon." She paused. "Do you have a gun on you?"

"I'm an officer. What do you think?" Jim said.

"Whatever happens, don't use it on me — I won't attack," she said. "Although it might be a little embarrassing when I change back, so I'll go into the bathroom and you'll need to hand me my clothes — if you're not too shocked."

"So I get you out of your clothes? On a first date?" He raised his eyebrows.

"You won't feel you're lucky when you see me." She paused. "Promise you won't shoot."

"Promise you won't bite."

"Deal."

At that, she concentrated, knowing full well that he didn't believe her. As she changed, she heard him yelling her name, but she couldn't answer. When the dizziness subsided, she looked up and saw Jim standing plastered against the wall with his gun out.

"Kira? Kira!" he was shouting.

Kira nodded once. She turned toward the bathroom and trotted off. Once inside, she changed back. "Jim, could you hand me my clothes?"

Silence greeted her.

"Damn, are you still there?"

"Yes. Barely."

"I told you I wouldn't bite."

"Are you in human form?"

"I can't speak as a wolf," Kira said in exasperation. "Can you bring me my clothes? It's cold in here."

Jim walked over to the bathroom and she peered out. His face was pale. "Look, I know I shouldn't have done that," Kira said. "But Alaric is running out of time."

"Alaric?" Jim asked, handing her the clothing. "Is he your boyfriend?"

"No," Kira said. "To be honest with you, I barely know him. But he's in charge of the Denver werewolf pack."

"There's a pack?"

"Yeah," Kira said as closed the bathroom door and she slipped her clothes back on. "Damn, I really didn't want you to know all this. I was thinking I was so close to having a real boyfriend."

"So, how do you know this Alaric?" Jim asked.

"I turned into a wolf on the full moon. Those bites turned me into a werewolf."

Jim sounded relieved. "So, you're not used to this."

"Hardly," Kira said, walking out of the bathroom. "Well, you can tell the guys at the precinct you got me out of my clothes on a first date."

"Not funny," he said.

"You can put your gun away."

"What?" Jim looked down and saw he was still holding it. He holstered it. "Sorry."

"It's okay. I would've too. It's a big shock," she said. "Anyway, Alaric saved me from some werewolf thugs. He had escorted me home. Somehow, one of your men caught him." She paused. "I suspect he didn't want to hurt anyone."

"I think he would've — they darted him seriously," Jim said. "They've been giving him water and food with tranquilizers in it to keep him under control." He paused. "Look, are you sure that wolf is, is..."

"A werewolf? Yeah," Kira said. She thought about telling Jim about the telepathy but decided against it. It was bad enough he knew about the weres.

"Why doesn't he change back?"

"Yeah, right, a naked man in a locked cage with no way out. He'd do it if he had no choice — and at this point, your friends at Animal Control are probably keeping him so doped up, I doubt he could do much of anything."

Jim nodded slowly. "Well, if he's the leader of the wolfpack, why don't they rescue him?"

"I went to Cathal earlier — he's second in line and he's not going to do anything to jeopardize his promotion. And none of the other werewolves are going to step in and help him without Cathal's approval."

"Nice group," Jim said. He paused. "Cathal? You mean Cathal Murphy?"

"You know him?" Kira asked.

"How many Cathals do you know?"

Kira shrugged.

"The guy's been arrested a few times, but managed to get off," Jim said. "You're running with some tough thugs."

"Werewolves," Kira replied. "Suppose I handed Cathal over to you and had something that you could make stick?"

"What about this wolf pack loyalty?"

"They have none — and I couldn't care less what happens to Cathal. But I do care what happens to Alaric."

"Okay, okay," Jim held up his hands. "Let's get dinner. I promised you a nice dinner — and I'm not going to renege — werewolf or no. We'll talk about Alaric over dinner, okay?"

"Okay." Kira grinned. Maybe not all was lost.

I don't get it," Kira said as they walked downstairs. "You should be disappearing right now, never to return."

Jim grinned. "You don't get rid of me this easily."

"Really? Maybe I've been hanging out with the wrong people. I didn't know cops were so difficult to dissuade," Kira said coyly.

"It might be the badge." He shrugged. "Maybe it's my past. There are legends of skinwalkers with my people. I guess I don't find it all that strange."

"Strange enough to pull a gun on me." Kira gave him a sidelong look.

"I was startled."

"Yeah, that's one word for it."

"You want dinner or not?" He looked at her.

Kira laughed. "Of course."

"Then, don't argue. I like a woman who's a little on the wild side," he said. "I just didn't realize how wild. You like Italian?"

"Yeah," Kira said.

"There's a great Italian restaurant not far from here. Have you been to Maurice's?"

"No, haven't tried it yet — it's a bit pricey and I'm on a budget until I get another gig," Kira admitted as they walked outside. "The life of a contractor." She sighed. "I need to get a real job."

"Your buddy Will Tagura didn't need one."

Kira raised an eyebrow. "What's that supposed to mean?" They started walking.

"You hang out with some rather unscrupulous characters," Jim said. "Cathal Murphy..."

"I don't hang out with Cathal..."

"Will Tagura?"

"Spaz? He's harmless."

"Spaz." Jim shook his head. "Your pal 'Spaz' is wanted by the FBI for identity theft, stealing government property, cybertheft and other assorted crimes. And you tell me he's harmless?"

"Maybe harmless isn't the right word. Mostly harmless."

"I ought to take you in for questioning," Jim remarked. "Instead, I'm showing complete lack of judgment and taking you out to dinner."

"Thank God for male hormones, eh?" Kira grinned.

Jim laughed. "You've got me. Now, what was Will — er, Spaz — doing here in Denver?"

"I don't know," Kira said. "He had some gig at *Axioms* to fix their holes in their wireless — can't say as I blame them with the kids I've seen around here with PDAs and palm tops."

"No, what was he really doing here? You know, he was making not much more than minimum wage and some free food. What's more, he was under a stolen identity."

"Really? Spaz? Never seemed like the type."

"He was your buddy."

"Back at MIT." Kira shook her head. "Ten years changes a lot. Don't know what he's gotten himself into except some Internet stuff."

"He went by John Powers on his credit card. Everyone knew him at *Axioms* as Will, but he told them that was his middle name."

"Look, I don't know. He was agitated when I emailed him about Cathal. Said I was getting involved in something I shouldn't."

"Did he know about your, er, *affliction*?"

Kira smiled slightly. "No, I didn't tell him about *that*."

"So, he didn't know about the werewolves?"

"No, or if he did, he did a good job faking it." Kira cocked her head to one side as they walked. "You think he did?"

"Maybe. Maybe not." Jim looked at her as if considering her. "Your eyes were a different color when I first met you."

"Yeah, that's before I turned into a wolf. Charming, isn't it?"

"Contacts would change that," Jim remarked. "It'd also be less conspicuous."

Kira nodded. "Spaz noticed my eye color — you think maybe he knew what had happened to me?"

"Maybe. Maybe not," he paused.

"Why all the interest in Spaz? Have you found him yet?"

"My partner is tracking down his address. Last I heard, he had a possible address and is going to check him out." He paused. "In the meantime, dinner and hopefully good conversation." He stopped and Kira looked up to see that they were standing in front of Maurice's.

"You don't get that lucky," Kira said as Jim held open the door. "There's still Alaric."

"So, there is," Jim said. He walked up to the receptionist. "We have a reservation. The name is Walking Bear."

"Yes, sir, right this way," the woman said and seated them both.

"Is there any way you can get Alaric released into your custody?" Kira asked after the waitress handed them menus.

"I could try," Jim said. "But Animal Control is a whole separate division of the department. Let me give Wendy a call over there. Maybe she'll release him to me." He glanced at the menu. "Order any wine you'd like, and I'll have the chicken parmesan and a salad with Italian dressing. I'll be back in a few."

Kira nodded and Jim stood up and walked outside. He flipped open the cell phone. The waitress came by with a bread basket, took their orders, and left. Kira looked out the window to see Jim pacing and frowning as he spoke into the phone. At last, he glanced at Kira, heaved a sigh, and came back in.

"Damn department," he grumbled. "They won't do a damn thing without paper filed in triplicate."

"And meantime?"

"Meantime, your wolf buddy gets the needle." He sighed. "Kira, what do you want me to do?"

"Break him out — or I'll do it."

"Kira!"

At that moment, the waitress came back with their orders. Kira looked down at the veal parmesan, not hungry anymore. "Look, I know what you're saying," Kira said. "But I can't let him die and Denver is going to have a lot of explaining to do when they jab a needle into what they thought was a wolf and it turns out to be a human."

"They change back?"

"Yeah," Kira said. "Haven't you seen those old werewolf movies?"

"Okay, Kira," he sighed. "I'll free him — provided that he really *is* human. He's got to prove that to me."

"There'll be no problem there. So what do we do?" she lowered her voice. "Break in?"

"No, with a key," Jim replied. "Cops don't break into their own buildings. I just need to stop by the precinct and get a building key."

"Oh." Kira felt disappointed. She sliced a piece of the meat, twirled the mozzarella around it and ate it.

"Don't worry; I'm going to get into a lot of trouble as is with this wolf." He cut into the chicken.

At that moment, Jim's cell phone beeped. "Hang on." He raised a finger as he saw who it was on caller id. "Hello? Yeah, go ahead. You found what?" He winced. "Yeah, I'm with her. No, I don't think she has any idea. Thanks."

Jim hung up the phone. "We've got a bigger problem now."

Kira frowned. "What?"

"That was my partner. He found Tagura's residence. There's been a sign of forced entry, a struggle, and blood everywhere."

35

Are you sure it was Spaz's apartment?" Kira asked, her stomach roiling at the news. Spaz was kidnapped? But how? And whose blood?

"Pretty sure — lots of smashed computer equipment was inside," Jim said, standing up. He put down the cash for both their meals and a tip. "Box this up and take it home. I'll come by and pick it up."

"But what are we going to do?" Kira asked. She stood up when Jim did, but then found herself at a loss. *What do you do when your college friend disappears?* she wondered.

"*We* are not doing anything. *You* are going home and waiting for me until I call," Jim said. "I've got to go."

"That's it?" Kira asked, feeling her temper rise and the hackles along the back of her neck rise with it. "You can't tell me to do anything."

"Yes, I can. I know your secret."

"Asshole," she hissed. "Who's going to believe you?"

"You're going home — and that's final." He turned and left her alone in the restaurant.

Kira eyed her food mournfully. Her appetite was gone now. She had the waiter put the food in boxes, numbly watching him as he did so. What could she do? She didn't even know where Spaz lived.

She thanked the waiter and walked out of the restaurant with a bag of food.

Why did life have to become so complicated? she asked herself as she walked back to her apartment. A little over a month ago, life had been so different. Now she was unemployed and broke, her best friend was dead, another friend and a possible boyfriend were both in trouble, and on top of it all, she had a propensity to turn into something dangerous and hairy.

It was enough to send a girl shopping.

Spaz, where are you? she wondered. They found blood there — could it have been his? Or maybe not. It might not even have been his apartment. Even so, Kira was filled with dread. Who would have wanted to hurt Spaz?

Spaz had been agitated about something. He was worried about Kira using the Internet. Jim had said that Spaz was wanted by the FBI for cybercrimes. What was he mixed up in?

"Patience, patience," Kira muttered. She paused as she entered the apartment building, then she ran upstairs and unlocked the door. After tossing the food in the refrigerator, she sat down at the computer. "Fuck patience. I'm going to kill something."

She put on the headset and at once jumped headlong into the Enchanted Forest.

The Forest was dark, as though Spaz had written a Night and Day routine. In spite of this, Kira found she could still "see" with her eyes as she walked through the forest. Maybe it was the programming or something else.

The help function was no longer running. At the moment, she doubted that seeing Spaz in his electronic form would help much. It would remind her too much of what Jim had said. Instead, she walked down the path that winded its way through the Forest. She went on for some time, not seeing anything except more trees.

This is boring, she thought. She had hoped she could find something that would clue her in to where Spaz might have gone.

Well, girlfriend, it depends where you're looking.

Kira halted and looked around. *Who's there?* she said, hoping that her voice was menacing enough. She turned around but saw nothing but trees. *Show yourself!*

You're practically looking right at me, the voice said. It was fairly high-pitched and even a little squeaky. Kira looked around but saw nothing. *Cold.* The voice said.

She turned back.

Warm, the voice said. She took a couple steps forward. *Warmer.* She kept moving as the voice said, *Getting really hot.* A few more steps. *Cold again. Are you blind?*

Kira made a face and stepped backwards. She looked to the left and saw nothing but the tree. To the right was a tree as well, but this one had a lizard on it. *Are you that?* she said and tried to point with her hand. To her surprise, instead of a hand and arm, she was looking down at a paw and foreleg of a wolf. She gasped and jumped back. *I'm a wolf.*

The Forest usually chooses the avatar, the Lizard said plainly. *Actually I think it's Spaz's idea of a joke. I ended up a lizard; you're a wolf.*

You know Spaz? Kira asked sharply.

Yeah, doesn't everyone? the lizard asked.

Kira frowned. She walked around the tree-trunk eyeing the lizard dubiously. Now that she looked at it, she could see it was a large iguana-type creature with large purplish spots across its hide. *I've never seen a lizard your color.*

Like it? I added that bit of programming in, the lizard said, puffing out just a bit.

Yeah, I guess, Kira said. *Who are you?*

Lizard, the Lizard said.

*I know **what** you are,* Kira said. *I was asking **who** you are.*

That's my nick. Lizard. It's also my avatar, Lizard said. *Surely you've been in chat rooms and on blogs?*

Yes, grumbled Kira. She never really liked the secrecy of the Internet that much, and here in the Enchanted Forest, it appeared to be even more questionable. *So, you know Spaz?*

Yeah, but everyone knows him.

Have you seen him?

Lizard cocked his head and Kira became envious of the EPRE software. By the way it looked, it had to be enhanced for it to mimic the emotion so well. *Not in several days — why?*

I don't know, Kira said. She didn't want to tell anyone that she knew about Spaz's disappearance just yet, and was reluctant to talk to a stranger about it. *He said he was going to contact me but didn't. So, I thought I would ask.*

And he gave you a headset, Lizard observed.

Kira frowned. *How many headsets are out in RL?*

The Lizard grinned and showed its teeth. It reminded Kira of an alligator's teeth. *That's the mystery, isn't it?* He paused. *Happy hunting.* With that, he disappeared.

Kira frowned as he left. She didn't know what to think of Lizard and couldn't tell if he was a friend, an enemy, or someone completely neutral. She wondered how this person knew Spaz and how he got his headset. What's more, she wondered what she ought to do to find him.

She continued down the path, not really expecting to find anything. She knew she ought to get back and try to contact Jim. After all, with each hour, Alaric would be closer to a jab with that needle. She was getting ready to turn back when she saw movement through the trees. She hesitated for a moment. If she ran through the Forest, would she find her way back?

I can always take off the headset, she reminded herself. She turned left into the darkest part of the Forest, hoping to catch a glimpse of whatever it was she saw move. She did not see the dark shadow following close behind her.

36

Kira could see the shadow move before her. She wondered what kind of commands she could use to determine what she was seeing or whether there was really something up ahead. She ran quickly, hoping to catch it. As she ran, she caught a glimpse of what looked to be a white horse's flank. She launched herself toward it, only to find it disappear as if it were nothing but vapor.

Kira halted and stared into the darkening forest. She didn't know where she was, so she paused and assessed her situation. *Command?* she asked tentatively.

Okay, came a reassuring reply.

Help? she asked.

Help not available on this machine. Try man.

Kira looked perplexed. *Hostname-a*

Treacle HP-UX 13.1.2.5a HP 9000 PA-8900 64

Kira frowned again. She was in a computer she didn't recognize, but it had to be somewhere off the backbone. She was considering doing a traceroute when she heard a low growl. She turned around in time to see a huge wolf with glowing red eyes leaping at her.

Kira leapt aside as the jaws snapped in mid-air. She turned and sunk her teeth into the creature. Hot blood flooded her mouth. Kira wanted to gag, and nearly let go. Was this a program? The wolf turned and slashed at her. Kira yelped as pain ran down her neck. She ripped the headset off and once more was in her apartment.

It was dark, and only the quiet hum of the computers' fans broke the silence. The monitor flickered and filled with another screensaver — this time, a swarm that changed color with each movement.

She felt sick and shaky. She was panting and drenched with sweat. The taste of blood still lingered in her mouth. She stood up to go to the mirror, but her legs wouldn't move. Instead, she felt all wobbly. She closed her eyes and stumbled forward. Her neck hurt so much, she was sure she had a gash. As she staggered to the bathroom, she felt what little dinner she ate rise in her gorge. She lifted the toilet seat and heaved her guts out. When she finally couldn't throw up any more, she pulled herself up and looked in the mirror.

There was no sign of an attack or any sort of injury. Her eyes were swollen and her face was red from throwing up, but beyond that, she looked normal. She sank back down to the floor and felt the cold linoleum next to her face.

Why did she always have to learn the hard way? she asked herself. Kira felt stupid. It was her curiosity that always led her into trouble. *Curiosity killed the cat,* she reminded herself. She had no idea what it did to a werewolf, but she knew it wasn't good.

Her mind went back to the white, horse-like thing. She had only caught a glimpse of it before the werewolf attacked. What might it be? She felt that she should have recognized it, but what exactly it was, she couldn't say.

When she felt steady enough, she stood up. The werewolf thing had been a shock; she remembered Spaz said something about werewolves in the Enchanted Forest. Well, now she knew and would have to be more careful. She washed her face and took a sip of water. As she dried her face with a towel, she glanced at the stick-em digital clock she had put on the mirror. It said 11:25 pm.

"Shit!" She walked out of the bathroom, still unsteady. Alaric was still in Animal Control and she was losing precious hours. She got some more water and opened the fridge. It wouldn't do for her to go after Alaric on an empty stomach, even if it was still a woozy one. She popped her leftover dinner in the microwave. While it was cooking, she went back to the bathroom to search for something for her stomach. After a quick search, she found a bottle of Pepto Bismol, opened it up and took a swig. The pink peppermint flavor made her want to gag, but she forced it down and then drank more water. If she was going to break into Animal Control, she had better do it at her peak.

The microwave beeped and she pulled out the veal parmesan. She and ate it and the fettuccini ravenously. Unsatisfied, she went back to the fridge for Jim's untouched chicken parmesan. She warmed that up, too, and ate it.

She wondered what this would do to her figure, but she guessed that as a werewolf, she burned a lot of calories. Wringing her hands, she tried Jim's cell phone but only got a voice recording.

"Jim, this is Kira..." she began. *Your werewolf girlfriend?* A nasty voice inside her head added. "Look, I've got to get Alaric out of Animal Control. Can you meet me there?" She was beginning to feel sick again. She gave him her phone number and hung up.

Oh yeah, that will really work, the voice inside her said. *Now you'll just get arrested for B&E.*

Kira ignored the voice, grabbed her keys and what little cash she had, and called a cab. She walked downstairs, glaring at Trevor as she passed him in the hall. He acted as though he didn't see her, but she could smell the change in his body's odor. It smelled like fear.

Good, she thought. *He ought to be afraid. How dare he turn his back on the pack's Alpha.*

She stopped herself. *Where did that thought come from?* She shivered, not really wanting to know. The whole concept of an Alpha was completely alien to her, and yet, a part of her accepted it. *No*, she told herself firmly. She would rescue Alaric, but not because he was Alpha. She would rescue him because he was in danger of being killed. And, she had to admit, she liked him a lot. Even if he was a werewolf.

As the cab pulled up and she got in, Kira wondered what she was getting herself into this time.

Alaric paced in the small cage. He had changed back to his human form twice, only to find that he could do even less as a human than he could as a wolf. He had tested the steel bars both with hands and teeth, but they were strong, tempered steel — there was no way he could break them. The lock, too, was case-hardened steel — without a tool, neither his teeth nor his hands could do anything with it.

So, he had resolved himself to pacing back and forth. All the hope he had left was Kira's promise to bring help. She *had* promised she *would* bring help. Would she talk to Cathal? And would Cathal show proper pack loyalty as his Beta? Alaric had never had a lot of faith in Cathal or in Cathal's loyalty, but now he didn't have much choice. Kira couldn't get him out alone. And with her cop boyfriend...

Now, that rankled Alaric. He snarled and slashed at the cage before catching himself. What did he care if Kira had a boyfriend? Alaric hardly knew her. Yet, he was attracted to her. She was beautiful both as a wolf and a human. She was tough-minded, too. And he could tell the attraction was mutual.

And yet, and yet... she was there with the cop. He didn't know the exact relationship between them, but their body language and pheromones told him they were more than just friends. Alaric didn't want that. In the old days, he would've killed the man for being so bold as to try to steal his mate, but these weren't the old days. Werewolves had to be careful because Normals had the means to kill them. It wasn't just silver anymore. Regular bullets did nothing, but there were other weapons available to the Normals now that would kill even a tough creature like a werewolf.

He paced the cage again. It had been hours since he had seen Kira. He wanted desperately to believe that she would be coming back for him like she'd said she would, but part of him knew that she might not. His last resort was to simply turn human and come up with a plausible story about a crazy man who had stolen his clothes, taken the wolf and locked him in the cage. He didn't think anyone would really believe it, but what other way was he going to get out of this cage except through a lethal injection?

There would be questions, of course, and perhaps an arrest, but when it was investigated, nothing substantial would turn up. The werewolves would be safe. He would have to face a few dings to his pride and maybe an arrest record, but he would still be alive.

Suddenly, he heard something outside the building. The dogs in the shelter started barking wildly. Alaric tried to listen, but to no avail — the barking was too loud. He then heard a loud screech as the door was ripped off its hinges. The dogs continued to bark, but then fell silent as whatever it was started walking toward him.

Alaric waited, cocking his head and listening intently. Footsteps came from the hall and he waited as the person entered the room.

Alaric turned into a human. "Cathal. Thank Hecate, it's you."

Cathal flipped on the light switch; a sardonic smile crossed his face. "I see your girlfriend was right — you did get caught." He tsked and shook his head. "Careless, Alaric."

"Yeah, well, sometimes it happens," Alaric said warily. He could smell alcohol on Cathal's breath; the man was drunk. "So Kira sent you?"

"No, not exactly," he said. "She asked me to come here and I told her no. You see, I like being Alpha."

Alaric set his jaw. "You can't be serious. That would be a breach in pack law. You would betray me?"

"There's nothing to betray, Alaric," Cathal said. "I never swore my loyalty to you or to anyone. I've always been an outsider and I've always gotten what I want — my way."

With that, he produced a gun. Alaric changed into a wolf again and Cathal laughed. "Do you think I'd bring lead bullets?" He pulled six bullets out of his pocket. They gleamed in the light.

Alaric's wolf gaze narrowed. *Silver bullets?*

"I had them specially made for you long ago — only I never seemed to find the right time to use them." He flipped open the revolver and began chambering each one. "It won't matter what form you're in, Alaric. You'll be dead either way."

Alaric lunged at the bars and grasped them in his teeth, pulling at them frantically. Drunk or not, Cathal was going to shoot him and at this distance, Alaric knew he wouldn't miss.

Spaz awoke to sheer agony. He was lying down on his side, bound and gagged. They had covered his eyes so he couldn't see, but he could move his left hand a bit. When he tried to touch his right arm, he felt the dirty bandages and the bloody stump beneath. Pain shot up his arm, his tongue pressed against the gag in a silent scream and he blacked out.

Spaz didn't know how many hours had passed when he finally awoke again. He had soiled himself and he was still in terrible pain but his thoughts were clearing. He had known that Cathal had joined the wolves, but he never thought his old friend, Randy Green, would've gotten involved the way he had. Somehow, the wolves had nudged him over into something more sinister and more deadly.

They weren't going to let Spaz live — that, he was sure of. Having a real wolf or dog bite off his hand was proof of this. They wanted to keep him alive long enough to gain access to the rest of the Forest and to sell it off to the highest bidders. Once they cracked the codes, they could go anywhere and do anything with any computer hooked into the Internet. The net within the Net gained them access into some of the most sensitive computers in the world.

The Forest didn't have access to all the computers in the world — just the ones hooked in to the Internet. But if they had just one system — even just one system with a firewall — the entire network was vulnerable. The Forest didn't access DOD machines; the government had kept most of the sensitive machines on private networks, eschewing any hookup to the Internet, even with so-called ironclad firewalls. Paranoia in this case was good. But there were enough systems hooked in—bank computers, financial computers, computers with information worth millions of dollars — that it was quite possible to finance a small country or even a large one with what could be gleaned from them. Then there were the hook-ins to utilities and vital government machines that could be exploited, or cause everything to come to a grinding halt.

Randy was looking for the codes to sell to the highest bidder. Or maybe he was now with the highest bidder. The wolves had to be a terrorist organization.

He closed his eyes and focused. It was useless to try to look out with the blindfold on, anyway. Spaz could sense the *hi-rFreq* band even here — he wasn't so far from the Forest that he couldn't feel it. He let himself drift; if he relaxed, he could almost see the entrance to the Forest.

Within his mind's eye, he could see the Forest appear around him. Every box had a backdoor for him. He had to somehow contact the police, but without a real voice and a real location, a 9-1-1 call would be considered a hoax at best.

Randy was a moron, Spaz decided. A dangerous moron but

a moron nonetheless. Randy had never thought about how *hi-rFreq* could affect people's thought patterns, especially once a person became aware of them through the headsets. When Randy had left Northrop, he disappeared. He had taken not only the plans for *hi-rFreq* but also the prototypes for the headsets.

Randy had given the headsets to Spaz first. They worked perfectly and Spaz had known they were the final piece of his Enchanted Forest. But Spaz had noticed a change in his perception each time he had worn the headset. And then he had noticed that after many sessions, the headset's influence still lingered. Spaz could still access the Enchanted Forest without it for a while. It was almost as if the frequencies of the headset didn't just pick up thought patterns, but modified them as well. Randy had never noticed it, even though he was an accomplished RF guy and a brilliant inventor. And now he was playing with dangerous criminals.

The wolves had discovered the Forest first. There was something within them that allowed them to pick up the *hi-rFreq* and see the Forest as it was. Spaz had never believed in mental telepathy or any sort of telekinetic powers, but he couldn't discount them now. The wolves' mental structure seemed to be arranged to pick up these odd frequencies.

Spaz decided against his usual avatar. If the wolves found him now, they'd know he could access the Forest from his confinement—more than that, they would know he was searching for help. And they would kill him for it. He pulled up his various avatars and settled on one. He became a white unicorn with a glistening pinkish horn and pale, luminescent goat hooves. He trotted into the woods, hoping his disguise would be enough to fool the wolves.

It wasn't long before he was on the pathway toward the city network. From there, he could send a text message to Kira, or maybe to the Denver police department. But at that moment, he saw a wolf standing beside a large tree. It was next to a gecko — a gecko! — Spaz turned and fled.

He could sense that the wolf had seen him — or a part of him. He ran as fast as he could. Before he knew it, he was back inside his prison, lying on the floor, bound and gagged again.

Spaz wanted to cry, but he was too dehydrated and no tears would come. He lay there wishing he were dead.

38

The door was open. It sagged against broken hinges where something powerful had ripped into it and pounded massive dents against it. Kira took a sharp breath inward and stopped. Her heart was pounding in her ears and her mouth was dry. Could she have gotten to Alaric too late?

Somewhere inside, she heard the barking start up and then fall silent, as if snuffed like a candle. Kira shivered. She knew the dogs' reaction was to a werewolf. Maybe Alaric's wolves had come to save him?

Cold comfort, she thought. She really didn't think the werewolves were so charitable. They were more likely to gloat because he was gone and they could scrap over the Alpha position. Or to make sure that he was gone for good.

Kira hesitated. Should she go in? She was strong enough to take on a human, but she doubted she could take on a big male werewolf. A male's werewolf-augmented strength would be greater than hers. She could easily be caught again, like when she had met the werewolves in the alley. Only this time, there would be no Alaric to come to her rescue. He would watch helplessly as the other werewolf tore her to pieces.

Her cell phone began to play its cheery tune and Kira snarled as she hit the button to mute it. Who in the hell would call her now? More importantly, who had her number? The number flashed before her but she didn't recognize it. Was it Jim?

She slid back. *The werewolf would've heard the phone ring.*

Her position compromised, Kira stood for a moment in indecision. The number was still flashing at her urgently for her to answer the call. If she answered it, she would give away her position. She hesitated. She should go back, call Jim, and get help.

The number still flashed urgently. She pressed the button to answer.

A scream echoed from behind the door. It sounded like an animal in anger or rage. Kira's heart raced and the wolf part of her leapt into action. As a human, she would've run, but she wasn't quite human now. Something more primal took hold of her. A pack member was in trouble and it was up to her to help him. With a snarl, she leapt forward.

Alaric! she shouted mentally.

The lights were on in the shelter as she ran through the door and past the cages in the shelter. Kira stopped dead in surprise and the cell phone fell from her hand.

Cathal Murphy was standing before the cage. His eyes were bloodshot and his face was flushed. Even from this distance, he reeked of alcohol. He held a revolver in his hand. Alaric, still in wolf form, was snarling at him and tearing at the bars, his mouth bloody and foaming from the exertion.

"I see your girlfriend decided to come to the rescue," Cathal said, his voice slurred. He turned to her. "Over there! Now!"

"Leave him alone, Murphy," she said, trying to steady her voice. Seeing the gun made her quaver. "You know you've got nowhere to go."

Kira, Alaric's voice spoke in her head. *Do as he says.*

Kira started to move toward Alaric. "I thought we couldn't be injured by bullets."

Silver bullets, said Alaric.

"Silver bullets?" she repeated. "You can really make those?"

"Yes," Cathal said. "Now, move over there."

Kira shivered and walked beside Alaric's cage. "What are you doing, Cathal?"

"Shut up." He pointed the gun at her.

Kira shut up.

You're stinking drunk because you don't have the courage to do this sober, Alaric said.

"You're such a sap, Alaric," Cathal said. "I could kill you anytime."

"You kill Alaric and you'll be in for more than you bargained for," Kira said.

Kira, shut up, Alaric said.

"No," Kira said. "You think you're going to kill the wolf in the animal shelter and get away with it, Murphy? What happens when people find the bodies?"

"They won't find yours," Cathal said. "And they'll simply assume Alaric is some crazy person."

"Locked in a wolf cage with a bullet through his heart?"

Thanks, said Alaric sarcastically.

"Yeah, something like that." Cathal raised the gun.

Traitor! Alaric shouted.

"What happened to Spaz?" Kira asked suddenly.

"Spaz?" Cathal blinked.

"Yeah. Will Tagura, or whatever he calls himself to you."

Alaric cocked his head at her. Something indecipherable gleamed in the back of Cathal's eyes. Kira didn't like it, whatever it was, but it was proof that she had gotten to him.

"You know Spaz?" Cathal asked.

"Yeah, he and I are old buddies," Kira said. "Is he still alive? He came to see me."

Kira... Alaric's voice was a growl in her head.

"Were you his operative?" Cathal asked. "I figured you and the other girl..."

"Susan," Kira corrected him, trying to keep her voice steady. "Her name was Susan."

"Susan — had something to do with the Enchanted Forest," Cathal said. "Did you?"

"Is Spaz still alive?"

"For the time being," Cathal said. Kira's throated tightened, but she kept herself steady. "What do you know about it?"

"Enough," Kira said. "Spaz and I worked on the architecture."

Kira... Alaric's voice was almost pleading.

"So, you could give me what I want?"

"Give me Spaz and we'll talk," Kira said. "Alaric too."

Cathal's eyes narrowed. "I don't think you have anything..."

"You shoot us both and you won't find out..."

"Halt! Police!" Jim's voice came from the doorway. His gun was out and just barely visible.

"Goddamn bitch!" Cathal roared and swung the muzzle toward her. But Kira leapt at him as he raised the gun. The muzzle blast exploded by her ear and the gun discharged into the ceiling. Suddenly, Kira was no longer gripping a man's arm, but was knocked over by a black wolf. In an instant, she shifted to her own wolf form and started biting anything she could.

Blood and fur were everywhere. She felt Cathal's teeth sink into her flesh just as she had when the wolf had attacked her over a month ago. Instead of being terrified this time, Kira was enraged. She bit hard and pulled, tasting blood and relishing the sweet revenge.

Gunshots rang out and Kira felt several hit her body and bounce off. They stung like hail. Cathal's teeth had sunk into her neck and he shook her like a rag. Pain exploded through her but she held on and kept conscious, scratching and snapping at whatever she could reach. She tried bracing herself against his body with her four legs; tried pushing against him, but to no avail. He was too powerful.

Jim was hovering over them, reloading. He was covered with blood splatter. He aimed at Cathal's head.

"Don't bother!" she heard Alaric's voice. "Normal bullets won't hurt him — get me out!" She could barely see Alaric from the corner of her eye — he had transmuted back to human form to communicate with Jim.

Jim turned and fired two rounds into the padlock. The door swung free, and suddenly Kira and Cathal were both knocked sideways, bowled over by the great black wolf. Next to Alaric, Cathal looked small. The Alpha ripped into Cathal's throat and his teeth pulled massive chunks of flesh. Blood spewed everywhere, falling on her like hot rain. Kira tried to raise herself from the ground, but she was in terrible pain. She groaned as the fighting wolves leapt off her and watched as Alaric dragged Cathal to the ground. She felt warm, reassuring hands touch her and when she looked up, she saw Jim's face.

"You okay, Kira?" he whispered.

Kira whined as her vision began to dim. *Help me,* she thought as she tumbled into blackness.

39

Alaric transmuted back into his human form and gazed on Cathal's dead wolf body, covered in blood. He picked up the revolver.

Jim raised his weapon. "I'm a friend of Kira's."

"So am I," Alaric said. He turned and emptied the rounds into the wolf. He turned back to Jim and tossed the gun down. "So, you know what we are."

"You just killed a man," Jim said.

Alaric shrugged and picked up Cathal's clothing. "I killed a wolf. That's what your report will read," he said as he slid the jeans on. He paused. "How is she?"

"Not good — she's lost a lot of blood," Jim said. He pulled the bandages from the first-aid kit on the wall and pressed them against her neck. Kira groaned but did not open her eyes.

"Let me see," Alaric came over and frowned. He flipped up her gums and pressed against them. They whitened and stayed gray. "She's going into shock — I've got to get her to Megan's."

"Who's Megan?"

"A werewolf vet," Alaric said. "How did you know we'd be here?"

"Kira left the phone line open when I called her. I had a hunch she'd come to get you."

"No wonder she was talking," Alaric said. "Bright girl — she knew to keep Cathal talking as long as she could."

Jim glanced at the black wolf lying on the floor. "Isn't he changing back?"

"No," said Alaric. "Most do, but he was born feral with wolves in Canada. That's his normal form."

Sirens echoed in the distance. "Great — you called for back up?" asked Alaric as he scooped Kira up in Cathal's leather jacket.

"Of course," Jim said.

"Look... If they find me, she'll never get help — I need to get her to the vet," Alaric said. "We'll be at Megan's vet hospital on Sixth Avenue — you know where that is?"

"Yeah, I do," said Jim. He reached into his pocket and handed Alaric his keys. "My name is Detective Jim Walking Bear — I already know you're Alaric Kerr. My car is out back — take it." He paused as Alaric stared at the keys in his hand. "You know how to drive?"

"Yeah," Alaric said. "Help me get her to the car."

They walked out the back. Alaric was still barefoot, but didn't seem to notice. Jim led him to the red Corvette, and Alaric unlocked the door. "If you don't come get me in an hour, I'll have your name across all the radios. I need to know how she's doing."

Alaric laid her gently in the passenger seat. He met Jim's gaze with his brassy stare. "Give me your phone number — I'll call from Megan's if I'm delayed." Jim handed over his card as Alaric climbed into the driver's seat. He started the engine and pulled out as the police cars parked along the front.

═══⧼⧽

Kira groaned, and Alaric glanced beside him. She had lost a lot of blood — more than he had seen most wolves lose and survive.

Stay with me, Kira, he said to her.

The drive to Megan's was relatively short. Megan was in

Southeast Denver, practicing in one of the old Victorian homes off of 6th Avenue. He could get there in less than fifteen minutes.

Despite his worry, and his fear that Kira might die, Alaric wondered what her relationship with the cop was. He had known nothing about the cop, and yet Kira seemed to have told Walking Bear everything about him and the werewolves. This was dangerous, Alaric reflected. He glanced at Kira. She seemed to be on better terms with Jim than with him. The cop even had a Corvette. A Corvette! It rankled Alaric, despite himself.

He pulled up to Megan's, hopped out, and pounded on the door. Nothing. He looked at the time and snarled. Of course, she'd be a wolf now. It was a little past two am — Megan wouldn't be arriving to work until sometime after six.

Damn, damn, damn, he thought. *Why in the goddess's name did it have to be so difficult?*

"Kira," he whispered in the wolf's ear. "Can you become human?" Denver General was only a few blocks away — if she could change into a human, she could be treated. He'd take the consequences — whatever they were — for bringing her in. "Change, Kira, it's the only way I can save your life."

Nothing.

Suddenly he felt a presence. He turned around to see the flitting image of a werewolf in the shadows down the block. Without a second thought, he turned into a wolf and leapt after it.

The wolf squealed in terror and began to run when it saw Alaric bearing down on it. *Wait!* roared Alaric. *I am Alpha!*

The wolf halted and lowered his head, turning his belly toward Alaric. *Forgive me, Alpha.*

Find Megan Olson now! Alaric roared at him. *She must come immediately! A life is as stake!*

I obey, the wolf said and skittered off.

Alaric raised his head and howled. Within that howl, he demanded that Megan come back. He returned to the car and transmuted back to human form, sliding his clothes back on. He sat with Kira, stroking her fur as he held her.

Now, he had to wait.

It was maybe fifteen minutes when he heard the pad of paws. He looked up and saw Megan approaching, still in her wolf form. *It's Kira,* he said. *She saved me from Cathal.*

Megan nodded once and went around back. She came out a minute later in human form, still buttoning her blouse. "Damn it, Alaric," she said. "You scared the piss out of John back there."

"He should be scared," Alaric replied. "I'd have killed him if you hadn't come."

"The whole pack is in an uproar," Megan said. "We heard you'd been captured by Animal Control, and then Cathal took over..."

"And no one thought to bother rescuing me?" Alaric said, his eyes narrowing. "No one except Kira."

Megan did not meet his gaze. "None of us were strong enough to stand up to Cathal and his wolves."

"I may let you live if you can save her." He opened the car door and scooped Kira into his arms.

Megan's face became ashen as she looked at Kira. "Damn it. She's lost a lot of blood. Bring her in."

He carried her to the door and Megan unlocked and opened it. "Should I have brought her to Denver Central Vet?"

"No, they would've killed her," she said. "Dogs don't have the same blood types as werewolves. One of the joys of having human genetics running around with the canine ones." She flipped on the lights and led him through the waiting area and into the back room. The surgery table stood clean and empty. "Put her there. What's your blood type?"

"I don't know," he said. "Don't you have blood available?"

"Yeah, I do — I have werewolf donors all the time — but she may need more than what I have on stock. Go to the fridge and pull out O-negative werewolf," she said. "I'll type her later."

Alaric opened the refrigerator and found several packets of blood. "There's O-negative human..."

"No, she's a wolf — she needs werewolf blood..."

Alaric searched. In the back, he found a couple of pints marked

O – Were. He held it out. "This it?"

"Yeah," she said. "She's going to need more than that. Get on the phone and call up Jim Smith — he's my O-neg donor."

Alaric handed her the plastic pints and looked around the phone for an address book.

"Damn! I wish Mike were here!" Megan snapped. "Turn on the computer and look in Outlook Contacts. Call Mike Fowlkes on his cell phone and tell him I need him now. Then call Jim Smith."

Alaric felt helpless as he dialed the phone and barked orders to the werewolves' voicemail. He then came over to watch as Megan began stitching Kira's wounds. "How is she?" he asked tentatively when Megan offered no information.

"She's make it," Megan said. "I don't know how that asshole missed her jugular, but he did. He missed the carotid too." She shook her head. "Lucky, lucky girl." She finished sewing up the wound and pulled out a syringe. "You know if she's allergic to penicillin?"

He shook his head.

"Dare not chance it then — we'll go with something else," she said. She smeared a slide against some of the blood and went over to the microscope. "Well, she's lucky. Your girlfriend's were-transformation is complete. If she were just a Normal, she'd be dead."

"Girlfriend?" Alaric said sharply.

Megan turned and grinned. "Don't play coy, Alaric. She wouldn't have come after you if she hadn't some feelings for you."

Alaric turned to gaze on Kira's face. "I guess not." He paused. "How long before she regains consciousness?"

"Might be a while," Megan said. "She's lost a lot of blood and needs to rebuild. I need to type her — and you — to see if there's a match. If there is, you can donate blood — assuming you're up to it. Otherwise, we'll use some of the blood in the fridge and let her body make up for the rest. I don't think Jim's coming any time soon — I hear he's dating a cute bitch in Englewood. Mike won't check his messages until the morning either." She paused. "Have you ever thought of setting up a kind of 9-1-1 for werewolves?"

Alaric cocked his head. "No, I hadn't."

"We need one," she said. "Mike and I have been working on the plans. He wants to set one up for Montana, too." She paused. "Nice Corvette, by the way. Whose car did you take? That wasn't yours."

"Damn!' Alaric pulled the business card from his pocket. "A cop named Walking Bear — he's going to be angry if I don't call." He dialed the phone, uncertain what he would say when the cop answered.

40

While he waited for backup, Jim tried to clean up the evidence as well as he could. It was almost impossible. Alaric's fingerprints would be on the gun with Cathal's. Cathal's blood would be mixed with Alaric's and Kira's. Jim knew he'd have some explaining to do.

But the truth was too weird even for him. He wondered if werewolf blood looked like wolf blood under the microscope. Probably not, he suspected. The only thing he had going for him was the fact that there weren't any human bodies. Otherwise, there'd be a full-blown investigation.

"Police!" shouted an officer.

"Kevin?" Jim shouted back, hardly believing his good fortune. It was his partner. "It's me, Jim. Coast clear."

Kevin opened the door tentatively and holstered his gun as he saw the blood and the dead wolf. Kevin O'Dell was a big man with red hair and freckles. He had been Jim's partner for three years. "Shit, what happened?"

Jim shrugged. "I got an anonymous tip that someone was going to try to let that wolf out. You know, from the attacks?"

"Shit," said Kevin. He picked up the gun that lay by Cathal

with a gloved hand. "Shot the pooch before he could get it out?"

"Yeah, something like that. He shot at me," said Jim. "Nice guy."

"Did you hit him?"

Jim shook his head. "I don't think so. He fled on foot."

While the investigative team looked for clues, Jim spent the time filling out paperwork. There were going to be discrepancies in the report and the evidence, but it couldn't be helped. The truth was just too bizarre. He'd deal with it when the time arose. If they were lucky, they'd only get a good set of prints from Cathal's hand. If not, Alaric would be a suspect too. But it served him right — Alaric had murdered a man.

And now Jim was an accomplice in the murder. But was it a murder if you killed a werewolf in wolf form? Or wasn't it? Alaric was one of them, and he seemed to not think so. He could arrest Alaric on charges of killing Cathal Murphy — but it had been self-defense right up until Alaric had double-tapped Cathal in the heart with silver bullets. Cathal probably wouldn't have lived anyway, though, and even if he had, he would've most likely gotten the lethal injection that had been meant for Alaric.

"Hey Jim, you know this wolf has been bitten?" Kevin was kneeling by Cathal's body.

"Really?" Jim said casually.

"Yeah. It was grabbed by the throat — I thought you said there was only one wolf."

"That's all I saw, but I came in late," Jim said. "Maybe we should get the Animal Control officers to check the other cages out. Maybe there's more than one wolf that's missing."

Martha came in the door. Her brown hair was disheveled and she looked as if she had just woken up. She halted when she saw the blood and the dead wolf. "Oh my God," she whispered, her face turning pale. "What happened?"

"Jim got an anonymous tip that someone was going to try to free the wolf," Kevin said. "He came down and caught the suspect in the act."

"The perp shot the wolf," Jim said. "We exchanged fire."

"Did you hit the son of a bitch?" Martha asked.

"No."

"Damn," she said. "I would've recommended you for a metal."

"We need you to check the other dogs," Kevin said. "There are bite marks on it."

Martha's eyes widened and she turned and went to the clipboard hanging on the wall. Pulling it off the wall, she started going through the cages to see which dogs were missing.

Jim's cell phone rang. "Walking Bear," he said.

"Yeah, this is Alaric. I'm at Megan's," Alaric's voice came through the receiver.

Jim's stomach knotted. "How is she?" he whispered, turning his back to the others and walking a few paces away.

"She's getting transfusions. Doctor says she'll make it."

"When can you pick me up?"

"After Ms. Vampire siphons a few pints of blood from me for her." There was an uncomfortable pause. "I'll be there as soon as Megan says it's okay to drive."

Jim frowned as he hung up the phone. By the sound of things, it could be an hour or more, or all night.

He was in the front office working on the paperwork with Kevin when the Corvette passed by outside, turned the corner and parked in the back. Jim excused himself and went around back to find Alaric sitting in the car. Alaric got out and handed him the keys.

"How is she?" Jim asked.

Alaric shrugged. "Megan says she's lost a lot of blood, but Cathal didn't hit anything vital. She should be awake and around by tomorrow."

"You're kidding?" Jim said. "After all that?"

"Werewolf," Alaric said. "We heal faster than normal humans."

"Even though she was bit?"

"Even though," Alaric said. "You know where Megan's is?"

"Yeah, on Sixth Avenue. I'm going. You want a ride?"

Alaric nodded and walked around to the passenger seat. Jim

got in, started the car and pulled out of the alleyway. Both men were quiet for some time as Jim drove.

"You know, I didn't thank you," Alaric said when the silence became uncomfortable.

"Actually it was Kira's idea," Jim said, without glancing at the lycanthrope. "I didn't believe her when she said you were human."

"Not quite human," Alaric said with a sharp laugh. "None of us really are."

"Kira seems human to me," Jim said.

"That'll change over time," Alaric said. "Each day she'll become more and more werewolf."

"That's not very comforting," Jim said.

"It is reality. Many have tried to reverse the process. No one has been successful."

"What if you weren't born one, but bitten?"

Alaric shook his head. "The result is the same. You become one of us. And nothing in heaven or on earth can change that."

41

Kira found herself standing in a silent forest of lodge pole pines. It was dark and cold here — the trees grew together so densely that she couldn't see the sky or anything beyond the forest. Nothing grew in the shade of the ominous pines. Only a scattering of evergreen needles and pinecones coated the forest floor.

Kira was in wolf form. She padded silently through the darkened woods, looking for something. What it was, she wasn't quite sure. When she tried to concentrate, her head and neck began to hurt. She tried to paw her neck with a foreleg and pain shot through her. Strong, invisible hands gripped her legs.

Don't let her scratch it, a familiar woman's voice said.

Kira looked up, and the canopy of trees melted before a brightly glowing ball of light. A whine escaped her lips as the ball grew and expanded, blotting out the forest in a blinding flare...

Kira opened her eyes. Her neck throbbed unmercifully as she lay on a blanket in the Very Bright Place. Two men were sitting beside her: one whose scent was powerful and wild; the other, warm and earthy. Both scents were familiar and remarkably comforting.

"Is she coming around?" one voice spoke. It was masculine, and very familiar.

"I think so," said another male voice. Again, there was a familiarity she couldn't place.

The light was bright and intense. Kira wanted to close her eyes and wish the entire scene away. The wolf within wanted to return to the dark, cool pines. And yet something was pulling her back to the bright light and the pain. And the world of the living.

Her mouth was dry and her throat hurt too much to be able to speak, even if she could have spoken as a wolf. The stale metallic taste of blood still burned in her mouth. She felt weak and as she moved a bit, she could feel the prickle of the IV tubes that snaked their way down into her veins.

"Kira?" came a voice. "It's Alaric."

Alaric. The name floated in her barely-conscious mind. *Alaric?* The vision of the handsome black wolf appeared in her mind. Then the fight with Cathal came rushing back to her and her neck ached. Cathal had nearly killed her.

"It's okay, it's over," Jim said. "Cathal is dead — he won't be attacking anyone again."

She raised her head. *It can't be,* Kira said. *I was attacked by a gray wolf, not a black one. The wolf who attacked the transient was the same, I'm sure of it.*

Kira's eyesight began to fade. The dark forest was returning, cool and inviting.

"Kira! Kira!" Alaric said. "Stay with me. Are you sure it wasn't Cathal?"

But Kira was already running free in the cool darkness beneath the lodge pole pines.

Alaric watched as Kira sank back into unconsciousness. His jaw tightened — he hadn't expected Kira to tell them that he had killed the wrong wolf. Not that killing Cathal had been wrong. Cathal had been a thorn in Alaric's paw for far too long, and proved his disloyalty by attempting to murder Alaric and Kira. Cathal might not have been the wolf who attacked Kira and killed her friend, but he had been sure that Cathal was one of the rogue wolves. But Alaric still had another wolf to find.

"What did she say?" Jim asked.

Alaric met the cop's steady gaze. "She says it wasn't Murphy."

Jim glanced at the sleeping wolf and then back at Alaric. "Are you sure?"

"She says that the wolf who attacked her was gray. It attacked a homeless guy too."

"Then you killed an innocent man," Jim said.

Alaric laughed.

"What's so funny?"

"Cathal was many things," Alaric said, "but he was not innocent. He was involved in this somehow, I am certain. He may not have killed Kira's friend, but he probably gave the orders to do so. Even if he didn't, he would've killed me and he would've killed Kira, and your 'law' and justice system would not have been able to hold him. It's best that he's dead."

"Werewolf justice?"

Alaric shrugged. "Call it what you like — it's effective."

Megan entered the room. "You two still here? My patients will be arriving soon and I've got to get this place cleaned up."

Jim stood up and checked his watch — it was almost 4 am. "Do you need a ride back to..." His voice trailed off.

"To wherever werewolves go?" Alaric remarked. "No, I don't. I'll be returning to *The Grey Wolf*." He paused and eyed Jim suspiciously. "So, what are you saying in your report?"

"I already wrote it up," Jim said. "A crazy man shot the wolf and escaped. Not exactly a lie by my reckoning."

Alaric chuckled and nodded. Despite himself, he liked the

cop — even if he could tell the man had designs on his future mate. That would change; it always did once the Normal had enough of the werewolf lifestyle. He bent down and ran his fingers through Kira's fur. "Rest, little one. Megan will take good care of you," he whispered. *Beloved.* He looked up at Jim. "If you need me, come to *The Grey Wolf* in LoDo. You know where that is?"

Jim nodded. Satisfied, Alaric shifted. The wolf floundered in the clothing for a few seconds, and then trotted to the door. Megan opened it for him and he traveled out into the night.

Jim hesitated and glanced at Megan, who nodded and left the room. He knelt down beside Kira and stroked her fur.

"Kira," he whispered. "Kira. I don't know if you can hear me but if you can, I want to tell you that you're a special lady." He noticed that her ear flicked, and hoped she could understand him. "Listen, I know this werewolf thing is difficult and Alaric says it can't be cured, but I don't believe it. You don't either — I can tell. Maybe you can come with me to the Cheyenne reservation. Their medicine is strong and they may have something that will stop you from being a skinwalker."

He looked down at her. "Kira, I find you very attractive. I've never felt this way before about any woman." He stopped, at a loss for words. *What was this foolishness? Was he going to tell her he loved her? He hardly knew her!* "Get well, Kira," he said lamely. "I will see you when I get off tonight."

He stood up and turned to leave. As he did, he was met by Megan.

"I don't think it would work out," Megan said. "She's like me — a werewolf now."

Jim was too tired to argue. Instead, he walked past the vet, out the door and back to his car.

Kira found herself standing in the forest of lodge pole pines again. It looked remarkably familiar — something she had seen sometime before. She walked slowly and deliberately through the dark forest in her wolf form, as though searching for something.

Damn, it seems so familiar, she thought.

Why shouldn't it be? came a voice.

Kira nearly jumped. She looked up at the tree to see a green gecko. *Lizard?* she said tentatively.

Hiya sis, the gecko said.

Kira frowned, sat down and looked up at the gecko. *I'm in the Enchanted Forest?*

Where else would you be, sweetie?

That's impossible! Kira said. *I didn't link to it.*

Lizard said nothing, but watched her with its odd eyes. It scuttled down the bark, still out of the way of her wolf teeth.

Kira pondered her predicament. *Command mode?* she said tentatively.

Okay, said a disembodied voice. *Command?*

Shit! Kira looked upwards into the forest canopy. Was she really in the Enchanted Forest?

- 193 -

I don't recognize that command.

No, voice recognition off. Kira turned to look at Lizard, but he was gone. There was something about the Lizard she didn't like. He didn't seem to offer her many answers.

Then, her senses prickled. She felt something coming toward her. Then she heard the howl.

Her hackles rose and she took off, but now she didn't know what to do. In real life, she could pull the headset off and that would be that. But here she didn't have a headset. Instead, she had somehow tapped into the wireless network without any devices.

The forest shifted and she saw them coming after her. Three werewolves loped toward her; their eyes were red and their tongues lolled in anticipation of the slaughter. Kira turned and ran — the wolves were terrible and she didn't know what would happen to her if they did get hold of her. Could they kill her or just mentally screw with her? She didn't want to find out.

Suddenly her avatar changed from wolf to human. To her surprise, she was naked and cold, and her skin prickled with goose bumps. Try as she might, she could not change back to her wolf avatar and her two legs were hardly fast enough to evade the three werewolves bearing down on her.

The forest grew darker and the trees changed to a mixture of deciduous and coniferous. Kira kept running, but slipped on the damp ground and fell. When she looked up, she found she had fallen in front of a large cyber yew tree in the middle of the forest. Right beside her stood the largest wolf she had ever imagined.

The wolf was a female with gray fur that shimmered almost silver in the cyberworld. She had red glowing eyes and her teeth were bared in a snarl. She was bigger even than the male werewolves Kira had seen in the real world.

The three marauding werewolves halted when they saw the She-Wolf. She snarled and leapt at them, her jaws closing on one and snapping its neck. The other two fled in terror.

The She-Wolf shook the carcass twice and then dumped it unceremoniously on the ground before Kira. Kira shivered and shrank away as the wolf came toward her. The She-Wolf lifted her lip. *You hate me, don't you?* the wolf said plainly in Kira's mind.

Raw fear filled Kira's throat and she backed up as the wolf approached. Kira's head spun and she tried to focus on changing into a wolf, but she couldn't. There had to be some way of escaping the Forest.

Funny, you would want to transmute now that I've confronted you, the wolf said.

Who are you? Kira's voice was choked with fear.

Who do you think I am?

I don't know. Even as she said it, the thought came to her. *You're me. I'm going crazy.*

Not exactly, said the She-Wolf, *but you will be if you deny me.*

Kira stared at the wolf. That thing was her? She couldn't believe it. Even in wolf form, Kira was never that large. *What are you?*

A manifestation of what we are. The Forest gives me a chance to take form without the transmutation.

How can I still be connected to the Forest?

Through me.

You?

The wolf sat down and licked her paws, turning her dark gaze away from Kira. *The DNA mutations—a part of your cells that mimic what they're told to do. The headset...*

Kira closed her eyes and shivered. Spaz's headset didn't just put thoughts into actions; it fed information back into the brain. In its bizarre way, it was modifying thought patterns. But how far did it modify brain patterns? To a point where her brain could pick up on wireless transmissions and find a route into the Enchanted Forest by itself?

The werewolf side of you makes you capable of doing this, the She-Wolf said.

Could a Normal human do this?

Maybe, the She-Wolf replied. *Some have the latent ability, but most don't. Maybe over time, even those with monkey brains could figure it out.*

Hey!

The She-Wolf grinned a toothy grin. *I don't see what's so superior about humans.*

Kira frowned. She didn't like the way this conversation was heading. *Go away. Leave me alone.*

I can't, said the She Wolf. *I'm part of you.* The She-Wolf faded from her thoughts and Kira was back in the Forest in wolf form.

The sun shone through the skylights at the vet's office and onto Kira's face, both warming her and waking her up. She lay for a while not quite cognizant of her surroundings, but aware of the smells and the feel of the place. The sharp scent of bleach and the animal smells wafted through her nostrils along with the smell of cool, fresh air from the city. The air was cool, but the blanket she was lying on was warm. She could feel the prickle of needles in her skin and hear the slow drip of the IV.

But there were other sounds, too, and other movement. A woman entered the room, lifted Kira's eyelids a bit and peered into her glassy eyes for response. Kira shifted uncomfortably, smacking her dry lips. She was thirsty and her neck ached — but less now.

"Doctor — she's coming around."

Kira pondered the words. They made no sense to her addled mind and she dwelled on each word as though individually, the words had some importance. They had great significance, didn't they?

A woman came in and Kira knew she was familiar but didn't know why. Kira lifted her head — would the woman bring her something to drink?

"Easy, Kira. Let's take a look at those wounds before we move around."

Kira blinked. The woman carefully picked at something along her neck. Kira tried to look down at her neck but couldn't. The woman's name was on the tip of her tongue — why couldn't she remember it?

"Ah, it's almost healed," the woman said. "How do you feel?"

Kira tried to speak but a whine came from her lips.

"Use your telepathy," the woman said.

Telepathy? Kira paused. The words were nonsensical and yet meant something to her. As she looked dumbly at the woman, the incident of the night before came back to her. *Megan?*

"Yeah, that's right, it's Megan," the vet said. "Your wounds are almost healed. By nightfall, your fur will have grown back."

Kira blinked. *You mean I'm completely healed?*

"You're a werewolf," Megan said. "You've made the complete transformation — otherwise you'd be dead. Cathal really tore you up good."

A panicky thought seized her. *Alaric?*

"Don't worry, you saved him," Megan said. "He and that cop brought you in."

Jim?

"Native American guy — real cute?"

Kira relaxed and closed her eyes. *That's him — he's been looking for the rogue wolves, too.*

"How much does he know about us?" Megan asked.

Kira hesitated. What could she say? Everything? Would it really matter now that Jim was helping them? Kira gave a noncommittal shrug. *Alaric needed help. He was willing to help us.*

Megan considered Kira for a while, and then shrugged. She knelt down and began removing the IVs. "Do you feel well enough to stand and change back?"

I'm thirsty, Kira replied.

"One clean bowl of water coming up," said Megan. She stood up and took a bowl from one of the cupboards, and poured some water into it from the water cooler. As she laid it on the floor for Kira to drink, Kira looked at the bowl suspiciously. "Don't worry!" Megan laughed, seeing Kira's expression. "I wash those in the dishwasher."

Kira began lapping the water up. The water was cold and washed away both the burning sensation and the taste of her own blood. When she looked up, Megan was holding a stack of clothing. She walked into the bathroom and laid the clothes on the sink. "Your cop friend brought them when he came. I had the techs wash and dry them."

Kira was touched. *Thank you.* Megan turned on the light inside the bathroom and Kira stood up slowly. She was hungry and a little wobbly, but after a few moments, she found she could walk. She peered inside the bathroom — there was a shower, and towels and soaps were laid out.

"You can take a shower, if you'd like."

What about the wound?

"I don't think it will be much of a problem," Megan said. "Check it out in the mirror. In the meantime, I've got to get back to clients." She paused. "Oh, and lock the door. Fred comes by with deliveries and while I don't think he'd intrude, it's better just to keep away unwanted surprises."

With that, she shut the door, leaving Kira alone. Kira closed her eyes and began the transformation. It was slower than usual, and a bit painful — probably because she had been seriously injured. As she became human, she looked at her neck. She could see the redness and bruising where the bite marks had been, but otherwise the skin had healed. She touched the newly formed skin and shivered as she felt a small prickle of pain. Not quite healed, but almost.

The first wolf bites had taken nearly a month to heal. Now, her werewolf body was doing what had taken her normal body a month, in less than a day. She turned around, locked the door and then turned on the shower, letting the water run until it built up some steam.

She closed her eyes and stepped under the spray, ignoring the first shock of the water on her tender neck. Kira knew she should be frightened, or at least freaked out. Instead, something inside her seemed to wash away the pain and fear as surely as the water washed away the dirt and grime from the previous night.

Kira had saved the life of the Alpha of the Denver wolfpack. She had never saved anyone's life before, as far as she could remember. But then, until she had gotten wrapped up in this whole werewolf thing, she hadn't been nearly killed, either. Twice, she added mentally as she rinsed the soap from her body. She picked up the shampoo and grimaced. It was a pro-groomer's shampoo for dogs, with a light apricot scent. She shrugged, poured some in her hands, and lathered.

As she did, her mind went back to separating the events from last night. Jim had told her that Spaz was missing and that he and his partner had to investigate Spaz's apartment. Kira frowned. There had been no time for Jim to tell her what happened to Spaz during their confrontation with Cathal Murphy. She remembered Alaric carrying her to a car, and then darkness. She remembered the dreams of running as a wolf through the Enchanted Forest. She remembered her encounter with the She-Wolf and how she saved Kira from the werewolves. It had been a dream, she decided. Nothing more. People couldn't access the Enchanted Forest through the *hi-rFreq* band — that was impossible. It would require a human to be able to sense a type of broadcast wavelength.

There had been something else — a voice through all of it. Jim's voice. He had promised her something. She tried to remember, but couldn't. She sighed. Maybe it was for the best.

Kira rinsed and reached out of the shower to grasp a towel. As she did, cold air assailed her nostrils and could smell pine forest. She groaned. The air conditioner in the veterinary clinic must have gone on. She dried her hair and then wrapped the towel around her and stepped out.

She was standing in the middle of the Enchanted Forest.

44

Kira stared at the Forest in shock. She wondered if she was hallucinating. It would have made more sense if she was, but she knew that she wasn't. The Forest was transposed onto reality; she found if she concentrated on either one, the other would fade slowly from her consciousness as though one of the two worlds was melting away. She closed her eyes and envisioned the Forest, and it snapped into view. She could smell the pines and the feel the cold wind on her face.

As she looked down, she could see that her avatar had taken the form of a wolf again. She trotted forward, puzzling over the Forest. Could the She-Wolf have told her the truth — that a werewolf could pick up the frequencies of the network and somehow make sense of it?

Kira had needed the headset to see the Enchanted Forest at first, but maybe she wouldn't have needed it if she had known what to look for. She wasn't as in-tune with this werewolf thing yet, and maybe it just came naturally for some bit-headed weres. Maybe the *hi-rFreq* was similar to the telepathy that the werewolves used. After all, there had to be some type of scientific explanation for how and why werewolves existed. And how the bites infected werewolves.

After a few attempts, Kira shut down her mental link with the Forest. She'd have to talk to Alaric to find out how much he knew about it, and she'd have to tell Jim what she found. She doubted he'd be happy about it, but he had to know what was going on.

Kira got dressed and stepped out. The clinic was busy. Two vet techs were in the room: one was filing folders; another was cleaning the teeth of a dog under anesthesia. They were both young women, wearing scrubs — barely out of high school, by the looks of them. The woman filing folders had blonde hair tied back in a bun. The other had short brown hair and was wearing safety glasses as she worked on the dog's teeth with a cleaner. Kira noted how foul the dog's breath was.

"Where's Megan?" Kira asked as they looked over.

"Dr. Olson's in with a client," the woman who was filing said. Kira noted her badge said "Trisha."

Megan walked in carrying a folder. "Trish, I want you to send the Smiths home with amoxi-drops for their cat..." She paused. "Kira, great! That cop fellow is back and wanted to see you..."

"Jim?" Kira said.

"Yeah, that's his name. He's kinda cute for a Normal but really, Kira..."

Kira fixed her with a stare and then glanced at the two vet techs. Trish was smiling unabashedly, but the other tech was trying hard to look uninterested.

"Oh we're safe. Trish and Amy are werewolves, themselves," Megan said. "It's not a big deal — I screen my help carefully."

"I bet."

"Anyway, your cop is out in the waiting room." Megan sat down at the computer and began entering the label.

"Ummm," Kira said.

Megan wheeled the chair around. "Yeah?"

"I want to thank you. Don't I owe you something?" Kira knew she couldn't pay, but maybe the vet would take a payment plan.

"Alpha got it," Megan said, a slight smirk crossing her features. "If you owe anyone, you owe him."

"Hmmm, thank him for me?"

"You can do that yourself, sweetie," she said without looking up. "He left a message — he wants to take you out to dinner at six. He'll drop by your apartment to pick you up."

Kira's eyes went wide. "Alaric left the message?"

"I wouldn't refuse, if I were you."

Kira said nothing. Instead, she walked out into the waiting room. An elderly woman waited with a cat in a carrier, a young family (a husband, wife and a toddler) sat with a Golden Retriever puppy, and teenager sat with her mixed breed. Jim was in a chair off by himself, looking bored but flipping through a copy of Tuft's *Your Dog*. He glanced up and grinned. "You know, they have a really interesting article on canine flatulence in here."

Kira stifled a laugh. "Thanks for dropping by."

He stood up and gave her a quick kiss on the cheek, much to her surprise. "How could I not see my favorite werewolf?" he whispered in her ear.

His earthy smell filled her nostrils. It was relaxing and yet heady for her. "I thought I was the only werewolf you knew."

"I got to meet quite a few last night," Jim said. He met her gaze. "Are you okay?"

Kira nodded and pointed to her neck. "Completely healed."

"I wouldn't have believed it even happened if I hadn't seen it myself," he said. He glanced at the clients in the waiting room. "Let's get out of here and get some food. You hungry?"

"Famished," she said.

"Good, I have news about your friend Will Tagura," he said as they left.

He's what?" Kira stared at Jim as she settled down with her bowl of chicken and dumplings in a quiet corner of the café. It was well past lunchtime, and most of the patrons were staying in the front part of the café and ordering carry-out, so Kira and Jim had found a seat toward the back where they could talk. "Spaz can't be dead. I know he's not."

"My partner went up to the place where Tagura lived. The family he rented from was murdered and all his equipment was smashed. The Secret Service has been called in and they're trying to retrieve the data off the hard drives, but whoever did this was good."

"They wiped the disks?"

"No, they smashed them to bits. All we've got are fragments, which makes the chance of piecing everything together virtually nil. And they found some bizarre headsets — smashed, of course."

Kira fell silent.

"Tagura is dead, Kira. We're pretty sure of that."

The words hit her hard. *Spaz dead?* She couldn't believe it. *No, he couldn't be. He just couldn't.* Tears formed in her eyes. *No, it just couldn't happen.* "Why?" Kira asked, feeling a cold, hard lump settle in her throat. "Did you find his body?"

"The family died from animal bites."

Kira felt her face drain of blood. "Rogue wolves. They could've kidnapped him."

"There's no ransom letter or demands. Why would they keep him?" Jim looked at Kira for a response, but she was silent. "We're doing DNA testing on the bodies now. It won't be long before forensics pick up some of that weird wolf DNA again." He paused. "Kira, you're not being honest with me."

Kira said nothing. Instead, she poked at her food with a fork. Tears fell from her eyes into the chicken dumplings.

"Do you know what Tagura was up to?"

"Sort of," Kira said sheepishly. "He told me right before he disappeared." She paused. "Look, I think you're wrong. If the wolves had killed him, they would've left him."

"What was Tagura doing before this?"

"He and the other spiders from MIT had created something — a net within the Net. A virtual spider's dream."

"What in the hell is a spider, besides something you squish?"

"Spiders are what you might call hackers," said Kira. "Andrew Burt coined the term — people were using the term hacker wrong, when they meant crackers. The truth is, spider is a much cooler term and pretty much describes what happens. Most spiders don't do much — they slip through the cracks of the machines they visit. Some just lurk and don't do anything; others just spin webs and go about their business. You're not usually aware of them until after they've gone and you're left to clean up after them. Occasionally spiders become disruptive or even downright dangerous."

"And Tagura created something useful to spiders?" Jim said. "Christ, I'm just getting used to the idea of werewolves."

"Not funny," Kira said. "Spaz figured out how to create a second Internet that piggybacks onto the holes on IP." She saw Jim's blank expression and shook her head. "No offense, but it's little wonder the cops are stymied."

"But you said that spiders usually aren't dangerous."

"Not usually, but there are enough of them who are," Kira

sighed. "Which is why you can never really trust their intent and you always have to have a lock-tight network and system. Problem is, you can have someone on the inside who sets the computer up for security holes. I found some of those at Intermountain and started closing them off."

Jim paused. "You think someone might have found out?"

"Yeah, I thought it might have been Cathal Murphy. After all, he was a network puke and he had access to root of all the machines present."

"But?"

"But Cathal is a black wolf. The wolf who attacked me was gray."

Jim frowned. "So how does this all work?'

"It's really simple — it's based on the OSI layers." She paused, seeing his confusing. "Open Systems Interface — there are seven layers."

"Seven?" Jim said. "Couldn't they just have one?"

"No," Kira said. "Of course not. At the basic level is the Physical Level — that's the hardware where the ones and zeros exist."

"Okay," Jim said cautiously.

"The second layer is the link layer — it often occurs in the hardware too but other times in the operating system. It uses datagrams..."

"What?"

"Datagrams — they're like the postal service," she said. "They send electronic packages of data, but there's no delivery confirmation. They simply are addressed and sent. It's very fast, but it can have errors."

"Okay," said Jim, "why is this important?"

"They are the backbone of a network. Those packets are what other protocols are based on — like TCP/IP and UDP."

"So, they use the link layer to take control?"

"Yes, if they can," Kira said. "They've build their own protocol, and in some places, their own network. Net within the Net. They set up the program to piggyback off IP's holes. So, machines that have these holes have code within the very drivers, and even in the

Ethernet and Fiber Optic drivers. Incredible, really. You'd think that it would take a corporation or a think-tank the equivalent of Bell Labs to come up with this."

"Who did?"

"Spaz. He is a fucking genius."

"A dead genius," Jim reminded her.

The words hit her hard again. "No, Spaz can't be dead. He just can't."

Jim shifted nervously. "Look, Kira, I doubt Tagura acted alone on this. He had to have had help to get into places like Intermountain, wouldn't he?"

"Yeah," she said. "Spaz was mostly a device driver geek but he had a lot of network knowledge. Still, he probably would've gotten with our group from MIT."

"What are their names?"

"Danni Jones, Randy Green, Tom Sullivan," Kira said. "And then there was Susan and myself."

Jim opened his pad and wrote the names down. "Anyone else?"

Kira shook her head. "Not really. Those were the MIT spiders. But hey, that was ten years ago."

"Do you have contact information for them?"

Kira shrugged. "Just some old addresses from my address book on my computer. I hadn't been in contact with them for almost ten years. Only Susan and I stayed in touch because we were both sysadmins, you know?"

"Well, it'll be a starting point," Jim said. "You really hadn't stayed in contact with Tagura?"

"No, he just showed up here in Denver."

"Don't you find that odd?"

"Spaz…" She shrugged. "Well, you'd just have to know him. He'd pop out of thin air, you know? Sometimes when you least expect it."

"Look, Kira, I know how you feel about this, but I'm going to have to report the werewolves and this net within the Net thing."

"No," Kira said. "You can't. You'll start a race war."

"Race war? Hell, Kira, they already have." He frowned. "No matter what you or Alaric want, these werewolves are killing *people*. Now, I've kept this secret because you asked me to and because I figured no one would believe it, but forensics is starting to ask questions. They've seen the DNA and they know we're not dealing with a normal case. Now, why do you think these werewolves are willing to kill over this Net thing?"

Kira glared. "You'll get nothing from me if you tell anyone."

Jim shook his head. "I want you to know how serious this is. It's going to come out sometime — sooner or later."

"No one will believe you."

Jim nodded. "It's doubtful, but then again, I've got a real live werewolf in custody."

"What? Are you arresting me?"

"I ought to," he said. "But other than your screwy DNA, I've got nothing other than what you've told me. And you're right, no one's going to believe in a wolfman." He paused and met her gaze. "Besides, this is getting personal for me."

A knot filled Kira's throat and her mouth went dry as she looked into those dark brown eyes. She understood his meaning all too well. "But I'm one of *them*."

"I know, but you didn't want to be, did you?"

"No," Kira said. "My life has pretty much been screwed up since last month. I could use a break."

"I've got the perfect place for that. There's a beautiful place in Montana I could take you — no networks, no nothing. Just forests and mountains and sky. I'd love it if you came with me."

Kira smiled. "Sounds beautiful; I'd love to."

Jim grinned. "Really? That was the easiest date I've ever made."

"Yeah, well a geek can't be choosy; especially when she's a werewolf."

She looked up at Jim, but he was looking past her, distracted. Kira glanced around. Two werewolves, obviously Cathal's thugs, had entered the café.

46

Kira stiffened. The two men had the typical look of
Cathal's henchmen, wearing dingy black leathers and
oil-smudged t-shirts with *Lobos Solitarios* logos across
them. They wore their hair tied back in ponytails that
were somewhere between black and gray, but so dirty that she
couldn't guess what color their hair might actually have been.
One wore a red paisley bandana to hide his balding pate.

Jim was about to stand up, but Kira laid her hand on his arm.
"Don't," she whispered. "If they change, you won't be able to
harm them."

"I need to take you to fancier restaurants," Jim replied. "They'd
have real silverware there."

"Nice. Is there another way out?" she asked. "They're looking
for me."

"Just out the back way," Jim said.

"Great. If anything happens, meet me at my apartment."

"What are you doing?" He glanced at the two werewolves as
they started walking toward the back of the café.

"Hoping I don't have to transmute," she said. She got up and
started toward the back.

"There she is!" The balding werewolf shouted and sprinted

toward Kira. Kira ran but instead of trying to make it to the door, she saw the Ladies room and ducked into it. It had a deadbolt that she snicked closed with some satisfaction.

Just as the werewolf passed the booth, Jim casually stuck out a foot. The man tripped and went down, skittering across the linoleum. The other werewolf stopped short and, seeing Jim's smirk, wheeled on the cop.

"You think that was funny, Monkey?" He drew himself up to full height.

The werewolf with the bandana tried the door to the Ladies room and found it locked. He pounded on the door hard. "Let me in, Bitch!"

Jim stood up, towering over the werewolf by a good three inches. "Hilarious," he said. "Why don't you pick on someone your own species, like Neanderthal?"

The werewolf's expression turned into a snarl. "I'll take you down and take you apart. You don't know who you're dealing with."

"Actually, I do, and you're under arrest." Jim flashed his badge. "For threatening a police officer."

The werewolf leapt at Jim, but the cop turned and sent the man face first across the table, sending dirty dishes and tableware scattering everywhere. Jim pounced on top of the man, pulling one arm behind his back and cuffing him. Suddenly, the hands and arms grew smaller and hairy.

A woman screamed from the front of the café.

"Shit!" Jim glanced over at the other werewolf and saw it was changing too. He drew his gun.

A smaller gray wolf exploded out of the Ladies room. Kira went right for the transmuting werewolf and chomped it in the neck. The half-man, half-wolf's scream turned to a gurgle as she tore away chunks of his throat. His thrashing ceased and the man/wolf's body went limp.

Kira leapt back, horrified to watch the man's eyes turn glassy as the life drained out of him. She stepped over the widening pool of blood and snarled at the other werewolf.

Jim slammed the man's head against the table. "You can either come with me quietly or suffer the same fate as your buddy, okay?"

The werewolf nodded.

Jim called for backup on the radio. When he looked for Kira, she was gone.

Hunger. Hunger burned in the killer once more. He had fed, and yet was not satisfied. He could never be sated — not as long as there were humans to kill. He licked his lips in anticipation of the hunt tonight. It would be grand. Tonight he would finish the job he had started over a month ago. The girl would die, and with her Tagura's only chance would die, too.

Monkey blood was sweet to his tastes. Tagura was beginning to break. Soon, he would have what he wanted...

⌇⌇⌇

Kira felt sick to her stomach as she shimmied into her clothes and exited the café through the back door. A glance back showed her that Jim had handcuffed the other werewolf and was reading him his rights. She wanted to throw up. She had killed a man. What's more, she had ripped his throat right out. Jim hadn't handcuffed her yet, but it was only a matter of time. He'd had seen her werewolf side, and now he would know what a terrible creature she had become.

She wanted to cry and throw up all at the same time. There was no way he would help her now that she had murdered a man. She heard sirens and looked around frantically. It wouldn't be long before he would put out an all-points-bulletin on her and have her arrested for murder.

She walked through the alleyway in a daze. Back on 16th Street, she caught the Mall shuttle. It was crowded, and she stood and looked at each of the faces of the people who stood and sat on the bus. There were a couple of men wearing Sun Microsystems polos. Several white and African-American kids were on their way home from school, sharing the latest tunes on their iPods. A woman was dressed in a three-piece suit; there was a mom with her toddler in tow... How many of them would she kill now that she was a werewolf?

Kira didn't have the answer. She had never killed anyone — never had the desire to kill anyone. She closed her eyes. She could still taste his blood in her mouth. It was awful. She was afraid she'd never get the taste out.

Suddenly, she was no longer on the bus, but in a Forest. It was green and the scent of pine was overwhelming. Once again, she was the wolf. Once again, she was free.

The wolf gave her the ability to sense the *hi-rFreq* waves emanating from transmitters from Intermountain Telecom. It gave her the ability to leave this world and go someplace else. Someplace private and safe.

She stared into the dark forest and a whimper escaped her lips. She wanted to leave the real world for good. Here in Spaz's world, she could be quiet and have peace.

"Market Street."

The voice pulled her back to the real world long enough for her to exit the bus at Market. She stood for a while, dazed in the sunshine.

The Forest was cool, dark, and seductive. It was like night; her sun was the moon now and the bright orb of day was something that was only tolerated. Kira blinked at the sun. She wanted to flee the sun and run into the eternal night...

"Lady, you okay?"

A voice broke Kira from her reverie and she turned to see a man staring at her, perplexed. He was maybe in his fifties, and wore a work shirt and jeans. Guessing by the tools on his belt, he was an electrician. He had a slight accent — Brooklyn?

"I'm fine, thank you," Kira said, her voice sounding a bit dreamy. She shook her head, trying to shake the feeling. "I'm fine," she said again, meeting his gaze. "Just got caught in a thought."

"Okay," the guy shrugged and moved on. Kira started down the sidewalk toward her apartment. As she did, she jumped as she felt a light touch on her arm.

It was the old homeless woman. "Be careful, Light Walker. You were not meant to walk in darkness. The Evil One pursues you — seek help in your animal guides."

Kira stared at the old woman. She was wearing the same tattered coat and bandana, but this time she had a cart a few feet away. Not a shopping cart, but one of those granny carts she had seen older women use to push their shopping along the sidewalk. She leaned on her cane.

"How do you know about me?"

The woman smiled. Some of her teeth were missing. "Do you have some change for an old woman?"

Kira fished in her pockets. She only had some pennies, a dime and a nickel. "I'm sorry," she said, holding them out.

"That will do," the woman said. "Come with me." The woman leaned heavily on the cane as she tottered over to her cart.

"What is your name?" Kira asked.

The woman looked up sharply. "Why do you wish to know, Light Walker?"

"You know my name," Kira said. "I'd like to know yours."

The woman grunted and nodded. She turned and began rummaging in her cart. "I have many names. Many, many names. But you may call me Verdandi."

"Verdandi," Kira repeated. "Haven't I heard that name somewhere?"

Verdandi pulled out her coffee can and set it by her feet. "Put your coins in, Light Walker."

Kira tossed the coins in with a clink. They rattled against the side. "How can you help me?"

"I can protect you against evil." She pulled out a piece of wood and held it for Kira to inspect.

Kira looked at the wood. On it was inscribed writing she recognized, but couldn't read. "Viking runes?"

"Powerful magic," the woman said. "Powerful magic — they will protect you."

There were three. "*Ansuz, Laguz*, and *Uruz*. Give me your hand."

Kira held out her hand. Verdandi dropped the wood into her palm and closed her fingers around it. Then she turned Kira's hand over and rummaged in the tattered coat. She pulled out a marker.

"What are you doing?"

"Bindrunes — very ancient magic. These are the most powerful — the Alerunes are to protect you against all evil, both in the physical and spiritual realms. To activate them I must inscribe a rune on your hand."

Kira nodded, puzzled. The woman was crazy; that she was sure of. But what harm did it do for her to go along with this? "Okay, what do you do?"

Verdandi pulled the cap off. "It will sting a bit." She began to chant in a language Kira had never heard — perhaps it was sheer gibberish — and marked her hand.

The pen burned like fire and Kira yelped, pulling away. But Verdandi was a lot stronger than Kira expected and held her hand firm. The mark of *Naudhiz* burned on her hand. Then, the mark faded from her skin.

"What the fuck?" Kira gasped. The piece of wood in her hand was gone, too.

Verdandi smiled and released her hand. "Find your friend, Light Walker. He needs your help. Your animal guides can help you."

"Spaz?" she said. "Jim told me he was dead."

"Not dead. Not yet. But his thread is beginning to unravel.

You can save him. The Forest is your path. But beware. There are wolves there."

Kira stared. "How much do you know?"

"I see much. Don't go home. Danger awaits you there."

Sirens wailed in the distance and Kira turned to look. She was still on the corner of Market near the bus terminal, blinking in the bright sunshine. When she turned back to speak to Verdandi, she was gone.

Kira walked toward her apartment, her mind reeling with the information Verdandi had given her. She would've normally thought the old woman was just some crazy homeless person, but the past month had taught her that appearances were deceiving. She had become a werewolf, had met two very handsome men, had lost her job, had rescued both men, had been severely injured, and now had killed a man. What was a witch, after all that?

Her throat tightened as she thought about the man she had killed. She really *had* killed a man. Yes, she had done it in self-defense and to save Jim, but it was murder nonetheless. And what would Jim think of her now?

The sounds of sirens interrupted her thoughts again and she saw an ambulance turn down Market and head toward her apartment. Turning the corner of Wazee Street, she stopped and stared.

Police cars lined the area in front of her apartment building. A news truck from 9 News was already on the scene. Kira remembered Verdandi's warning. She closed her eyes and immediately accessed the Forest. Suddenly she was no longer on Wazee but somewhere in the darkness of the Enchanted Forest.

I need the Denver 9 News computers, she shouted as she loped down the path.

A panel opened up and she was able to read the access choices as she loped through the Forest. It took her a moment to realize that she was not only looking at the website, but at the direct feeds from the main computers. It included the streaming video, real-time.

Pull up live feed, Kira said. She halted.

A woman news reporter was standing in front of the apartment. She was a dark-haired, petite woman that Kira had seen on the news before. The camera panned to paramedics treating a man with spiked hair for bruises and lacerations.

Trevor, Kira thought.

A cop knelt beside Trevor as the paramedics were treating him. He was saying something.

Increase volume, Kira said. If she strained, she could just "hear" them.

"I don't know who they were," Trevor said. *"Owww!"* He tried to bat away the paramedic's hand. *"Look, they broke in and smacked me around. When I came to, they'd already ransacked Kira's place..."*

Shit! Kira said as the shock settled in. *What about her computers? What about her books?* She shuddered as she thought about what would have happened if she had been there. Could she have handled several werewolves on her own? She somehow doubted it.

Maybe the old woman was right. Maybe Spaz *was* still alive. But why would the rogue werewolves be looking for her?

"Kira?"

A voice broke her from her contact with the Enchanted Forest and her reverie. She turned to see Alaric standing beside her. She smiled, despite herself.

"What's happening?"

"Somebody attacked Trevor and ransacked my apartment," Kira said tonelessly. The whole situation seemed surreal.

"Are you all right?" Alaric looked her up and down. Kira could help but feel pleased that he cared so much.

"Fine, fine, I was just getting back," she said.

Alaric gave her an odd look. "How do you know what happened, then?"

"It's a long story... but I think you need to know."

Alaric looked into her eyes, his own mirroring his concern. "All right," he said. He took a step toward her apartment.

"No," she said. "Let's not go there just yet."

"Okay," Alaric said. "How about a walk then?"

Kira nodded.

Alaric grinned and offered her his arm. Kira found herself grinning too, despite everything that happened. She took his arm and let him lead her toward the park.

As they walked, Kira told Alaric everything she knew about the rogue werewolves and the Enchanted Forest. Alaric remained silent but attentive as she told him about the ability to enter the Enchanted Forest at will without the headset. She finished up by telling him about Spaz's possible kidnapping and the two rogue wolves that had come looking for her.

When she finished, she noticed that Alaric had said nothing. They had stopped in Commons Park, where she had first met him. He was frowning as he motioned her to sit on the bench, and took a seat beside her.

"Did I do something wrong?" she asked tentatively as he squinted into the sun. She looked around. A few kids on skateboards were at the opposite end of the park showing off some new maneuvers.

"No, it's not your fault," Alaric said, at length. "I wish I had more time to bring you fully into the pack." He gave her a half-smile and shrugged.

"I don't *want* to *be* in the pack," Kira said.

"I'm afraid that's not your choice," Alaric said. "When you became a werewolf you became a member of my pack."

Kira glared. "You can't order me around." She began to stand up.
"No, I can't."

Kira began to walk away, but stopped. "What?"

"I don't believe anyone can," Alaric said. "Order you around, that is."

Kira blinked at him. "What's that supposed to mean?"

He shook his head. "When Normals are bitten by a werewolf, it changes them..."

"No kidding."

"No, I mean, it changes them not just in their body — but in their mind as well. The inherent personality of the human is amplified to merge with that of the wolf. I don't know how to describe it, but in essence, you become what is core to you."

"You mean if you're a nasty, mean son-of-a-bitch deep down inside, that's what you'll become?"

Alaric nodded. "Only more so."

Kira frowned. "Then it takes away all vestiges of civilization. Great."

"In a Normal, yes. In those of us who are born lycanthrope, we've come to grips with that personality. It is ourselves and we work very hard to deal with the Normals culture."

"I see," said Kira. "So I'm going to change into something I'm not."

"No, you've changed into something you always have been, but never let show."

"And what might that be?"

"An Alpha."

Kira stared at Alaric. His face was earnest and without deceit. She wanted to argue; wanted to tell him that he was full of shit. And yet, she could sense the She-Wolf inside her nodding slowly. *I am Alpha.*

Alaric smiled slightly and turned away to watch the kids on their skateboards. "I know it's hard to accept, but I know you sense it as much as I do. You just won't admit that you're that strong of a person. Which is odd, because you are that confident and strong."

Kira snorted.

"That's why I can't order you around. That's why no one can."

Kira put her hand on her hips and stared at him. "Okay, let's say I am Alpha. I don't want to be. I just want to be Kira. Computer geek with a comfortable job, preferably in Southern California..."

"You don't like Colorado?"

"What do you think?"

Alaric nodded and chuckled. "Yeah, I guess you've had it rough."

"That's one way to put it."

A silence ensued. Kira sat down beside him. Alaric was lost in thought.

He sighed. "Kira," he said at last. "I can't change what has happened to you. As far as I know, no one can. I regretted not bringing you into the pack because you've put the entire Denver pack in a precarious situation. Your cop friend knows more than he should..."

"I don't think he knows enough."

"You've put him at great risk — not from me," he added when she shot him a look. "No one under my command will attack him. But, not all werewolves are under my command. That rogue wolf who attacked you will try to change over and attack him. Assuming your cop friend isn't killed, chances are, he'll be bitten. Do you want him to end up like you?"

Kira turned pale. "I didn't think of that."

"No, but I have. And there are many among the lycanthropes who fear having a Normal know our secrets. Certainly, there have been stories about our kind throughout the Normals' legends, but those stories are relegated to myths, at best. It's the stuff children tell around the campfires at night to scare each other. What would the Normals think if they knew we really did exist?"

Kira grunted noncommittally and shook her head.

Alaric gently touched her chin and she looked into his eyes. "How did you feel after you were attacked?"

"Frightened. Scared shitless."

"Now take those feelings and put them in the entire city of

Denver; the entire state of Colorado; and the entire United States. How do you think people would respond if they knew their deepest, darkest fears were real?"

Kira said nothing. Sure, there would be those who would accept the werewolves as people, but they would be in the minority. Most people would think of werewolves as the demon creatures who ripped people's throats out every full moon. And Kira couldn't be sure that she was not in agreement with them.

Alaric cocked his head. "What would you do if you were me?"

"I'd have better control over the wolf pack." As soon as she said it, she saw Alaric's expression darken and immediately regretted it.

"And how would *you* control them?"

"I don't know, but I would find a way." Kira said.

Alaric chuckled. "It's not as easy as you think."

"Perhaps not."

"Are you willing to give it a try?"

Kira raised an eyebrow. "What are you proposing?"

He grinned. "You're an Alpha; you're smart. What do you think I'm proposing?" He leaned over and kissed her.

It was nothing more than a kiss, but it sent a shockwave through her body. Despite herself, Kira pulled away and stared at him. "You have a lot of nerve."

"Yes, I do." He pulled her close and kissed her again, his tongue sliding into her mouth this time. Kira slid her arms around him and kissed him passionately. When he pulled away, she opened her eyes and saw the same pleased grin on his face.

"Why did you do that?" Despite being angry, she couldn't muster enough energy in her voice to show it. Her words came out breathless.

"Because I think you needed it," Alaric said wryly. "As much as I did."

"I don't need anything," Kira said.

"Ah, but you do," Alaric said, stroking her hair. "You know, you're a very beautiful woman — I'm surprised no one's caught you by now."

"Maybe I don't want to be caught."

"I don't think so." He kissed her again and she responded eagerly to his touch. He pulled away suddenly. "A woman who isn't interested wouldn't show such enthusiasm."

Kira felt her face redden, and Alaric laughed.

"It's okay, Kira," he said. "I feel the same way. Now, why don't you show me this Enchanted Forest the rogues are so interested in, and maybe we can catch dinner and see what's happened to your apartment?"

50

"It shouldn't be this hard for you," Kira said in exasperation as Alaric shook his head a third time. "I don't get it. You're a lycanthrope. You shouldn't have any problems connecting." They were still sitting on a bench in Commons Park. The kids on the skateboards were gone now, leaving them alone.

"Maybe there's more to linking up with the Enchanted Forest than just thinking about it," Alaric said. "You told me you were introduced when you activated the headset."

"Yeah, but that was different — I didn't know what I was actually looking for besides a net within the Net," she said. "You know what I'm talking about."

"Not really," Alaric said. "I'm not really technical. Maybe we can go back to your apartment and find the headset."

Kira shook her head and sighed. "It'd be gone — zip, nada." She closed her eyes and slumped back on the park bench. "Damn it, I didn't even have business insurance. I bet the insurance company won't cover my computers."

"We ought to go and see what's gone. And see how Trevor is. He can tell me who attacked him."

"No. I *killed* a man, remember?"

"You were defending yourself and defending the cop," Alaric

said. "And seeing as you were a wolf, I don't know how the cop can implicate you."

"Werewolf DNA has been splashed all over the crime scenes," she said. "He told me that forensics was asking questions."

Alaric fell silent.

"He doesn't have a plausible story — he doubts people would believe him."

"That's the only thing saving our butts right now," Alaric said at last. "Damn Cathal!"

"Cathal wasn't in charge," Kira said.

"What? He was my second."

"He was too dumb. Everything points to someone else pulling the strings."

Alaric cocked his head. "Why do you say that?"

"Susan and I were attacked by a gray wolf."

"Yes, you've said that. It could've been one of Cathal's henchmen."

"I don't think so. The wolf was almost as big as you," Kira said. "Second, Spaz is missing. The cops think he's dead, but I don't think so."

"Why?"

Kira hesitated. "You wouldn't believe me."

Alaric frowned. "Why don't you try me?"

"An old woman told me he was still alive, but in great danger."

"An old woman?" Alaric said sharply. "Verdandi?"

"You know her?" At once Kira felt relieved and perplexed. "I thought I was losing my mind. I mean, she knew me and knew my name. She knew what had happened to me. I'm so glad you've met her."

"I haven't exactly met her," Alaric said. "But I have heard of her. Others have seen Verdandi." He fell silent and chewed his lip in what Kira guessed was worry.

"What's wrong?"

"I wouldn't have expected a Norn to take interest in you."

"A Norn?" Kira stared at him. "You mean like a Fate?"

He nodded. "She's an AEsir."

"A Norse goddess?" Kira laughed. "Surely, you don't believe..." Her voice trailed off as she saw the seriousness in his eyes. "Look, my parents are archaeologists. I learned all about these old religions growing up. I have respect for them, but..."

"You didn't believe in werewolves either," Alaric said. "Look, Kira, this is serious if a Norn is paying attention to you. Strange forces are at work."

"You're telling me," she muttered. "What am I going to do if you can't *see* the Forest?"

Alaric stared at the skyline of Denver for a while. "How about if we use our telepathy."

"How?" Kira asked.

"I could see what you're seeing and perhaps even figure out what you're doing to get there." He paused. "You'll have to not fight me when you feel my presence in your head."

Kira hesitated. A man she was highly attracted to wanted to rummage around in her mind. How much would he see in the few moments before he latched onto the Forest and began to see it, himself? For all she knew, he already had access to the Forest and this was some trick to get her to open her mind to him.

But...Kira couldn't sense Alaric's presence in the Forest. By how he acted, she doubted he had really experienced it. And it wasn't if she had Jim to go back to. Despite what Alaric said, she doubted that he would look at her as anything other than a murderer. And then there was her apartment....

She closed her eyes. She didn't want to do this. She trembled as she thought about letting someone — anyone — into her mind. In the course of a month, she had lost nearly everything she had. She didn't even have control of her body. She didn't have anything left to her except her mind and that was slowly being taken away from her.

"Kira?"

Alaric's voice was soft and gentle. Kira opened her eyes, met his golden ones and nearly melted. *Damn*, she thought. *The man of my dreams is a fucking werewolf.*

"Kira, you don't have to if you don't want to."

Kira sighed in exasperation. "What other choice is there? If you don't see the Forest, you won't know what they can do." *I have no one left to help me.* She paused. "You've got help me, Alaric. You have to help me find Spaz before they kill him."

Alaric nodded. "I'll try, Kira. You know I don't want anyone else killed because of the rogues — especially your friend."

"Okay. What do I do?" Kira said.

"Can you link to the Forest now?"

"I'm already linked," Kira said.

"Okay. Now think the way you would when you're trying to talk to me via wolf telepathy," he said.

Kira closed her eyes. She could see the outline of the Forest within her mind's eye becoming sharper and more real. The air was colder here and slightly rarified — she guessed Spaz had made this section mountainous. And yet, she could sense Alaric's wolf-presence nearby. All she had to do was reach out to him...

A day had passed since Spaz had tried to access the Enchanted Forest. His captors had given him some water and some stale crackers, but nothing substantial. They wanted him alive for the moment, but for how long remained to be seen. He felt miserable as he lay with his arms bound in duct tape and the bloody stump burning like fire.

Something had been nagging him about the wolf he had seen with Lizard. It had been smaller than the other werewolves and not as threatening. The werewolves he had seen in the Forest were usually huge menacing things with glowing red eyes, and blood dripping down from their teeth.

Spaz closed his eyes and focused on the Forest. He was getting weak and his link with the Forest was tenuous at best, but he had to find help somehow. Even if it meant popping out into the cops' computers and writing "help" across their screens. Within moments, he was galloping through a dark pine forest in the avatar of a unicorn.

No sooner had he appeared than three werewolves materialized before him, their eyes red and their maws dripping with blood. Spaz turned on his hoof — a maneuver impossible in the real world — and vanished from sight. But the wolves already had a lock on him, and they dogged his every move.

Spaz ran from machine to machine, faster than thought. He sent out an email to the Denver police but as the packet flew away from him, the wolves spun off daemons, smaller versions of themselves, to track down the email. The wolves were so quick, Spaz guessed that they were daemons themselves, not human-driven. They were programs set to search and destroy.

It was then that he sensed something else. One of the daemons sent out a *traceroute* toward him. Spaz tried to set up a firewall, but to his dismay, he found that his priority had been lowered. The werewolves had found part of the program he was using and had modified his permissions, so that he wouldn't have the strength to block them.

There was nothing to do except bail. If the werewolves found out where he was picking up the signal, it wouldn't take long before they realized it was him. Spaz pulled the plug and opened his eyes. Although he couldn't see past the blindfold, he was back in his cell again.

⚊⚊⚊🐾

Kira closed her eyes and concentrated. As much as she was afraid to let go, she was more afraid of Spaz dying. The rogue werewolves had killed too many people now, and she wasn't going to let them kill him, too. If there were any way for her to save him, she'd find it.

She reached out to Alaric and felt his presence at once. It was as if every nerve fired simultaneously through her body as she felt his power course through her. The She-Wolf seemed to relish in it; drinking in his consciousness as though it sustained her. Kira could do nothing except watch helplessly.

But, as overwhelming as he was, Alaric's presence became focused on her link to the Forest. As soon as Alaric appeared in her mind, he had disappeared.

"Alaric?" she said aloud.

"It's okay, Kira. I'm in. Look in the Forest."

And she did. Beside her stood a large black wolf. He was looking not at her, but all around at the Enchanted Forest. Kira knew what he was seeing.

The world had suddenly shifted for him. What had been a world of reality was now layered with something that looked like a shadow world; a world of binary ones and zeros that overlapped reality in a fuzzy image.

Kira faced Alaric in her wolf form. Only, it wasn't quite wolf form, but a binary approximation of such. He stared at her. "How did you do that?" he asked, and started at his own voice. It had a tinny echo to it.

You don't need to talk. You just need to think, Kira said.

"Like werewolves?" He tried to think his words. *How is this secure?*

Normally, it's not, she said. *Look around us.*

Alaric looked at the trees and saw flames erupt all around them. He jumped back, but there was nowhere to go.

Easy, Alaric, it's a firewall. Kira sounded smug even to her ears. She tried to tone it down. *It's a barrier between us and other machines and programs.*

How? Alaric was intrigued.

Using secure socket layer to encrypt our conversation, Kira said. *Spaz thought of everything. There are programs we can access that will allow us the basic security. It won't withstand a full-on assault of malicious code, but it's a start.*

But why are you a wolf?

Our avatars. We can be anything here. With that, she turned into a sexy anime of herself. *You like?*

I like you just fine the way you are, Alaric remarked. *I don't need a fantasy.*

Well, you're in the wrong place, Kira remarked, turning back into her wolf avatar. *The Internet is full of fantasy.*

So, what am I looking at? Alaric asked, surveying the binary landscape.

The Enchanted Forest.

Forest? Alaric said. *It doesn't look like a forest to me.*

Kira laughed. *You're seeing the bare bones.*

The bare bones?

Without skin, Kira said. Alaric looked puzzled. *Watch this,* she added, and called up the computer. All around them, a magical forest of trees sprang up. In one view, he was standing in the sunlight with Kira, staring out into Common's Park. But in another view — almost like a mind's eye view — he could see a pristine forest before him. The trees were flocked with snow and he could feel the cold wind in his face.

Feel? He looked at Kira, and she smiled. *Like it?*

This isn't real, he said.

Kira shrugged. *What is reality, Alaric? Is it what you see and feel? The Forest offers more reality than most people can imagine.*

Reality is life or death, said Alaric. *No one dies here.*

How do you know that? Kira asked.

Alaric hesitated. He didn't have an answer for that. Could people die here, as in the real world? If so, did this make this second existence just as real? He found he couldn't answer that, either.

Even if you can't answer it for certain, Kira said, *can't you see how important this interface would be?*

Alaric nodded slowly. *This interface makes the Enchanted Forest more accessible to anyone who uses it.*

The ultimate reality trip.

Alaric shut down the link. "Maybe for some people — not for me." The Forest and all that surrounded him vanished, and he stood facing Kira in the park.

"It's wonderful," she said.

"It's dangerous," Alaric replied. "You told me that our werewolf senses allow instantaneous access into the Enchanted Forest."

"Yes," Kira said and stopped. "The Enchanted Forest has links into everything."

"Financial institutions, communications — all at the speed of thought?"

Kira laughed. "That's pretty slow. You could get everything you want with a program."

"But you need to know what you're looking for, isn't that correct?"

"Well yeah, unless you have some AI code which can modify its programming." Kira looked at Alaric skeptically. "Are you suggesting that Spaz was doing more than just a cool interface for the Forest? I mean, the money on the design would be enough to kill anyone for."

Alaric nodded. "True, but think. The rogues aren't interested in money. They want power."

Kira thought about this for a bit. "Okay, let's say you're right. Let's say the rogues have found some reason to want this interface. What would it be?"

"You're the computer expert. You tell me."

Kira leaned back. "Let's say it is power. I wonder how much access to the Enchanted Forest they have. They have at least a good portion of the backbone, through Intermountain."

"But do they have everything?"

"I doubt it. I suspect that the Enchanted Forest is as large as the Internet. There's bound to be areas the rogues wouldn't know."

"But Spaz would," said Alaric. "He's one of the architects of this thing?"

"Yeah." Kira paused.

"Listen, what if the rogue werewolves didn't have complete access? What if they simply had control over a few places and a few portals? Maybe there's more to this Enchanted Forest than just trees."

Kira looked thoughtfully. "Well, the rogues could hack into systems."

"How much easier is it when you're already there?" Alaric paused. "So the rogues might not be able to take systems that the government has not connected to the Internet, but what about other systems?"

Kira hesitated and brought herself back into the Forest.

Query Forest Map, she said to the command prompt after she brought it up.

What appeared in her mind's eye was a dizzying array of machines — many off the Intermountain backbone, but many others she didn't recognize. As the picture wrapped itself around her, Kira noticed a small menu at the bottom, similar to the Google menus: ***Approximately 1,200,475 hits. Page 1 of 240,095.***

Kira blanched. Alaric cocked his head. "What do you see?"

"It's huge," she said. "There's over a million that I can see. There could be many more. Spaz's program acts like a virus and tries to snake into any machine hooked into the Internet... which means the entire Forest is growing at a phenomenal rate." She paused and looked at him. "I don't know how deep it goes, but I'd wager you can get just about any information about anyone." She closed her eyes.

#*find / – network –print* | *grep "Kira Walker"*
#3572 hits

"Shit."

Alaric cocked an eyebrow. "What'd you find?"

"All my bank account records," Kira said. "Shit, I'm thirty-seven dollars overdrawn..." She shook her head sheepishly. "I thought I had enough money to cover that."

"Nice," said Alaric.

We need to shut this thing down now," Alaric said. "If you can get access to bank accounts and other personal information, it means the rogues can, too. It also means that they can finance their revolution with other people's money. So why would they still need your friend, Spaz?"

Kira frowned. "Maybe it's still access," she said.

"They can access the Forest the way we did."

"Yeah, but maybe they don't have the same access. Or maybe there's more to accessing the Forest than what we can do."

"Right now we have data access — what else is there?" Alaric asked.

"Let me ask," Kira said.

"Ask who?" Alaric said in puzzlement.

"Spaz," she said. When she saw his confused expression she grinned. "Spaz created a help program that looks just like him. Let me ask it." She slid back into the Enchanted Forest. *Help program?*

Spaz's smiling face appeared in front of her. *Can I help you?*

What's the security on the Enchanted Forest?

Please define security level

Shit. Command line interface.

Ready. Command?

Man security
No man pages on security.
Ready, command?

Kira felt like smacking her head against a wall. It would take all day for her to guess what the security levels were on the Forest. She glanced at Alaric, who was staring at her curiously. She shrugged. "It's not that intuitive."

"I didn't think computers were," Alaric said dryly.

Kira lifted her lip in an imitation of a wolf snarling. She went back to the interpretive interface and started looking at the NIS+ yellow pages and various security levels. Slowly, she began to unravel Spaz's design. There were protected databases on top of the various layers — most of which were encrypted in a way she couldn't readily access. With a few queries, she was able to determine that she had fairly high permissions, but wasn't superuser.

No one was, save Spaz.

Kira decided it was time to see how far she could get inside other computers. She chose a top bank on Wall Street and went in. The Forest changed from trees to skyscrapers. She was walking along what she imagined was Spaz's interpretation of New York City. The buildings loomed over her, gray and foreboding with a cold wind running through canyon-like streets.

And yet, Kira would've known in an instant that this was not real. There were no people here — no crowds, no cabs. She had been to New York City once, and this looked like nothing she had ever seen.

Pull up account information, she said.

Suddenly a firewall leapt up in front of her. A fiery message appeared in the flames.

You are not authorized to access this information.

The heat from the firewall forced her to take a step backwards. *Who is authorized?* she asked.

You are not authorized to access this information.

She rubbed her eyes and snapped back into the real world. To her surprise, it was getting dark.

"How long?" she said.

Alaric shrugged. "Almost an hour."

"An hour?" She stared at him. "And you waited?"

"I am patient," Alaric said. "But so are most predators. What did you find out?"

"Spaz has firewalls on the most sensitive stuff. He's a spider, but he wasn't stupid. He knew if someone else got into the real important stuff, someone might just figure out the Forest and find ways to shut him out. So he firewalled and passworded them."

"Are there ways around them?" Alaric asked.

"I don't know." Kira's stomach rumbled and blushed. "Sorry."

"No, we should get something to eat," Alaric said. "We'll go to *The Grey Wolf* and I'll have my wolves start searching for your friend."

"But what if they're rogues?" she asked. "Won't they alert whoever is in charge?"

Alaric shrugged. "I'll offer a reward," he said. "Some rogues' loyalty can be turned with a bit of money."

"I don't like the people you deal with."

"I can't always choose my own kind," Alaric said.

"Yes, but you can choose your lieutenants," Kira said. "Cathal was a poor choice."

"Cathal held the Commerce City pack's loyalty," Alaric said. "He wouldn't have been my first choice for second-in-command, but he held a lot of power. Still, I didn't think he'd go against pack loyalty and betray me."

"I could've told you he would," Kira said. "Cathal cared about nothing except Cathal."

Alaric smiled as she stood up. Kira found it both intriguing and disarming. "Perhaps we should discuss this over dinner. If we're to find your friend soon, I'd better send my wolves looking for him." He offered her his hand.

Kira took it and he pulled her into his arms. Before she knew it, he was kissing her. Her nostrils filled with his musky scent and she was overwhelmed with the passion in his kiss.

Alaric pulled away and grinned, leaving her breathless. "Let's get dinner. I'm eager for dessert."

53

The *Grey Wolf* seemed darker and more ominous as they entered it that evening. Several werewolves hung around the entrance as Alaric strode toward door, Kira's arm firmly intertwined in his own. As he approached, the werewolves took notice of him. Most were younger wolves, barely in their teens and early twenties. Many wore spiked hair and leather spiked dog collars.

Kira glanced at Alaric, who smiled ruefully. "They're into the rogue wolf look," he explained. "Most of it is just rebellion against their parents. Harmless really. Few are actually into it."

"Like that kid who tried to rape me?" Kira said. "I don't think it's *that* harmless."

Alaric considered her thoughtfully. "You think I should ban it?"

"I think you should be very careful," Kira replied. "But we may be able to use them." She paused as the She-Wolf inside her silently nudged her to act. She turned to Alaric. "Do you trust me?"

Alaric paused, his eyebrows raised slightly. "What do you plan to do?"

"I plan to have these kids find Spaz." She could feel the She-Wolf in her nudge her hard. Alaric nodded. Kira turned to the pack of teens and considered them.

She noticed one of the girls — about fifteen, by the look of her — staring at Kira. She met the young woman's challenging gaze with her own steady stare. The girl shrunk back, and then looked away.

"See? Harmless," Alaric said.

"I'm not convinced," Kira replied. She slid her arm from Alaric's and stepped forward. The girl withdrew a bit. "What's your name?"

The girl flinched and shivered, despite the warm breeze. She had crimson hair and pale white skin. Her leather top barely covered breasts which displayed tattoos of wolves running toward each other, facing her cleavage. *That had to have hurt,* Kira thought. Looking down the girl's body, Kira noted the leather miniskirt and the too high stiletto pumps. "Emily," the girl said in a hoarse whisper.

"Emily," Kira repeated. "Does your momma know you're out here?"

The girl blanched and trembled under Kira's steady gaze. "No."

"I didn't think so," she said. "Look, you tell your friends here that Alpha and I have something for you to do besides just hang out. There's a Normal who's been kidnapped by the rogues..." She paused. "You're not a rogue are you?"

"What do you care, bitch?" The teen beside Emily stared at Kira defiantly. He was a tall, lanky boy with a mop of dirty black hair and black makeup on his eyelids and lips. Kira turned to meet his gaze.

"I *care* because *Alpha cares,*" she said with a hint of a snarl in her voice. "The man's name is Will Tagura. He's also known by the nick of Spaz. Got it?"

The teen averted his eyes. "Yeah."

"What's your name, Pup?" she asked, and smiled as she saw him bristle at the insult.

"Tom."

"Good. Now, you, Tom and Emily, are in charge of this lot. I want you to find Spaz. Once you have, report back to either me or Alpha." She glanced back to see Alaric nodding slowly.

Tom bared his teeth in defiance. Kira looked up at him and circled slowly. "Are you challenging me?"

Tom looked down, caught her gaze and then moved away. "No, ma'am."

"Good. See that you don't," she said. "You can work for me, or deal with my anger."

Tom nodded. "What does your friend look like?"

Kira quickly filled the young werewolves in on the specifics of the man they were looking for. Many already knew the Enchanted Forest, and they understood that this man had created it.

Alaric nuzzled Kira as she watched the kids disperse. She turned and met his gaze. "I'm sorry if I overstepped by bounds."

"Not at all," he said. "Let's go inside. Felan makes a mean buffalo steak."

54

After dinner, Kira and Alaric took a walk through downtown Denver. The air was warm with a light breeze. No clouds hovered in the sky. Kira looked up at the gibbous moon that had been full only a few days earlier. The city lights obscured most of the stars, but Kira could pick out a few as they walked together toward Cherry Creek.

"It's a beautiful evening," Kira said, taking in the drowsy scent of the cottonwoods and Russian olives that grew along the banks.

Alaric smiled; his teeth gleamed in the dusk. "Yes, it is," he said. "I should take you to the mountains where you can feel the alpine breeze against your fur and smell the sage and tundra flowers. I know a place where the columbine, Indian paintbrushes, anemones, and buttercups fill countless meadows above the pine and aspen. It's amazing to see them in the summertime. I could take you where only the elk roam, along the fourteeners and away from people."

Kira closed her eyes, trying to imagine it as they walked. "Sounds lovely," she said. "I didn't know you were such a poet."

"Don't let that get out," he said, stopping and taking her hands. She opened her eyes. He was standing close to her; she could smell his wild, musky scent. It frightened and enticed her.

"I wouldn't want my reputation ruined."

"Don't worry," she said, thinking back on Cathal and the young wolf who had tried to rape her. "I don't think anyone would think less of you."

"Good," he said. "But I wonder what *you* think of me." He brought her hands to his lips and kissed them gently.

A pleasant shock ran through her and she smiled coyly. "I think you should take me to the mountains. I'd like to see them sometime."

Alaric hesitated, long enough for her to slide her fingers from his hands. "You've never been to the mountains?"

"No," she admitted. "Susan wanted to go, but we were also so busy with our work that we never had the time."

Alaric shook his head. "I have a home up there."

"You do?" She blinked. "What do you do, Alaric?"

"What do you mean?" he said, cocking his head in a very wolfish way. In the moonlight, Kira found it nearly irresistible.

"You have to do something to make a living. Megan is a vet; Trevor is a landlord..."

"Oh, money." Alaric waved his hand. "That's so mundane."

"And so necessary," Kira said. "Are you the owner of *The Grey Wolf*?"

"Part owner," he said. "But then, I own a lot of property."

"Land baron?" she teased.

"Yeah, something like that."

A silence ensued. Kira followed him into the park along the grassy path. She wondered where he was leading her. At last, they walked up a small hillside and he stopped. She stopped, too, and looked into his eyes.

He grinned wolfishly and took her hands. "I bet you've never seen the stars."

"I've seen them," Kira said, trying to pull away. "There's one there." She pointed to a bright star that outshone the city lights.

"Sirius," he said. "The dog star. Somehow very appropriate." He drew closer. "I'm talking *stars*, Kira. A universe of them. And to see you there, beneath that sky among the pines..." He ran his hand through her hair.

This time, she did not pull away when he touched her, nor did she flinch as he raised her chin to kiss her. He was warm and inviting as his lips pressed against hers. He pulled Kira close, and she slid her arms around him.

"Sounds beautiful," she murmured.

"As beautiful as you are," he said between kisses. His lips traced her jaw line and wandered down her neck. "You know I've wanted you since I first saw you."

"At *The Grey Wolf*?" she asked, pressing tight against him.

"No, since the last full moon," he said, gently nibbling her neck and sliding his hands over her breasts. "I knew you were beautiful in either form."

Kira lightly bit his jaw. "Is that so?" she said playfully. "Well, then, catch me!"

With that, she transmuted into a wolf and leapt from her clothing, leaving Alaric speechless.

Don't you want me? she teased again.

Suddenly Alaric was the great black wolf. He charged at her, but she dodged. She was fast and leapt right over him as he ran for her. Alaric tried to stop, took a tumble, and shook himself off as he got up.

Alpha, she called, twitching her tail. She ran toward the river and led him on a chase in the moonlight. Kira was amazed at how fast she actually was. While Alaric had sheer power and mass, she was quicker and more nimble; capable of evading a larger animal. Where he was strong, she was fast. Together they made an unstoppable team.

She led him up the banks toward City Park; the city a bright backdrop for their romp. Kira slowed down as she crested the hill and he caught her, grasping the fur along the back of her neck with his teeth. They rolled once, twice and then Kira found herself in human form, looking into Alaric's handsome face again.

He kissed her, this time holding her down to keep her from bolting once more, but in truth, she needed no such restraint. She groaned under him as she felt him enter her, and felt the shockwave of pleasure with each thrust.

Kira rolled him over, getting on top and gasping as the cool breeze prickled the sweat on her skin. He pulled her close — kissing her, running his tongue down her neck and laving her breasts. Kira screamed as pleasure rolled through her. Again, and again. She lost count after five, and still he was relentless. Alaric gripped her and rolled her over again; his body shook. A low growl rumbled in his throat and she felt his release. He collapsed, panting, on top of her.

For a few minutes, Kira lay staring up at the moon high above them. In the June breeze, she was beginning to grow cold again now that the exertion was over. She snuggled closer to Alaric to stay warm.

Alaric's eyes opened. In the pale moonlight, the gold glinted with amusement. "Again?" he asked.

Kira grinned back. "I wish! It's been so long."

A silence ensued as a strange look entered Alaric's eyes. He shook his head. "I forget, you've only become a lycanthrope recently."

"What does that matter?" she asked.

He smiled. "Nothing, beloved. Nothing." He ran a finger along her bare skin and she shivered involuntarily. "Are you cold?"

"Yes," she said. "Sorry."

"No need," he said, getting up and helping her up. "We'd best get moving — we made enough noise to attract unwanted eyes." He gazed at Kira. "You are beautiful."

"And you are incredible," she said. "Had I known love could be like this..."

He flashed his charming wolf grin before transmuting. *I'm not bad as a wolf lover either*, he said.

She laughed and turned into a wolf. *I'm already going to be sore tomorrow.*

She heard Alaric's deep throaty laugh come from his wolf body as he started back toward Cherry Creek. *Get used to it*, he said. *I'm not letting you go.*

They ran quickly, returning to their clothes like two fleeting shadows. As she picked up her clothes to dress, she found Alaric gazing at her.

She laughed self-consciously. "I'm sorry," she said. "I've never had a man who thought I was sexy."

Alaric bared his teeth as he pulled her half-naked into his arms. "That's a shame," he whispered in her ear. "But lucky for me." He began kissing her slowly down her throat.

"No, not here," she whispered. "Someone will see us."

Alaric pulled away, but only reluctantly. She could see he was ready to make love to her yet again. "Later?" he asked hopefully.

She grinned as she tugged on her shirt. "You bet!" She looked at her clothes and frowned. "I need to go back to my apartment and see what happened. At least I'll need a change of clothes." She shivered. "But suppose the police are waiting for me?"

"They won't be," Alaric said, taking her hands in his own. They were warm and comforting to her. "I told you, your cop friend isn't going to implicate someone who just saved his life."

Kira felt queasy. "Are you sure?"

"Positive," he said, brushing her hair back. "No one is going to believe that you're a werewolf, and he knows it. Certainly not without proof."

When they were dressed, Alaric turned to her. "Let's go to your apartment. We'll see if anything they took might provide a clue to where your friend is."

Kira walked beside Alaric, her arm laced in his. She stole curious glances at him. He was a handsome man and a great lover — it puzzled her that he didn't have a wife and kids already. Her own situation, she could understand readily — when you were a contractor geek, you didn't find many meaningful interpersonal relationships. Not when you were always moving to a new city for a new job. Occasionally geeks could find someone to marry, but if they married normal people — that is, not engineers — they often ended up divorced within five years.

Kira remembered that all too well. When she had run into Tim Smith from her first job, he had filled her in on what had happened to everyone in her group; all ten engineers had gotten divorced. Kira couldn't blame their spouses, either — when you worked sixty-hour weeks on a regular basis, family life suffered.

She felt a soft touch to her chin. Alaric was looking into her face. "Why so pensive? We'll find Spaz."

She smiled. His golden eyes glinted even in the darkness. "Oh, I was just thinking." She paused. "I never really had a decent relationship with my line of work."

"You're a programmer, right?"

"Sort of," Kira said. "I'm a systems administrator. That means I'm responsible for making sure everything runs right. But you know, once I fix the computers, they usually don't need me. So, I go where the jobs are." She sighed. "Only, there aren't any jobs. The damn dot-com bust."

Alaric looked sideways at her. "You don't need to leave anymore..."

"I do if I'm going to make a living," she said. "I don't expect Trevor..." She stopped as Alaric gripped her arm. "What?"

Alaric pulled her away. "By Mani, what sick bastard...?"

Kira turned and looked despite herself. On the ground was the half-eaten body of Megan Olson.

56

Kira found herself shaking. Bile rose in her mouth as she stared at Megan's naked corpse. She was barely recognizable. Even through the smattering of blood, Kira could see her features and strands of blonde hair; but it was her *smell* that Kira recognized — she hadn't even realized she had associated a smell with Megan. The werewolf part of her was enraged; the human part made her throw up.

The werewolf that had attacked Megan, had fed on her. Her throat was ripped out and considerable portions of her torso and organs were gone. The werewolf had slashed her face and stripped much of the flesh away from her right arm. Kira turned away and lost her dinner and continued until there was nothing but dry heaves. She felt Alaric's arm around her back.

She wheeled around. "What kind of person does this?"

Alaric's face was grim. "A psychopath," he said. "No werewolf feeds on another. It isn't done."

"Well, evidently this one didn't get the news." She closed her eyes and found herself crying. "Why? What did Megan ever do?"

"I don't know, but there's another body under that tree."

Kira looked up. She could just see the mangled body of a large man lying on his side. Even in the scant light, she could tell he had been brutally mangled. Alaric walked over to the body and came back shaking his head. "It's Mike."

"Mike Fowlkes? Megan's cousin?"

"Yes." Alaric looked grim. "Do you have a cell phone?"

"Yeah, who do you want me to call?"

"You know that cop friend of yours?"

Kira felt a pang of fear. "Won't he...?"

Alaric shook his head. "Call him. We need help."

⚊⚊⚊ ⧢K

Kira shivered as she waited for Jim. She sat maybe twenty feet away from the body, watching Alaric as he snuffed the air and the ground, still in human form. She guessed that since he'd been a lycanthrope all his life, many of those same senses spilled over from his wolf side.

Jim had sounded anxious when she called. His voice had been mixed with worry and relief. The first thing he had asked was if she was all right. Kira smiled, despite herself. He actually *cared* about her. She gave him her location and hung up the phone.

Despite it being a warm night, sitting not far from Megan's and Mike's corpses made her skin rise in goose bumps. The stench of death was overwhelming to her lycanthrope nostrils. She could smell blood, urine and excrement mixed with the reek of torn bowels and raw meat. As a werewolf, she knew she should've been excited by the carrion smell, and yet the wolf part of her was outraged. Maybe because Mike had stood up for her. Maybe because Megan had been like her.

Like her. Kira blinked back her tears and stared at Megan's hair. Megan was blonde haired and about Kira's size. Same weight and close enough in age. Kira paused as she tried to remember Megan's form as a wolf. She was a little smaller than Kira — but in the dark, would anyone even notice?

Surely, a werewolf could have distinguished between Megan

and Kira — or could he have? If he didn't know Kira or Megan well enough, perhaps their scents might have even been confusing. After all, Megan hadn't been born a lycanthrope — she had been bitten. Just like Kira, only not as violently. Did Normals who were bitten smell like werewolves or did they have a different scent? Maybe they smelled too much like humans.

The implication was too unnerving for Kira to ponder. Could the rogue wolf have been looking for Kira and mistaken Megan for her? And when he attacked, had he realized he had the wrong girl, but been forced to go through with it because Megan might have known of him? And maybe Mike was a witness, so the rogue wolf had to kill him too. Kira guessed that a veterinarian who worked on werewolves pretty much knew the entire pack. They probably knew their murderer.

A scent Kira had smelled before was mixed in with Megan's scent. It was the scent of the murderer. She closed her eyes, shivering involuntarily. She wondered if she remembered the smell from her attack, but quickly reminded herself that she had still been a Normal before the full moon. So, where had she smelled this wolf?

Sirens stirred her out of her reverie. Alaric stiffened and headed back to her. "Don't worry," he said. "Let me handle it."

The first car that pulled up was none other than Jim Walking Bear's. He brought out his flashlight and swept its beam in their direction, flashing it briefly over them. "Kira? You okay?"

"Yeah, okay," Kira said in a voice that didn't sound convincing to her ears.

Jim walked up to her and wrapped his arms around her shoulders. His lips pressed against hers and she felt herself respond to him. For a moment, there were just the two of them. She felt safe with him, as opposed to with Alaric, who enticed the wolf. "I was worried about you when you fled. Are you okay?"

A small noise pulled her out of her reverie and they broke apart. Kira turned; Alaric stared at them both. She opened her mouth to say something, but found that the words had left her.

"What happened?" Jim asked. He turned, and his flashlight's beam fell on the gruesome discovery. "Oh my God."

"It's Megan Olson and Mike Fowlkes," Alaric said quickly. "A rogue wolf killed them."

"The werewolf vet," Jim said, the official police mask sliding back over his features. Two cops came out of their police cruisers and joined him. "The victims are over there — I need you to search for evidence." He paused. "I'll be back in a moment to get your statement," he said to Kira before turning to go with the two officers.

Alaric came up behind Kira and gripped her shoulders. As she turned to him, she saw the anger smoldering in his eyes. "I don't want you seeing this man any longer."

Anger welled up in Kira. She turned to him. "What? You can't order me around. I don't belong to you."

"Actually, you do," Alaric said. "Wolves mate for life. By lycanthrope laws, you're my mate."

I'm your *what*?" Kira didn't even realize she was shouting. "You've got to be god-damned fucking kidding me!"

"No, I'm not," Alaric said. "When we made love, you became my mate."

"Bullshit!"

Alaric looked affronted. "You didn't object earlier."

Kira felt her face flush. "Well, yeah you're a great lover and that was really great, but..." He voice trailed off as Alaric's gaze narrowed.

"You're my mate," he said. "You will not see that man again." There was a hint of a growl in his voice. Kira was both frightened and enraged by his tone.

"You have no right to dictate to me how I should act or behave," Kira said. Her voice took on the ominous tone of the wolf. "Last time I checked, this was America and people don't belong to other people..."

"You're my mate."

"Bullshit. I didn't stand at an altar or in front of a justice of the peace. I didn't say any vows."

"I thought you loved me."

Kira felt her throat tighten. She looked into Alaric's gold eyes, angry and earnest.

"Kira," he whispered.

She turned and fled, heedless of the cries from Alaric — or from Jim.

≡≡≡ᴣⰍ

Kira ran, her mind whirling with Alaric's words. *You're my mate...* How could she be? Sure, they had sex. Great sex. Wild sex. But that didn't mean you were married. She liked Alaric a lot. She felt that she could even love him over time. But marriage? What was that? She'd settle down and have — what? Kids? Puppies? Or — what did the Boy Scouts call wolf pups? Cubs? Her mind strayed to a kid she had known growing up — his name, she remembered uselessly, was Mike. He had proudly shown her each of his Cub Scout badges as he had earned them.

But Alaric was no Cub Scout. She doubted he even knew what merit badges were. And now he was saying she was his wife. *His wife!* Kira wondered what Susan would've said if she had heard that. She wondered what Spaz would've said.

Spaz. Kira felt a pang of guilt. She didn't know where he was or whether he was even alive. Verdandi said he was, but she was just a crazy old woman. Wasn't she? Alaric didn't think so. He had called her a Norn — one of the Norse goddesses of fate. Like she believed in Norse goddesses?

Kira ran blindly, not really paying attention to where she was going. She was only aware of her breath, rising and falling raggedly in time with the pounding of her feet — and the pounding of her heart. It took a while but eventually she came to her senses.

She was following the bike path back to Lower Downtown. The air along the Platte River was cool and humid, but she was sweating from the exertion. She caught movement to her right as she slowed down, but saw that it was just a homeless man on the ground, curling up with his tattered blanket. Kira kept moving until she got her bearings. She was maybe a mile or two from Auraria and not far from Commons Park. She could try to go home, if she wanted to, but she didn't really know what to expect there.

Kira shivered and looked up at the stars. Her life had become awfully complicated since the werewolf attack. She had become someone she really didn't want to be. Like it or not, she was now a werewolf. Despite her denial, she knew the wolf was changing her in ways she never wanted. She had killed a man, had almost been killed several times, had nearly been raped, had met two dangerous and exciting men — and she had made love to one of them. Her best friend was dead and her only other friend from college had been kidnapped and might be dead. It was enough to piss off a saint, as her mother used to say.

Kira felt a pang of guilt. What would her parents say if they learned their daughter was a werewolf? Her dad would probably be excited and ask all about the transformation. She could hear his voice in her head: *"But what does it feel like?"*

She grinned despite herself as she imagined her mom's voice answering: *"Now, Arthur, that's not really appropriate..."*

Kira stifled a laugh. No, the werewolf thing would only be a curiosity to them, where other parents would be horrified. Hell, her dad might even buy a wolf cage and kibble for her transformations, thinking to make his daughter safe from possible injury.

The thoughts were warm and comforting. With so much of her past stripped away, Kira felt alone and powerless.

"You're not really powerless unless you choose to be."

Kira nearly jumped. She turned around to see Verdandi rummaging in a garbage can Kira had passed not more than a few seconds ago. "You weren't there," she said, her voice sounding oddly loud and accusatory in the quiet night. From somewhere toward LoDo, she heard a siren wail.

"No, I wasn't," Verdandi said, looking up. Even in the dark, her blue eyes seemed to glow. "You've gotten distracted, Kira. Do you want to save your friend or not?"

Kira blinked. "How do you know about my friend?"

Verdandi shrugged. "How does a Norn know about anything?' She clucked her tongue. "What a waste — there's half a Frappuccino in here." She held up a Starbucks cup.

"You see the future?"

"I see much," she said. "If you don't find Spaz, the evil ones will win. They will kill him. They've already killed your other friends."

A lump filled Kira's throat and she felt her mouth go dry. "Who? Who is dead?"

"Danni Jones and Tom Sullivan."

Kira stared. How did the woman know her friends' names? If her mouth had been dry a moment ago, now it was like sawdust. "How do I find Spaz?"

Verdandi shrugged. "Spaz gave you the portal. Use it. He searches for you."

"For me?' Kira asked.

The old woman went back to the trashcan. "Look at this," she muttered, shaking her head. "Half a sandwich. How wasteful."

"How will I know Spaz is there?" Kira pressed.

Verdandi said nothing, still rummaging. Kira gripped the old woman's arm. Verdandi looked up, her bright blue eyes staring hard. "You'll know." At that, Kira's hands closed on nothingness; Verdandi slowly vanished, like mist in the air.

58

Kira stared at the spot where Verdandi had been. Before, she had only half-believed the old woman was more than what she appeared, but now she knew otherwise. She had never believed in supernatural beings, skeptical when her dad would tell her about his conversations with ghosts and spirits at archaeological digs, but now she wasn't so sure. She had always thought he was joking with her, but...

"Maybe not," she muttered.

She looked around and saw that a homeless man was approaching her. Normally she would be terrified, but now she wasn't. "Spare change?" he asked.

She smiled chagrined. "Sorry, I have nothing." She walked by and continued on toward LoDo. She couldn't stay at her apartment now, as far as she knew, but she decided she at least needed some things from it if she was going to rescue Spaz.

The sky was lightening in the east, giving the sky a rosy glow. Not quite pink and not quite orange, Kira thought. The high-rises obscured the actual sunrise, but Kira could see the orange glow on their mirrored glass and on the mountains in the west. She took a deep breath of the air and enjoyed the sensation of the wind prickling her skin. She was beaten but not down. She was still alive.

The traffic was beginning to pick up as she made her way through the streets to her apartment. She still had her apartment keys and let herself in. She went up the stairs and paused at her apartment door. Marks along the door and door jam made her hesitate. The rogue wolves had used crow bars to pry the door open, but someone — presumably Trevor — had repaired the latching mechanism and door posts for it to lock.

Kira studied the door. It was a lousy job and one she doubted she would have problems forcing open if Trevor had changed the locks. She fit her key in and opened. The door groaned and she turned on the light.

Then, she turned it off again. But that didn't work. Her werewolf vision was good in the dark.

The entire apartment had been ransacked. Her Sun computer and PCs were smashed to bits; the monitors had been ripped from the workstations and the flat screens had been shattered. As she walked in, she smelled urine — both human and wolf — throughout the room.

She stared, blinking a few times. Turning off the light hadn't lessened the trauma, but it helped to stop her from focusing on any one thing. Thousands of dollars in computer equipment was destroyed. All her programs and customizations were gone, as well as all her disks and notebooks. She had been meaning to do a backup for some time and save it all off-site, but with the lack of income, she hadn't done so. Now, she was regretting that decision.

She was also regretting her lack of renter's insurance, but she doubted it would've covered this. One look at the thousands of dollars of equipment, and an agent would've laughed in her face and called the place a business.

The couches and furniture were smashed or ripped up with the stuffing spread around as if it had snowed. Her clothes, too, were strewn about the place. They were also the source of the urine smell. Assuming they weren't ripped up, she might be able to wash them and get out the stink and the glass — if she wanted to.

The only thing that remained untouched was that gawd-awful jade plant.

Kira stared at the ugly thing and grimaced. She wondered if it was like wolfsbane. She walked over to it and touched the bulbous leaves. They felt fake and even plastic-like, but the plant hardly repelled her — except through its sheer ugliness. Maybe the rogue werewolves had already thought it was damaged enough.

Kira looked around her apartment a little longer, finding the mattress slashed and pissed on, and the pillows ruined. The drawers had been turned out of her dresser and smashed, but she spied a small Altoids box amid the wreckage. Opening it up, she found her last $20 bill.

"*Yuppie Food Stamps,*" Susan used to call them. Kira cached the bill in her pocket and headed out of the room. She needed someplace to get her thoughts together and look for Spaz. Preferably someplace without werewolves.

She knew just the place. She turned and left the apartment, not caring if the door locked. As far as she was concerned, her whole life was gone now. What she did now wasn't for herself, but for Spaz.

If Verdandi was right, the wolves were killing off her friends; she would soon be their victim, too, if she didn't save Spaz. It didn't matter if she knew nothing about the development of the Enchanted Forest — she had a connection to Spaz, and that was all that mattered.

Kira entered Uncommon Grounds as the techno-geeks began their daily migration from the coffee shops to their workplaces. Kira felt out of sync, watching two men wearing HP polos and Dockers, complete with cell phones and handheld Internet devices on their hips, walk out of the coffee shop with their large lattes. She caught a snippet of their conversation as she passed.

"We should be able to do that installation next week," the brown-haired, slightly balding admin was saying.

Kira smiled as she watched the other admin — who looked to be just out of college — nod sagely and sip his latte as they passed her by. She walked in, ordered a mocha latte and brought it to the back of the room. The sign on the door indicated that this was a *hi-rFreq* hotspot for Intermountain Telecom. That was what she needed. That, and peace and quiet.

She glanced at the people in the back of the shop. Geek 1 was busy on his laptop. No threat. Geek 2 was embroiled in a conversation with Geek 3, who was working on his PDA. All were harmless. She sat away from all of them and held her cup in both hands. She focused on getting into the Enchanted Forest.

And suddenly she was there. She stood in a grove of aspens,

looking up at a mountain range — or a good facsimile of one. She was back in her wolf avatar and loping through the fields.

Google Danni Jones, she said.

531 hits, the Forest replied.

Plus death, Kira said, holding her breath.

57 hits.

Shit, she thought. *Name sources.*

The Seattle Times, the...

Stop. Pull up The Seattle Times.

A window appeared, hovering in the Forest. Kira read the news article in disbelief: a network and computer designer named Danni Jones had been killed almost a month ago in an execution-style shooting. She pulled up Tom Sullivan's name and found he had been shot in a Washington, D.C. hotel. Randy Green appeared as a missing person in the police databases.

Kira unplugged from the Forest and stared into her latte. It had become cold and bitter. She drank it anyway and stared ahead. She was alone in the back of the café now. The air conditioner switched on, chilling her.

Danni, Randy, Tom... Spaz knew he was next. He probably hadn't thought that Kira or Susan would've been in danger, since they hadn't kept in touch very well since graduation. It had been ten years, but the werewolves were thorough. They had looked for anyone who might be associated with the Forest.

But why kill those involved in the creation of the Enchanted Forest — assuming Danni, Randy, and Tom even had been? Had they been commissioned to create the Forest? It didn't seem like Spaz to create something like this under someone's paycheck, but she couldn't be sure. For all she knew, Spaz had created the Forest but had kept the truly dangerous areas locked out with his own codes. Maybe the werewolves had had enough, and those with the knowledge and the ability to entering the Forest were killing to gain the power it represented.

Too many questions and too few answers. She needed to find Spaz, and fast.

"Where in the hell are you, Spaz?" Kira muttered. She plugged back into the Forest, wandering aimlessly, hoping she would find some trace of him.

In her wolf avatar, nothing dared approach her even in the darkest part of the Forest. She checked the IPs and found that she was in the heart of the Intermountain Telecom systems. She checked her links on Mini and learned that her access was still safe. As long as she had Mini, she could still hop from machine to machine, having used NIS to propagate the passwords throughout.

She looked at the Enchanted Forest, and mentally studied the layout. Spaz was a fucking genius, she decided. The Forest was complex, and yet so simple. At its simplest stage, she could hop from machine to machine with no usernames or passwords — the entire system was built on the link layer and the sockets used to establish a connection of sorts. Being lower than the transport layer (TCP), it wasn't without its faults, but the verification was sophisticated.

But where would she start? The entire world was a massive river of data that she couldn't possibly hope to trace. She could trace individual datastreams, but it would be like finding the proverbial needle in a haystack.

Unless the needle wanted to be found. Kira tried to relax first and read the streams of data as they flew by her. Surely Spaz had to know that his invention restructured thought patterns. He'd had the longest exposure to the headsets. Even if he wasn't a lycanthrope, she guessed he would've eventually experienced the change at the neuron and synapse level. So, it stood to reason that he would be able to get to the Enchanted Forest or even the Internet. But how would she find him? And how would she recognize him? If the rogue wolves knew he was capable of connecting without the headset, he would be dead.

Where did a kidnapped needle in a haystack hide so he would be seen? Her She-Wolf avatar was a bit intimidating. It was time to choose an avatar that Spaz would know.

Follow the Yellow Brick Road.

Of course, Spaz knew that she had learned of his penchant for Oz references. She considered each of the characters and deliberately chose the one that would leave no doubt as to what she was. She morphed herself into her chosen avatar and began to walk. The Forest grew darker as she walked. She continued to walk down the path, keeping her new eyes on the look-out for possible werewolves. She would be ready for them with her weapon raised.

Are you a good witch or a bad witch?

Kira swung around and almost laughed. The Good
Witch of the North appeared beside her. *If I only had
a heart,* she said.

But Oz didn't give nuthin' to the Tin Man, Glinda said.

That I didn't already have, Kira grinned despite the metallic
skin. She lowered the ax. *You're alive.* She set a firewall around
them and they changed into avatars closer to their appearances.

Barely, sweetie, said Spaz. *Jesus, Kira, I wasn't sure you'd figure it
out. But I see you've got some talent with this.*

It's the werewolf thing, Kira said. *I wouldn't have gotten it quite
as fast if I hadn't been bit.*

Spaz stiffened visibly. *You're one of them, aren't you?*

Not intentionally, Kira said. *I was bit, remember?*

Shit, Spaz said. He fell silent.

Shit, Kira said. *Your hand...*

Yeah, Spaz said. *I'm one of you, aren't I?*

*Next full moon... but I don't think they're going to let you live
that long,* she said. *Where the fuck are you?*

I don't know, Spaz said. *A warehouse, I think.*

You don't know?

I was blindfolded and kinda indisposed. You know, the pain thing.

Did they put you in a car?
Yeah.
How long?
Maybe 15 or 20 minutes.
Kira sighed. This was beginning to feel like Twenty Questions. *I wish I could see where you were.*
Well, you could see and feel what I do, Spaz suggested.
How?
Get inside my head, Spaz suggested. *The link works both ways if there isn't a firewall.*
Kira stared at him. *You're shitting me?*
Would I, girl? His expression was so earnest that Kira didn't doubt for a moment he was serious.
How do I do it? Kira was intrigued.
Open network, baby. Come on in. The IP addy is 255.255.255.255.
Broadcast, Kira thought. She pinged the broadcast address and Spaz returned an ICMP ping. Kira noted the address and plunged right in. Suddenly she felt pain burning along her right hand and she cringed. *Jesus, Spaz, this hurts!* She could see nothing, and smell little.
No shit, Kira, he said. *Can you figure out anything?*
Kira felt like shit, but she knew it was how Spaz felt. Despite the bravado, Spaz was scared and sick. When the wolf bit off his hand, he had shit his pants and passed out. They hadn't really cared for him — they were keeping him alive only because he knew how to configure the Enchanted Forest's interface for the werewolves. Both he and the werewolves knew he would be dead after his job was done. At the same time, he didn't want them to disassemble him piece by piece.
Kira frowned. Beyond the pain and the darkness, all she could really smell was his own sweat and bowels. It wasn't pleasant, but she knew what hell he was going through, now. His nose was nothing like hers, but Kira's werewolf senses had taught her how to analyze even a whiff.
Sniff the air, she told him.

She could feel Spaz's lungs fill with air as he breathed in deeply through his nose. She caught a whiff of the cotton bandana they used to gag him, and there was something else. Oily. Like machines. Or diesel. There was a strong acrid scent of steel.

You're by a bunch of machines, she said.

I could've told you that, Spaz said.

But you didn't. She paused as she caught another scent. Tar? Or was it creosote? *What the hell?* she muttered. At that, she heard— or rather felt—a rumbling beneath him. *Does this happen often?*

Spaz gave the mental equivalent of a nod.

You're by train tracks, she told him as she left his mind. *Maybe the stockyards or Union Station.*

You know where that is? he asked.

Yeah, she said. *Look, Spaz, I'll be there to get you. Hang on.*

No cops.

Yeah, sure, Kira said. *Can you hang online while I call in some backup?*

Backup? I thought you said no cops, Spaz objected.

Werewolves kidnapped you, she said. *I'm not stupid enough to take them on by myself.* She paused. *By the way, who kidnapped you?*

Cathal Murphy.

Cathal is dead, she said. *Who is in charge now?*

Some guy by the name of Bob Marks.

61

Bob *Marks?* Kira's head spun. *Are you sure?*

Yeah, you know him? he asked.

Dark hair, brown eyes, UNIX admin? Smug as hell.

That'd describe any UNIX admin.

Ha ha, Kira replied. *Try again.*

Yeah, that's him — the Intermountain werewolf. But he has gold eyes.

Kira sat back and thought in silence for a while. *Shit, Spaz,* she said. *This is big — really big.*

Spaz looked at her. *Can you help me?* He paused and his eyes went glassy. When they snapped back into focus, he looked scared. *Shit, they're coming. Got to go...*

With that, he unplugged.

Kira unplugged, too. She stared out the window of Uncommon Grounds toward Union Station. It was already noon by the clock at the café. She brought up Jim's number and dialed his cell phone. It went right into voicemail.

"Jim, this is Kira," she said. "Long story, but I got in touch with Spaz. The nearest I can figure is he's in one of the warehouses outside the old stockyards, or not far from Union Station. I'm going in. The werewolf's name is Bob Marks — I think he's the same asshole who killed Susan and bit me. Call me on my cell."

She set her phone to vibrate, then hesitated as she thought about contacting Alaric. She considered contacting him for help, but now his bizarre notion of making her his wife had made her reluctant. He would no doubt babble about her being his partner for eternity. He might even use his leverage to get her to promise to marry him if he rescued Spaz. Spaz was worth a lot, but not an eternal marriage to a werewolf.

Kira got up and tossed the cup in the garbage before heading out the door. But where to? What she was planning to do was stupidly dangerous, and she would need backup.

She walked over to the apartment building and reentered. Instead of going to her apartment, she went over to Trevor's and banged on the door. There was no answer. Kira pounded on the door again, this time more urgently.

"Go away!" she heard Trevor's voice from somewhere inside.

"Open this door now!" she shouted. "Or I'll break it down." She slammed her hand against the door and felt it shudder.

"Hang on!" she heard Trevor inside. He opened the door and peered out. "So, now you're the big bad wolf?"

Kira pushed her way into the apartment. Trevor was in pajamas. "Do you ever stay awake?"

"Look, I need my rest after the long nights."

"Right. You know where Alaric is?"

"You tell me, girlfriend. He's hot on you."

Kira felt her face flush. "Yeah, well, tell Alaric that Bob Marks is the wolf he's looking for."

"Why don't you?"

"Because I have more important things to do," she growled. Trevor averted his eyes from her stare. "Listen, Marks has got a friend of mine hostage. Now, I know you don't give a shit about me, but Alaric does. And if he finds out that you didn't tell him..."

"All right! All right!" Trevor's brow was furrowed but his skin looked pale. Angry but intimidated. "I'm getting tired of this, you know."

"Like I care?" Kira said. "Listen to me. I'm going to find Bob Marks — you know him?"

Trevor nodded. "Big wolf. One of Cathal's henchmen."

One of Cathal's henchmen? Or was Cathal on Bob's chain? Kira wondered. "Yeah, him. My friend is somewhere in an abandoned warehouse near the railroad tracks. I'm going to have to find him. Tell Alaric I'm out there."

"It's going to be tough for even Alaric to find you."

"Yeah, well he can fucking try."

Trevor shot her a glance that would've fixed a lesser werewolf, but not Kira. She lifted her lip in a bare-teeth snarl and Trevor lowered his gaze. "All right," he said. "I'll tell him."

"Good. Now get going. I need to find my friend." She turned and left him growling behind her.

62

As she walked down the hall, she wondered if she should turn into the wolf. The wolf was strong and powerful—capable of handling herself in most situations. Kira stood for a moment in hesitation. She hated being what the wolf was; it seemed as though each time she changed, Kira became a little closer to the animal she didn't want to be. It frightened her to lose her identity in that way. And yet, the pull of the moon was strong.

You can't resist me, the wolf said in her mind. *You know you are more powerful with me.*

I don't want to be you, Kira said to her. *You will destroy what little humanity I have.*

You can't save Spaz without me, the wolf countered. *Without me, you will never rip Bob Marks' throat out.*

I don't want to kill him, Kira said. *I just want to save Spaz.*

Like hell you don't, the wolf hissed, her laughter menacing. *You want Bob dead as much as I want to rip his throat out. You cannot deny what you are...*

I can, Kira replied. She envisioned a large cage and she deposited the wolf within it. Closing her mind, she ignored the enraged screams from the beast. It hated her as much as she hated it — maybe more so. After all, she was the control behind it.

There were logical reasons for not becoming the wolf, especially now. As a wolf, she couldn't communicate with humans and she would be at risk if seen in her wolf form. She would probably need her dexterity to open doors — something wolves weren't good at. What's more, she would be without clothing. While the wolf didn't really care, Kira did. She'd have a hard time explaining this to Spaz, too, and while Spaz was only a friend, she knew that he could be a letch when he wanted. She could always change into a wolf later on if she needed to. She hoped she wouldn't.

She slipped outside and caught a whiff of another werewolf; she realized it was Trevor as he skittered away. She'd have to be careful, she decided, as she made her way deep into Lower Downtown, where the roads finally met the Platte River and where the railroad lines still ran. Even in the daylight, the area was dangerous.

Kira walked slowly, trying to take in her surroundings. This would be slow going, even using her werewolf senses. She looked around at the buildings that sat at the corner. The smells from the railroad tracks were overwhelming to her werewolf senses, but she tried to match what she had picked up from Spaz.

Hours passed as she walked, trying to pick up the remembered scent. It was all wrong, she decided, and her stomach growled reminding her that she'd had nothing but a lukewarm mocha latte. She walked along the warehouses beside the tracks, heading north and passing by homeless people, railroad workers, and truck depots. None of it made sense.

She hesitated and then tried to feel Spaz's presence. The wireless was weak here; virtually nonexistent, actually. Now Kira had a conundrum: how did she connect with Spaz where there was no wireless available?

The answer was simple: she couldn't. Perhaps that was the trick to finding him — a wireless relay had to be close enough for him to access it and for her to find it. Without Internet access, there was no way Spaz or anyone could hook into the Enchanted Forest.

"Wireless," she muttered. "Wireless. I'm looking in the wrong part of town." She pondered her predicament. Intermountain would set up their wireless around businesses. But here in the warehouse areas, there would be very little wireless. Where would there be both tracks and wireless?

She wanted to access Intermountain's link, but the signal strength registered as poor or nonexistent. She had to get back on Mini and find the maps of where the wireless was — and wasn't. Problem was, there could be a private network Spaz had tapped into inadvertently that allowed him to route into the Enchanted Forest.

That was it. The IP address of the access point might tell her where he actually was. She felt stupid for not thinking of it sooner. She had Mini as her point of contact, which meant packets had to run through a solid network link, which would have to be off the Intermountain backbone.

She walked back down the street. One mile. Two miles. Suddenly she had signal strength again. Kira hopped on board and was in the Enchanted Forest in no time. She logged into Mini and sent a daemon to grep for the network maps, redirecting the find command to the grep search feature.

She then considered the situation. Spaz could be anywhere along the miles of railroad tracks that ran north to south along the Platte Valley.

Kira? Spaz's voice came through to her.

You okay? Kira asked. She checked the IP. It came from the last gateway he had been on. Good. She did a *traceroute* on Spaz's address and came up with an IP address that made no sense to her. It was a network, not a subnet that had a computer on it. It was one of Intermountain's main wireless routers.

Yeah, they're gone. They told me I don't have much time.

I wish I had a better clue where you are.

In the warehouses off of Sixth and I-25. You know where that is?

How did you find out?

I overheard them talking. Kira, you've got to help me...

I'm there, Kira said.

S he's *where*?" Alaric said. "Did she say where exactly she was going?"

The Grey Wolf had suddenly become quiet. Felan polished the ebony bar and looked over at Alaric with mild interest. The other werewolves had figuratively pricked their ears and some cocked their heads in his direction. Alaric towered over Trevor by several inches, making the other werewolf shrink backwards toward the bar.

Trevor shook his head. "Just to find her friend, Spaz, and to confront Bob."

"Bob Marks," Alaric began to pace but stopped himself. "All this time, I thought the power lie in Cathal. But it was Bob all along."

"He's dangerous," Trevor said. "Can I go now?"

"No," Alaric fixed Trevor with a stare.

"Damn," Trevor muttered under his breath.

Alaric turned to the other werewolves. "I want you and all available werewolves looking for Bob Marks and Kira Walker. Now." He turned to Felan. "The bar is officially closed."

Felan nodded. "You want me to lock up?"

"No, I want you to stay here and direct any lycanthropes who might come by to search for Kira. Tell them she's in danger and they need to get word to me ASAP when they find her. If Bob is the rogue leader, he'll kill her." He paused and turned to the wolves. "Now, who is with me?"

It took a while for Kira to find a main road. She called a cab from her cell phone. It was getting dark and Kira's stomach was more than rumbling, but she knew she was running out of time. Kira took the cab to the warehouses along I-25 where the rail line ran beside the highway. It was dark here and the warehouses loomed all around her in foreboding silence.

The cabbie had looked concerned when she'd made him stop at the corner. "You sure you want to be here, ma'am?"

"Yeah," Kira said. "How much do I owe you?"

"Ten-fifty."

Kira handed him twelve dollars. It cleaned out her pockets. "Keep the change."

"You want me to wait?"

"No, I'll be fine," she said. She stepped out and breathed in deeply as the taxicab drove away. Deep within her werewolf senses, she caught a whiff of what she had smelled through Spaz. What was it? Oil, machinery, and creosote. She kept walking for a bit, following the scent.

On one of the street corners, she realized that Jim wouldn't know where she had gone. She pulled out her phone and dialed. It was a good idea to keep him in the loop.

"Transferring you to Intermountain Telecom, please hold...."

"What the fuck?" Kira said.

"Hello?" came a voice on the other end that clearly was not Jim. Nasal, and definitely female.

"Hello?" Kira said dumbfounded. "Who is this?"

"This is Margie with Intermountain Telecom. Our records show that the credit card you have on file with us has declined authorization..."

"Christ almighty!" Kira looked around the darkened streets. "It worked earlier."

"We just ran billing. Your credit card was declined."

"Look, lady, I have to get hold of Detective Walking Bear right now..."

"You must supply a new credit card or account number."

"Shit, doesn't that one work?"

"As I said," Margie droned on with complete indifference, "the credit card you have on file has declined authorization..."

"You need a new credit card? Lady, I'm in the middle of a warehouse district trying to find a kidnapped friend. The last thing I want to do is start pulling out my maxed-out credit cards to try to find one that might work..."

"We'll accept a checking account number."

"That's not the point!" Kira said. "This is important."

"You can always dial 9-1-1 without charge..."

Suddenly Kira felt something like a hot iron press against her throat. She yelped and dropped the phone as a hand grabbed her and pulled her close. She felt crushed against the body behind her. Her neck burned and kept burning and she wanted to scream, but a gloved hand clasped over her mouth. She wanted to bite down but the pain was intense.

"Ma'am? Ma'am?" The phone echoed through the empty streets.

"Kick the phone away," a voice behind her said.

It hurts... she whined.

It'll hurt worse if you don't do as I say. She heard the lycanthrope in her head.

Kira kicked the phone away. She could still hear the woman at the other end say, "Ma'am, are you all right? Ma'am?"

Good. I wouldn't move or scream, the lycanthrope said.

The voice in her head was familiar. *Bob?* she asked. The pain in her neck was intense, but she knew if she could get to the Enchanted Forest from here, she could alert Alaric or any of his lycanthropes. She started to make the link through the wireless...

Pain shot through her neck and she nearly collapsed. "Don't do it," Bob's voice came out in a hoarse whisper. "Now walk."

The burning pressure increased on her neck, forcing her upwards. *What is this?* she asked.

"Silver," Bob said. "If you resist, I'll slice right through your carotid."

Can you take your hand off my mouth so I can breathe? I won't scream.

"It won't do you any good anyway if you did. Nobody hangs around here besides the bums and the rogue wolves." He pushed her roughly forward. "Walk."

"Okay," Kira said. Her legs felt all wobbly but she forced them forward through sheer will. To do otherwise would mean more excruciating pain, and perhaps death. "Where are we going?"

"Well, you seem to be so interested in finding your little friend; I thought I'd reunite you."

"That's helpful," she said. "Saves me time looking for him."

"Yeah, I didn't expect him to be clever enough to link with the Forest," Bob said. "I thought only werewolves could, but I guess there's something even in monkey brains that can pick up the signals, if they're retrained." He laughed at his own joke. "Of course, it took you long enough to figure out what was going on."

"Your eye color had me fooled."

"It's a wonder what contact lenses will do," Bob said. He was leading her toward a dingy gray warehouse. In the dark, Kira could just make out the Intermountain logo on it. "It's our network room for the south side," he said.

"You held Spaz here?" she said. "Wouldn't someone find out?"

"Like who? All the network admins are lycanthrope — and rogues, at that. Cathal made sure of that."

"Shit," Kira said. She stopped at the door and a large man with dark hair and glasses glared at her. He looked vaguely familiar. Kira tried to place him but couldn't. Most likely he had been with Cathal in *The Grey Wolf.*

"So, this is the bitch?" he said. "The one who got Cathal killed."

"Cathal got himself killed," Kira said. "Alaric..."

"Alaric, Alaric..." Bob sneered. "Monkey lover." He pushed Kira into the big man's arms. "Take her in with the Lizard."

The lycanthrope half picked her up and shoved her through the door. For a moment, Kira was tempted to turn into a wolf, but then she felt the silver burn against her neck. "Don't try it. You'll be dead."

"Hi, Kira," came a familiar voice.

Kira halted. The man had been sitting at a console, but now he wheeled around and grinned at her. He was pale with blond hair. His once-blue eyes were now gold. "Randy? Randy Green?"

"Yeah. Lizard," he said.

Randy Green from MIT. One of the guys from Spaz's inner circle. She remembered him, Tom, Danni, and Spaz all sitting together laughing and talking about their pet projects. "Christ, what did they *do* to you?" she said.

"They gave me a choice," he said with a shrug. "I took what was most sensible — as you should have."

Kira felt anger well up in her throat. "You bastard. You betrayed a friend. Don't you know what happened? Susan is dead, and they're going to kill both me and Spaz. And it'll be *your* fault..."

Lizard blanched for a moment, but then his gold eyes hardened. "It's not my fault, Kira. It's a matter of choices — you just made the wrong one."

Bob laughed and pushed her forward. "Since you like the little jap, you can hang out with him for while."

He opened the door and shoved her in. As it slammed shut, Kira stumbled into the darkness and nearly retched from the stench. The place smelled of blood, bowels, sweat, urine, and fear. As her eyes adjusted to the dark, she saw Spaz curled up in a fetal position on a filthy mattress in the corner. He was bound and gagged, cradling what was left of his arm with his good hand and whimpering.

"Christ, Spaz," she said, coming over to him. She was half-filled with revulsion at the sight of him. What had they done to him? Her nose caught a whiff of something else — rotting flesh. Was he becoming gangrenous? The thought terrified her. Even if she managed to save him, there was a terrible chance that he might still die from the infection.

Kira? She heard his voice clearly through his link into the Enchanted Forest.

"It's me, save your energy," Kira said. She walked over and pulled the blindfold and gag off him.

"I feel sick," Spaz said. "I didn't mean for you to get captured."

Kira frowned. Despite her fear, she looked over the room. "Well, I'm not taking this lying down," she said. "What does Bob want from you?"

"The main encryption for the Forest," Spaz said. "They've been trying to wear me down and get in my head. So far it hasn't worked."

"The main encryption?" Kira asked.

"The software's locks require some very sophisticated keys. Without the keys, they don't have full access to it."

"Why don't they decompile it?"

"They can't get to it. It's the brains behind the Forest. They've tried tampering with it, but once they screw with a memory location, another piece of code wipes it out and reloads it. In fact, the whole thing is set up that way."

"Fucking genius, Spaz. And not even Randy can get at it?"

Spaz shook his head. "No." He paused. "Can you get rid of the duct tape on my arms?"

Kira approached slowly. "It's going to hurt," she announced after studying the tape.

"Like it doesn't hurt already?"

"Stay still," Kira said. She picked at the duct tape, trying desperately not to show her disgust. Her wolf sense of smell couldn't ignore the scent of rotting flesh and she wanted to gag. Her short fingernails had trouble picking at an edge of the tape. She worked for a while, cursing silently and listening to Spaz's raspy breath. Finally, she got her fingers around a piece. "This is going to hurt."

"Pull now."

Kira pulled and the tape snapped away. Around and around she pulled the tape. When it was at last on bare skin, she winced as she tugged. Spaz bit his lip so hard that he drew blood, but she had to hand it to him — he did not scream.

"I'm so thirsty," he said, licking his dry lips and closing his eyes. "Kira, what are we going to do?"

Kira looked around. There wasn't much here — they were in what she guessed had been a storage closet at one time. There was what looked to be a rack with an old router in it. The screws were out and it was half off the rack; worthless except as a boat anchor. She walked up to the door and listened.

"When do you think you'll have access?" Bob was saying. "We don't have a lot of time."

"I don't know," Lizard said. "I can't hack into any of it. He's a better spider than any of us — that's why he did the architecture."

"And if he won't tell, then he's useless to us unless you can hack his brain," Bob said. "And now the bitch has come looking for him, which means the cops and Alaric aren't too far behind."

"Why don't you use Kira?" Lizard said. "She obviously cares about him — maybe he'll spill to save her life."

Kira turned to Spaz. "The conversation is turning nasty. Can you run?"

"I can barely walk, much less run."

She closed her eyes. "Wait a second — can you get into Denver's police computers?"

"Yeah, so?"

"So, tell them where you are."

"I don't know where I am."

"But I do," Kira said. "Send a message to Detective Jim Walking Bear — I wish I had his number memorized."

"Home or cell?" Spaz said. "Why don't I just get hold of Denver Dispatch?"

"They won't know what they're up against."

"And we do?"

"Good point. Tell them we're at the Intermountain warehouse off 6th Avenue."

At that moment, they heard the click of the door unlocking.

Everything happened so fast that Kira couldn't keep track of it all. The doorknob turned. Kira found herself transmuted and flying toward Lizard and Bob in her werewolf form. Her teeth clamped onto Lizard's throat as she bowled him over. The She-Wolf took complete control and ripped the throat out of the man who had once been her friend, and she could only watch in horror.

Before she knew it, Bob was on top of her in wolf form as well, slashing his powerful canines into her neck. She screamed loudly as his massive teeth ripped through her hide. Instinctively, she raised her leg and shoved her shoulder between her neck and his teeth.

There was a loud thud and suddenly Kira was free. She looked up to see Spaz standing with a router in his hand, holding it by the handle. He had somehow found the strength to pick up a rack-mounted router and slam it into Bob. Bob shook his wolf head as though trying to shake off a headache. He snarled and leapt at Spaz. Spaz held up the router to try to defend himself, but was too weak and slow. Kira leapt at Bob and tore into his thickly furred neck.

"Run!" shouted Spaz.

Kira needed no urging. Despite the limp, she turned and ran.

Asshole! She shouted mentally to Bob. *You're a coward!*

Bitch! shouted Bob as he followed her. He chased her through the hallway and deep into the building. Most of the warehouse was empty except for some pallets on the loading dock that were marked as servers. The door to the dock was open and there was a truck pulled up to it.

"Hey, what's that?" Two werewolves in human form stood next to the cartons of computer equipment.

Kira didn't dare stop as she ran past them; she hit the loading dock, twisted to the left and leapt clear of the truck. Bob was right behind her. She noted with some satisfaction that he also had a limp.

A shot rang out, and she fell heavily, as though something had knocked the wind out of her. Her shoulder and chest burned as she struggled to get up and keep moving, but she couldn't. Her breath came out in rasps and gurgles.

Her head spun. She found herself in an ever-widening pool of blood. Bob, in his werewolf form, was gloating over her when she raised her head.

"Shall I kill her?" the lycanthrope said, pointing the gun at her head.

Wait, said Bob. *Make her suffer a bit for all the trouble she's been.*

You were afraid to challenge Alaric for Alpha, Kira said forcing each word out.

No, bitch. You haven't any clue what's been going on, have you? I knew I had to muster as many lycanthropes behind me as I could, so I began the rogue lycanthropes. And then, you and Susan showed up.

You were afraid we'd find the site, Kira said slowly. *We didn't, but you attacked us anyway. But you didn't expect me to live or for the cops to get there so soon.*

It was too close to the Mall. I should've known better. Bob paused and smiled a wolfy grin. *I won't make that mistake again.* He drew his lips back, ready to take the fatal chomp.

Kira snapped, catching the underside of his neck, her teeth slicing through fur, skin, veins, and arteries. Bob screamed in pain and rage, shaking his neck. There was another shot, but this time the bullet went wide. The lycanthrope went down as Spaz hit him with a spare piece of pipe.

Bob tried to shake her hold on him. His paws braced himself against her torn body. But the more he pushed, the more damage she did. His paws raked against her, but Kira still hung on.

Suddenly, Spaz screamed and dropped to the ground, rolling himself in a ball. From out of the darkness came what appeared to Kira to be an army of wolves. Werewolves. Leading them was none other than Alaric. He leapt on Bob, knocking him from Kira's grip, and tore into the werewolf. The other werewolves streamed into the building, attacking whatever they found. As Kira began to sink into unconsciousness, she thought she heard sirens.

66

Kira awoke to sunlight streaming in through the windows. She lay in a half-conscious state for a long while, vaguely aware of the scents of pine boughs and wood. At first, she thought she was back in the Enchanted Forest, and her mind filled in the trees and the darkness; but as she came to, she realized she was lying on a couch and wrapped in a blanket, close to a crackling fire in a fireplace.

Kira blinked as her eyesight became clearer. She was no longer in wolf form, but she ached all over. She wasn't naked, and for that, she was thankful. Someone had dressed her in a soft flannel nightgown. Kira winced as she looked at the flowers on it. She'd never have been caught dead in such a frilly thing, but then, maybe that's all they had.

She was in a cabin somewhere in a forest — perhaps even in the mountains. To her lower-altitude lungs, the air felt dryer and thinner here. The furniture was unmistakably masculine — hewn log furniture with strong plaid motifs. And wolves. There were paintings and photographs of wolves everywhere.

Kira craned her neck and felt a stab of pain. Feeling her neck, she touched sutures that ran down the front of her body. She was tender there and from what she could tell, she would have some pretty ugly bruising for a while. The last thing she remembered was Alaric tearing into Bob, and then sirens. Had the cops arrived?

The door to the cabin swung open and a cold breeze wafted through. She nestled deeper into the blankets. Alaric walked in with a bundle of wood in his arms and thumped his feet against the mat indoors, shaking off mud and dirt. "You're up," he said, grinning. "The doctor said you'd be coming around today."

"How long have I been out?"

"Only two days," Alaric said. "It was touch and go for a time, until you changed back to human form. You were really chewed up."

"Yeah," Kira said chagrined. "I hope I gave as good as I got."

Alaric laughed. "That you did. I just finished the job. You'd already ripped out Marks' throat." He turned and put one of the logs on the fire and stoked it.

"Where am I?"

"You like it?"

Kira nodded. "Homey."

"It should be. It's my home," Alaric said.

"I thought you lived in Denver."

He shook his head. "My businesses are in Denver, but my home is here. The forest calls to me, as it does anyone with werewolf blood."

"There's no link to the Forest here," Kira said after trying to access it.

"Nope — not close enough to the transmitters. I think the closest Intermountain antenna is on Lookout Mountain, and we're not in good sight range."

"Luddite," Kira said.

"No, I just know when to keep technology at arm's length." He left her to go into the kitchen. "You hungry?"

"Starved."

"Tea okay? My espresso machine's on the fritz."

Kira laughed. "Sure that's fine. Where's Spaz?"

"I'm not sure how much you remember. The cops came shortly after I killed Marks. The police captured your friend. We barely escaped with you."

"I'd imagine he's telling some pretty amazing stories no one will believe," Kira said.

"Nobody except that cop friend of yours," said Alaric. Kira noted the look in his eyes. "We'll have to figure how to get him out of jail before the next full moon. It'll be hard to explain when he turns into a wolf, and even harder when his hand grows back."

"Grows back?" Kira stared at him.

"Tagura's a werewolf now. He'll have the same recuperative powers you have. Werewolves don't stay maimed or we couldn't survive. The moon will heal him when it's full again."

"We don't have much time, then."

"No and he's in quite dubious company. You know Homeland Security wants him for identity theft, among other crimes?" The teakettle whistled and Alaric poured the hot water into a mug with a teabag. "Leftover sandwiches okay?"

"Fine. You're lecturing me on dubious company?" Kira smirked. "Two words: Cathal Murphy."

"I never said lycanthropes weren't a little rough." He brought the tea and sandwiches over to her.

Kira grabbed the first sandwich and bit in. She'd never thought ham could taste so good.

"So, would you like to tell me how you knew Marks was the one who attacked you?"

"Easy—Spaz told me." She chuckled at his look. "See, Spaz, along with all my MIT pals, had created the Enchanted Forest, but they needed a cool interface for it. That's when Spaz started learning about the *hi-rFreq* bandwidth that Northrop's Skunkworks had developed. Spaz wasn't the network guru — Randy Green was. They somehow positioned themselves as top contractors and got in."

"What about security clearances? Surely something would've shown up."

"Piece of cake for someone like Spaz. He hacked himself into the databases and made himself squeaky clean, and did that for Randy too. Somewhere along the way, they discovered EPRE,

TPRE, and CPI. That network was being used by the military for heads-up thought recognition, and the military refined the headsets. They came away from the contact with some pretty sophisticated equipment.

"One of the big things Spaz must have discovered but kept under wraps was that there was a certain amount of biofeedback with the headset. It could actually alter thought patterns and tap into latent telepathic talent in people. The same talent the werewolves exploit."

"A machine that can mimic our telepathy?"

Kira nodded. "I think Spaz kept that to himself. A few sessions within his Enchanted Forest brought him around to actually seeing the Forest in his dreams and eventually to his conscious mind. Who knows how many sessions he had before it happened, but it eventually did. The werewolves, however, accidentally discovered the Forest on their own. Its bandwidth is so close to the actual telepathic transmissions that I'm sure the werewolves who stumbled onto it showed others how to plug in, like I showed you.

"At some point after this, I think Bob Marks must have approached Spaz and Randy to make the Enchanted Forest more accessible for them, preferably through a big telecom who owned a huge portion of the Internet backbone. In truth, I'm really not sure who approached whom, but it was a bad match. Marks saw the potential and decided to exploit it."

"But Tagura had locked out the vital areas," Alaric said. "But I don't get it. Why wasn't the military after this?"

Kira chuckled. "The military probably had another name for the technology. Private companies come out with new bandwidths all the time. Give it an innocuous name and keep it below their scan. No mention of TPRE, EPRE, or CPI." She sighed and closed her eyes, cradling the tea mug in her hands. "I still don't know how you found me."

Alaric smiled wryly. "You're not the only one who can use the Forest."

"You?" Kira was impressed.

"Well, not exactly." He shrugged. "I had some of the werewolf geeks search for your appearance. We were able to track according to some Intermountain IP numbers. Bob wasn't the only werewolf at Intermountain, you know."

"I should thank you," Kira said. "Marks would've killed me."

"Anything for my mate."

"Alaric, I— I..." A guilty thought about Jim flitted through her mind.

"Shhh," Alaric replied. "We'll sort it out later. In the meantime, get some rest."

Kira let him take the mug from her hands. She didn't even object when he pulled the blanket over her shoulders and gave her a gentle kiss on the lips. Maybe it wasn't so bad to be married to the Alpha of a pack, she thought as she drifted off to sleep. At least until she figured out how to reverse the lycanthropy.